THE
NIGHT
WATCHMAN

**Center Point
Large Print**

**This Large Print Book carries the
Seal of Approval of N.A.V.H.**

THE
NIGHT
WATCHMAN

MARK MYNHEIR

CENTER POINT PUBLISHING
THORNDIKE, MAINE

This Center Point Large Print edition
is published in the year 2010 by arrangement with
Multnomah Books,
an imprint of The Crown Publishing Group,
a division of Random House, Inc.

The text of this Large Print edition is unabridged.
In other aspects, this book may vary
from the original edition.
Printed in the United States of America
on permanent paper.
Set in 16-point Times New Roman type.

ISBN: 978-1-60285-719-3

Library of Congress Cataloging-in-Publication Data

Mynheir, Mark.
  The night watchman / Mark Mynheir. -- Center Point large print ed.
    p. cm.
  ISBN 978-1-60285-719-3 (library binding : alk. paper)
  1. Ex-police officers--Fiction. 2. Murder--Investigation--Fiction.
   3. Orlando (Fla.)--Fiction. 4. Large type books. I. Title.
  PS3613.Y58N54 2010
  813'.6--dc22
  2009046415

To my mom, whose strength of character
and courageous spirit have been
an inspiration to me

ACKNOWLEDGMENTS

In over twenty years of law enforcement, I've had the opportunity to work with some incredible law enforcement professionals who have provided much of the fodder for my stories. When I first started investigating violent crimes, I partnered with an edgy veteran named George Santiago, who had the decency to take me under his wing and teach me how to be a detective. I'm greatly indebted to his wisdom in those early years, especially his knowledge of interviews and interrogations, in which he is a master.

I currently work with some great detectives as well as godly men—Sergeant Ken Arnold and Detectives Ernie Diebel, Louis Figuroa, Mike Pusatere, and Steve Hill—who make up the Violent Crimes Unit. Rarely does one get the opportunity to discuss deep theological concepts while on the way to arrest a murder suspect. The Violent Crimes Unit allows me to do just that. Mike Pusatere also provided his proofreading skills and love of mysteries to this project, for which I'm grateful. Major John Blackledge and Chief William Berger have also been incredibly supportive in my writing and my police career.

Rachel Savage has once again loaned her keen eye and willing spirit to this book.

My greatest appreciation goes out to my editor

and very good friend Julee Schwarzburg, who has helped me grow as a writer and a person. I'm also indebted to the many wonderful people at WaterBrook Multnomah Publishing Group, including Shannon Hill-Marchese, Tiffany Lauer, Allison O'Hara, Jessica Barnes, Joel Ruse, Lori Addicott, Carie Freimuth, Jan Walker, Kim Shurley, Stuart McGuiggan, Ken Petersen, Steve Cobb, and many others. They've made the writing of this book not only fun but also quite rewarding.

Lastly, I'd like to acknowledge the loving sacrifice of my wife and children, who encourage, support, and bless me through two very demanding careers. Lori, Chris, Shannon, and Justin—I love you with all my heart.

1

THE TWO MEN STALKING ME emerged from the shadows and then trailed me through the parking lot.

They lagged behind me about fifty feet. I slowed my pace, not that I wasn't as slow as a tree slug already, to see if they would overtake me or hang back.

They hung back. Not good.

Any human at a normal pace should have passed me by now. I could feel their eyes punching holes in me, waiting for the right time to move.

Since I wasn't up for dealing with any problems, I stepped it out as best I could. With a new-and-improved plastic pelvis and hip, along with ten months of physical therapy, I should be able to hobble a little faster. No such luck. The cane and gimpy leg would only go so fast. Grandma Moses on a pogo stick could hop circles around me.

Using the rearview mirrors on the cars parked along Lake Avenue, I kept tabs on my new friends without being too obvious, a little trick I picked up when I worked undercover. No need to give them more of an advantage than they already had.

The big one, a black kid maybe twenty years old, wore a white wife-beater muscle shirt and black jean shorts. Mini-dreads jetted from his head like a frayed ball of yarn. The other kid, probably the same age, was an anemic white with a tattoo sprawled on his neck and a shaved head that glistened under the streetlights.

With each glance I caught, they feigned like they were talking to each other, but I could sense they were planning to pounce. And why not? I was an easy mark—a crippled guy negotiating the Orlando streets alone at night. One more block to go until I was at work.

Eleven months ago I would have enjoyed this game of cat and mouse. But then I would have been the cat, a big hungry one ready to swallow those thugs like the rodents they were.

I hoped they were just playing a game.

I stole a furtive glance behind me, and my tails were nowhere in sight. I stopped and shifted all the way around. Gone. Must have headed up an alley. Maybe I was just losing my mind. Hadn't been out much lately.

I used to love the Orlando nightlife, the clubs and things to do; the pulse of the city at night energized me. It had changed so much in a short amount of time. Faster, meaner, a stranger to me. Like I was living on a different planet. I had grown up here, not long after Mickey scurried in, back when Orlando was more of a cowtown. Now it's a big city plagued with big-city problems.

As I approached the corner of Lake and East Jackson, Tweedle Dee and Tweedle Dumber raced around the corner right in front of me, both out of breath. They must have sprinted down the alley behind the store to cut me off just before I reached the intersection.

This wouldn't end pretty.

"Hey, old man." The ugly white kid checked up and down the street, like felons do when they're preparing to do something monumentally stupid.

His buddy invaded my personal space on my left. "How about some spare change?" he said with an accent, maybe Haitian.

"Don't have any change." I eyed possible escape routes, though escape wasn't likely in my condition. And I couldn't count on anyone to help me, or even to notice, for that matter. On this corner, in a city of over two hundred thousand people, I was on my own . . . as usual.

"Then give up your wallet, or I bust your head like your leg is." The black kid pressed in on me.

"Okay. Okay." I held up my right hand while leaning more on the cane with my left. "I'll give you my wallet. Just don't hurt me."

"Hurry up!" The white kid spit as he spoke, clenching his fists at his sides. "I ain't got all night." He was the alpha dog of the two. If they were going to attack, he would lead. He needed to be tamed.

I reached back with my right hand, brushed past my wallet in my back pocket, and slipped my hand up into my waistband. I let go of the cane. The brass handle clanked as it bounced off the concrete, echoing around us. Huey and Dewey beaded in on it, drawing their attention down for the second I needed.

I unsnapped my Glock 9mm from its holster, then drew it to eye level, setting my night sights on the white kid's forehead. A stupefied look crossed his face, which must be a regular event for him. He wasn't so alpha dog now.

"The leg's busted, scumbag, but my finger works fine." I gritted my teeth and leaned forward. "You wanna test it out?"

Both raised their hands. "We're just playin' around, man." The black kid glanced toward his partner, who peered down the barrel of my pistol.

"I'm not. You got ten seconds to run before I call the cops. Ten. Nine." They were half a block away before I hit five.

Retired cops can legally carry guns, even if they're medically retired. At least I had that going for me. If not, I'd have been a quick lunch for those creeps. I thought about calling Dispatch and reporting it, but something told me my new friends would think twice for a while before robbing someone again, and I didn't relish the idea of being listed as a victim again on an incident report with my old department.

I slid the pistol into its holster at my back, then snapped it in. I combed my fingers through my hair. The May air was thick and still. The adrenaline surge from the game with my buddies wasn't all bad. For the first time in a while, I felt alive, energized. Too bad it would die down soon.

My cane lay on the sidewalk, which shouldn't have been a big deal. But everything was a big deal these days. As I stood without support, I felt like I was balancing on a dry, cracked twig ready to snap at any moment, sending me crashing to the concrete. My own legs were under someone else's spell, because they certainly didn't obey me anymore. I used to be able to roundhouse kick a heavy bag so hard it would bend in half. Now I had to mentally prepare to bend over and pick up my cane so I wouldn't fall on my face like an idiot . . . or worse, a helpless child.

I shouldn't have been too worried, though. Me and my physical terrorist—I mean, therapist— Helga, had been working on this. Her name really wasn't Helga, but I liked to call her that. A linebacker-sized woman with viselike man hands, sweet Helga and I would rendezvous three times a week—whether I wanted to or not. (If I didn't go to my therapy and doctors' appointments, I didn't get my medical retirement checks.) I imagine Helga's former job was as an interrogator in a Russian gulag somewhere deep in Siberia, slapping, twisting, and pounding confessions from the prisoners. I've cried out for mercy more than once on her medieval torture table.

I drew in a deep breath, then exhaled as we practiced. I eased down, shifting all my weight onto my left foot while rolling my right foot on its heel, stretching it out. Throbbing bolts of pain fired up my leg then my spine, like multiple shots from a Taser. I wobbled as my fingers brushed the cane, as if I were petting the head of a snake. My middle finger caught the lip of the hawk-bill handle, then drew it into my hand. I stabbed the tip into the concrete and pressed myself up. What a production.

As I righted myself, I took a second to compose, the nerve endings in my lower half signaling their dismay and rebellion. I checked my watch. If I was gonna make my shift as the night watchman at Coral Bay Condominiums, I'd have to hustle. I'd hate to lose my new job. But then again, I didn't have much respect for someone who's never lost anything.

My name is Ray Quinn. Eleven months ago, I lost everything.

2

WHILE I USED TO WAGE WAR in the streets against felons and thugs, my largest battle now was staying awake for an entire shift. The height of last week's drama at the condo was when Mrs. Ragland's Yorkshire terrier left an unwanted deposit on the carpet in the lobby. In a short time, my world had disintegrated into this.

I navigated my way across Jackson Street to the glass double doors of Coral Bay Condos. The eight-story building was about twenty-five years old. The sign above the doors read Where Luxury and Comfort Meet.

I rapped my knuckles on the glass. The doors were locked from 8:00 p.m. until 5:00 a.m., and my shift started at 9:00. The second-shift guy, Hank Karpinski, was sitting in my chair at the front desk. Hank didn't move. I doubted he could hear me. He was easily a hundred and thirty years old and the only person on the planet I might be able to take in a dead sprint. I rang the door chime. His gray head bobbed my way, and I waved. He squinted, then pressed the metallic buzzer to let me in.

I pushed through the door. "How are things going, Hank?"

"Crazy as usual, Ray." Hank made his way around the counter. "Mrs. Campola is off her medication again. She's been mean as a snake all day, calling down and hollering at me."

"Sounds nice."

"Busy, busy, busy." The old man shuffled past me toward the door. "Watch Crevis tonight too. He's already here and fired up as usual."

"I figured." I eased into the cushioned swivel chair at the front desk, then propped my cane on the table next to me. Hank had kept my seat warm.

Four security monitors hung on the wall behind me, covering different areas of the complex—the front door, the back, the underground parking garage, and the elevators. The front desk faced the lobby and the glass double doors.

Two maroon couches were in the lobby, so residents could sit and talk. At night, they were virtually unused, which was one of the reasons I volunteered to work the midnight shift. I could sit back in my little kingdom, alone, watching the world pass by. Like a wrecked voyeur of sorts, my life was more of a spectator sport now.

The job wasn't too bad, though. I answered phones, buzzed folks in and out, watched the monitors, and called for help if we needed it (usually an ambulance, since many of the residents were elderly). The pay wasn't great, although it did supplement my retirement benefits. A friend suggested I pursue a second job, if for no other reason than to get out of my apartment more. He might have been right.

Stretching out my right leg, I massaged it, hoping it wouldn't cause me too much discomfort tonight. The walk and near rumble left me a bit sore. I needed to talk with management about letting me park on the premises. I thought parking a couple of lots away would give me some exercise, but now I wasn't so sure.

I pulled my *Sudoku Masters* book from my pocket, then flipped to my current puzzle. I loved a good puzzle. As a kid, I wore out a dozen Rubik's Cubes.

"Ray!" Crevis Creighton rounded the corner

16

from the first-floor hallway and burst into the lobby. "I got a new knife at the flea market. Wanna see it?"

So much for being undisturbed. "No."

He plopped his size-twelve hoof on the chair next to mine and drew a dagger from a sheath tied to his boot. Crevis's face lit up as he held the blade in front of him.

Crevis was my nighttime co-worker who walked the property while I manned the desk. I couldn't bring myself to say *partner* in the same sentence with Crevis; it violated all good standards of decency.

About my height, a good six foot, Crevis had a wiry build and was a little lighter than me (especially since I'd put on some pounds recently). With a bright red flattop haircut and long gangly arms, he resembled a spider monkey with a pencil eraser glued to its head—with all due respect to the little primates who might have a couple of IQ points on him. He was in his late teens or early twenties and had ruddy skin, pitted with acne scars like a wall-spackling job gone awry.

"Pretty cool." Crevis twirled the implement of war, mesmerized by the shiny dagger in a way that should cause concern to any person with even a rudimentary understanding of psychology. "Wanna hold it?"

"No."

Crevis held it out to me. I glared back at him.

"Okay, okay." He slid it back into its sheath and stood tall, his PR-24 police baton dangling on his web belt. The guy had every security gadget known to man on that thing—pepper spray, handcuffs, an expandable baton, plastic Flexicuffs, a flashlight, a Leatherman tool, and a Velcro pouch containing who-knows-what, and I didn't dare ask him.

"Wanna hear what happened at the flea market?"

"No."

"When I was looking at the knife case, these three guys were behind me. One of them started gettin' mouthy because he said I was standing in front of him. They all got in my face, so I stepped back, ready to go at it with them."

Crevis raised his hands and took a feeble karate stance. "I told them to bring it on. They just backed up and walked away. They were scared." Crevis planted his hands on his hips and puffed his chest out like it should have a large *S* on it.

"Lucky for them." They could have damaged their fists on his face.

"You know it." Crevis worked a quick series of jabs and hooks in the air, a triumphant smirk sliding across his uneven teeth. "They had no idea who they were dealing with. I'm a weapon of death and destruction."

This conversation needed to end. I glanced at the garage monitor and rolled my chair closer, seemingly fixated on the screen.

"You see something?" Crevis hurried around the

front desk and went shoulder to shoulder with me, eyes locked on the monitor.

"I'm not sure. I thought I saw a shadow or something move in the garage area by one of the vans there." I tapped the screen with my finger. Pausing a second for effect, I waved a dismissive hand in the air and leaned back in my chair. "It was probably nothing. I wouldn't worry about it."

"You never know. I'm on it." Crevis scampered down the hall toward the stairs, his gear rattling. "I'll call you if I see something."

Worked every time. One night I must have sent him to a dozen different shadows and movements. The kid had been lacquered in a healthy sweat before that shift ended. I almost felt sorry for him . . . almost.

After just a few minutes, Crevis crept past the garage camera, gazed back, and gave me a thumbs-up, as if I cared. Flashlight in hand, he slipped out of view. That should be good for a half hour, maybe forty-five minutes. His parents must have been hippies who ingested large quantities of narcotics in their day. There's no other rational reason why someone would name their child Crevis.

I positioned my chair so I could keep an eye on the monitors and the front door, then I returned my attention to my puzzle. Didn't want my back to the door; old cop habits were hard to break. One of the benefits of this job was lots of time for my Sudoku. I checked the puzzle pattern to this point and added two more numbers when the buzzer drew me to the front door.

An attractive blonde in her late twenties knocked on the glass and waved. She wore blue jeans and a white shirt, and her hair was in a ponytail. I'd never seen her before. Then again, I hadn't been working here all that long.

"May I help you?" I said through the intercom, resting my unchallenged puzzle on the desk.

"I'm here to see my brother."

"Did you ring his unit?"

"He won't answer. Please let me in." She rested a hand on the glass. "I'm worried about him."

I pushed the button, feeling a little guilty for not buzzing her in right away.

She hurried to the counter and leaned her elbows on it. "I'm sorry to bother you, but I haven't been able to reach my brother since yesterday. He hasn't answered his cell or house phone. This isn't like him at all." Her hazel eyes were a nice complement to her pretty face.

"What's his name?" I pulled the resident listing book from next to the telephone.

"David Hendricks."

I wasn't familiar with his name either. I found his number and picked up the phone. "I'll call his apartment." I got an answering machine with a man's voice, probably her brother, telling me to leave a message at the tone. I didn't leave one.

"Answering machine." I shrugged.

"Can you please let me in his apartment? He's a pastor and runs Outreach Orlando Ministries. He didn't show up for work today and didn't call in." Her voice cracked, but she caught herself and regained composure. "Something's wrong; I just know it."

After fifteen years of police work, I was pretty good at spotting trouble and troubled people. She was neither. I had the master key and would escort her up to his unit. I could have let Crevis do it while I attended to my puzzle, but even though I didn't know this lady, she'd given me no reason to subject her to Crevis.

"Hey, Crevis," I called into my radio. "You need to cover the front desk for a minute. I'm going to let someone in an apartment on the fourth floor."

"On my way." He was out of breath and no doubt running to the desk, as he did with every request.

She leaned over the desk and touched my forearm as I stood. "Thank you."

"No problem." I got my cane and started down the hallway. She followed.

"Everyone at the mission is worried. David is the most responsible person I know."

A pastor? Fifteen snarky responses piled up in my head like rush-hour traffic. I have a filter in my brain that's often "out of order" and allows whatever I think to flow way too freely across my lips. It's been my undoing more than once. But today, for some reason, I shut off the comments and

21

didn't tell the lady what I thought of pastors, religion, or anything else, for that matter. Didn't know how long the filter would keep working, so I'd best get this done and finish my puzzle.

"What's your name?"

"Ray." I fumbled with the keys in my hand. "Ray Quinn."

"I appreciate this, Ray." She scooted ahead of me to the elevator and pushed the Up button. "I'm Pam Winters."

I nodded. Different last name than her brother, no wedding ring, but a rather fresh indent on her ring finger. Must be a story there. I pay attention to hands. When I was a cop, it was a matter of life or death. The hands were what could cripple or kill you. Not to watch them was a dereliction of duty. Now it was just an annoying remnant of my former life.

We were on the fourth floor before I knew it. Pam exited first, well in front of me. I did what I could to keep up with her brisk pace.

She stopped at room 419 and knocked. No answer. I knocked. I didn't want to be jiggling the door with the key and have some goofy, scared resident pop a few rounds my way. Maybe this guy just wanted to be left alone for a day. I'd had whole months where I didn't want to be bothered.

Pam tapped her foot and then pounded on the door. "David. It's Pam. Open up. Are you okay?"

I waited for a second. Still nothing. I unlocked

the door and eased it open. "Mr. Hendricks, it's the night watchman. Are you all right?"

"David." Pam stepped around me as we entered the living room. No one was there.

The living room was nice with an open kitchen area. Nothing opulent, but not a bad place for a single guy. Sure beat my digs.

Pam walked into the kitchen and over to the phone on the counter. The message light flashed.

I stayed where I was because I didn't feel comfortable milling around someone's apartment. But I didn't want to leave her alone here either, just in case I was being duped and she was some crazed stalker chick or something.

She called to her brother again and then moved down the hallway toward the bedrooms. As she opened a door on the left, her scream could have peeled paint off the wall. I ran forward as best I could, nearly stumbling in the hallway.

Pam halted at the doorway, hand over mouth, another shriek tearing through the air. I stepped into the room and found out why.

I pulled my radio from my belt. "Crevis, call 911 now!"

"What?"

"Call OPD right now. We've got two people down." I switched hands with my cane and grabbed Pam by the arm because she looked as if she was going to faint.

"Tell them it's a homicide."

3

CRIME SCENE TAPE is like flypaper for busy-bodies; the second you put it up, they all come buzzing around and stick to it.

Coral Bay Condominiums' fourth floor was as packed as a Christmas sale at Penney's. Orlando patrol officers had cordoned off the hallway and were keeping folks back from the apartment. I didn't recognize any of the uniforms. They were probably new. I didn't ID myself to them. No need to go through that rigmarole.

Crevis mirrored the movements of one of the officers and echoed the commands to step back. He would be tough to live with after this.

The crowd at the end of the hallway parted as a tall African American detective lifted the yellow tape and passed underneath. Sergeant Oscar Yancey, my former boss, checked in with the officer manning the crime scene log.

Six-three with a sinewy build, Oscar sported his tailored gray dress shirt, slacks, and tie as if competing for best-dressed crime scene apparel. He'd win hands down. In his early fifties, Oscar was a cop's cop. Smart, diligent, tenacious. A good boss to have and solid backup when you're out with an ornery felon at two in the morning. No one messed with Big O. He'd been a sergeant in Homicide for a dozen years.

24

"Ray." Oscar smiled, hand extended. "Great to see you."

"Hey, Oscar." I walked toward him, leaving Pam still catatonic against the wall in the hallway. His hand engulfed mine. "How are Mimi and the kids?"

"Good." He nodded as he unbuttoned one sleeve and rolled it up. "We miss having you come around."

"Who's on call tonight?" I said before he could invite me to his house again. He'd been leaving messages on my machine about once a week. Sometimes I'd call him back, more often not. Didn't want to get into it with him again.

"Me." A shrill voice pierced me like an ice pick in the eardrum.

I didn't have to turn around. Detective Rick Pampas just slithered into the crime scene.

"What are you doing here, Quinn?" He looked down at my nametag and Coral Bay security shirt and let out a thunderous laugh. "You're a rent-a-cop now? This is priceless."

He sneered. His black hair contrasted with a pasty white face that just couldn't be punched enough. Two inches shorter than me and lean, Rick ran marathons for giggles. If he'd put half the effort into his cases as he did with his running, maybe I wouldn't have such a problem with him. He was also the second-best shot in the unit, next to me. I imagine my trophy was somewhere on his desk now.

Crevis hurried toward us and pressed in on the circle. He bumped me with his shoulder and nodded to Oscar. He wanted an intro.

I rolled my eyes. "This is Crevis Cretin."

"Creighton." Crevis seized Oscar's hand and wrestled with it. "I'm the one who called. I'm gonna be a cop. I'm testing now to go to the academy, so I'll be working with you guys soon." He hooked his thumbs in his duty belt and rose up on his tiptoes.

"That's nice." Oscar turned back to me. "Ray, what did you see?"

"I let the victim's sister into the apartment." I pointed to Pam. "She found them first in the bedroom. Two people down. I'm assuming the male is her brother. He was on the floor at the foot of the bed. There's a female on the bed with what looks like a gunshot wound to the head. A pistol's on the floor between them. Don't know the caliber for sure, maybe a nine mil or forty cal. I wanted to get the sister out of there, so we left the apartment and Crevis called."

Oscar ran his hand through his graying hair. "What's your gut tell you?"

"Didn't have enough time in the scene, so I can't really say. Whatever it is, it isn't good."

"So you've already been inside my crime scene, messing it up, no doubt." Rick drew a pair of latex gloves from his pants pocket and worked them onto his hands. "Not much has changed. You never could wait to pilfer through other people's cases."

"Give it a rest, Rick, and go survey your scene." Oscar dipped his head toward room 419.

Rick looked at me and shook his head with a stupid sneer. I knew what he wanted to say, and if he did, I would hammer him with my cane so hard I might actually knock some sense into him.

"You were a cop?" Crevis said, his face beaming.

"He was the best homicide detective who ever worked for me." Oscar flashed a patronizing smile my way. His eyes couldn't lie about the truth, though. "The man was good."

"You told me you worked in the circus and got hurt in a freak elephant accident." Crevis scrunched his mug and scratched his head.

I chuckled; I still couldn't believe the kid bought that story.

"Hey, Ray-Ray," Steve Stockton, Rick's partner, called from behind me. He ducked under the tape and meandered over to us.

Steve was a decent guy, albeit not the shiniest star of the homicide unit. He'd packed on the pounds since I'd last seen him. He'd been a cop for over twenty years, and I'd often pondered how much police knowledge had been lost in the doughy expanse between his ears.

"How ya holdin' up?" Steve slapped me on the shoulder.

"Doin' okay." I shook my head. "I'm sorry, though."

"Sorry for what?" He raised an eyebrow.

"Sorry you're still partnered up with Pampas."

"Ah, you two need to kiss and make up." Steve waved a hand at me. "It's been a tough year for all of us." Steve gave me the look, too, but avoided stating the obvious.

"Stockton, you need to talk with the deceased's sister," Oscar said. "Get a statement from her and see what we're looking at."

"Got it, boss." Steve approached Pam and introduced himself.

"Well, I've had enough fun for one night." My heart was pounding in my ears. The hallway seemed to be shrinking. For some reason, I didn't do crowds well anymore. It had been that way since the shooting. The psychologist said that could happen, but I didn't have to like it. "I'm going downstairs if you need anything."

"Why don't you hang out awhile? I could use your insights on the case."

"Nice try, Oscar, but I'd hate to miss any of the fun at the front desk. I've got a Sudoku puzzle down there just itching to be worked. The Coral Bay Condos can be a pretty happening place at night."

"Promise me you'll give me a call. We've got a lot to talk about."

"Yeah. I'll give you a buzz later this week. We'll do lunch or something."

"Promise?"

"Sure." I hated lying to Oscar. He's been good to me over the years, but I'm about as likely to call him as I am to return to kickboxing. That part of my life is over, and I didn't like reliving it.

Crime scene investigators Dean Yarborough and Katie Pham checked in. Katie was just starting the job when I retired, so I didn't know her well. Tall and slender with blond highlights in her dark hair, she was an attractive Asian woman. Word was, she did decent work.

Katie toted a gym bag filled with all the necessary crime scene accoutrements—latex gloves, fingerprint tape and cards, ample amounts of plastic and paper crime scene bags, gunshot residue kits, DNA and blood swabs.

Dean had his camera bag slung over his shoulder and was carrying an alternate light source case in one hand and a laptop in the other. He lived and breathed crime scene work—no girlfriend, no life.

Dean traded eye work with me as he passed but didn't speak. No surprise there. We never got along. I caught him surfing some Internet dating site at his desk one day and teased him about it . . . a lot. He hadn't forgiven me since.

Dean had a build conducive for crime scene work: short, thin, able to fit into places average-sized folks couldn't go—like a hobbit. The bespectacled CSI had, covering his balding head, a comb-over that fooled only him. He and Katie entered the apartment without so much as a word.

Pampas stepped from the open apartment door and beaded in on me. "Did you sign in on the crime scene log?"

I didn't answer him but gauged the range of my cane to his melon. I was a little far away, but that could be corrected with a single step, should I need it.

"Great, sign yourself out then, unless you want to run and get me some coffee," Pampas said.

"Since when did you ever stay awake at a scene, anyway?" My filter was off with Pampas.

He snarled. Time for me to go. I glanced back at Pam, who still leaned against the wall, talking with Steve. I'd seen that vacant stare before, too many times. Some unsuspecting relative finds a loved one in a gruesome, shocking fashion. The human mind is not programmed to process that kind of information. It usually leads to a temporary shutdown.

That being true, Pam was in full-blown disconnect. She stared at me with a look on her face that made me wish I hadn't seen it. That terrible pain. I knew exactly what she was experiencing.

"We need to go, Crevis. They've got a job to do."

As Crevis and I prepared to leave, the building manager, Mr. Savastio, made frantic hand gestures and talked boisterously with one of the uniforms protecting the crime scene. Crevis and I slid underneath the tape.

Mr. Savastio was in his sixties with salt-and-pepper hair and a swarthy complexion, made darker by a two-day growth on his face.

"Back in my country, policemen never treat citizen like this." Mr. Savastio poked his finger toward his feet as he squared off in front of the patrol officer. "I demand to see scene."

"He can't do that, Mr. Savastio," I said. "He's only doing his job."

"Ray," he said, sounding more like *Vay*. "Tell him I run this place and must be allowed to assess what is happening."

"He runs this place and must be allowed to assess what is happening," I said to the uniform in monotone. He chuckled; Mr. Savastio did not. I shrugged.

"Is damage bad?" Mr. Savastio said. "Will owner be able to clean the apartment and get it on the market? We have many people interested in buying these."

"I don't think this owner is going to be selling anything anytime soon," I said.

"Why didn't you two stop this from happening?" The manager pointed his little crooked finger back and forth between Crevis and me. "That's why we pay for security . . . to feel secure. Now this." He twirled in a circle with his hands in the air. "Crime scene tape. Policemen everywhere. This looks very bad."

"First, we were off duty when these people died," I said.

"How do you know that?"

"I can just tell, Mr. Savastio . . . trust me." I didn't think explaining how a human body decomposes would ingratiate me with him, so I let the comment stand. "The officers will clear out of here soon, and everything will go back to normal. We'll handle it."

He rubbed his woolly face. "I want full report in the morning. I do not like this, Ray. Not at all."

"Will do."

Mr. Savastio glared at the officer and hurried to the elevator.

I didn't want to listen to Mr. Savastio prattle on anymore, so Crevis and I waited until he left, then we ambled toward the elevators. Crevis kept checking over his shoulder, looking back at the scene. I couldn't afford to look back.

"You were a homicide cop," Crevis said as the door closed. "How cool is that? How many cases did you work? How many dead people did you see?"

Crevis peppered me with rapid-fire questions the entire ride down to the lobby. I'd never realized how long a four-floor elevator ride could be, nor been so thankful in my life to hear the *ding* of the destination floor. Crevis's gums hadn't even slowed.

"What's it like being a cop?" He moved in front of me, arms out like he was fixing to tackle me.

"Back off, Crevis. I'm not in the mood."

"C'mon, Ray. All I've ever wanted to do my whole life is be a cop. Tell me about it."

"You really wanna know what it's all about?" I stepped nose to nose with him. "You want all the dirty secrets?"

Crevis nodded, unable to speak, near euphoric.

"There's no other job like it." I jabbed a finger into his bony chest. "You'll give everything you have to help people who don't want to be helped. You'll try to save a world that doesn't want to be saved. And by the time your career is over, your head will be so messed up that you'll have to take medication to sleep because all the crud rolls through your mind, like a morbid movie playing over and over again. And if you live long enough to make retirement, you'll be a cynical shell of a man, begging to die just for relief. Heard enough yet?"

He wanted it, so I gave it to him—both barrels. He needed to understand what the job does to perfectly normal human beings. Well, I didn't know if Crevis was normal or if I ever was. I just knew what I was now.

Crevis stepped back and gazed at me in a pensive manner. Then he smirked. "Did you ever shoot anyone?"

"I'm thinking about shooting *you*."

"Do you have a gun on you right now?" He scanned me up and down as he side shuffled behind me. "Where is it? Can I hold it?"

"I'm going home. I'm done for the night."

"C'mon, Ray. Let's go get a burger or something. I want to hear some stories."

I'd give him some stories—scary and depressing ones that would keep him up late at night.

4

KEEPING AN EYE OUT for my two friends from earlier, I used the time it took to get back to my car to vent some steam. I needed to head home and get some meds or hang out with my friend Jim, who I was pretty sure would be paying me a visit this morning. He'd been a regular at my place since the shooting.

The sun just threatened to crest the horizon as I made it to my apartment complex, Hacienda del Sol, which bore no resemblance to the Coral Bay Condos. Just off John Young Parkway, Hacienda del Sol, a two-story horseshoe-shaped building much older than I am, is my little slice of heaven these days. About half of the apartments were occupied; many were being remodeled or were in various stages of decay. A pool sits smack-dab in the center of the complex with all the apartments facing it. Well, it should be called more of a pond than a pool since the pump didn't work. The water was a gummy shade of green—I swear you could walk on the patches of algae that floated on it—and the stench could make a landfill seem like a garden.

My one-bedroom apartment was on the bottom floor, so I didn't have to climb the stairs. I used to have a pretty decent place off Semoran Boulevard with a pool that was actually usable and a small gym. That was a lifetime ago.

I parked in the back lot just behind my apartment and hoofed it toward my door. The uneven, rusty gate to the middle of the complex groaned as I forced it open. The leg was done. I was done. When I push it too hard, I shake and wobble as I walk. My hip was gyrating so wildly I looked like a drunken Elvis impersonator.

I unlocked my front door and sighed as I crossed the threshold. It wasn't much, but it was home. I checked my phone for messages. None. I untucked my shirt and loosened up. I slipped the holster from my waistband and laid the Glock on the kitchen table.

I had a TV/DVD player across from the couch in the tiny living room and a small desk next to the wall with my laptop on it. A painting of John Wayne—the greatest action hero who ever lived —held a prominent place on the wall above my television. He's mounted on his steed and keeps a steady eye on the place. I own a copy of every movie John Wayne ever appeared in, all 170 of them, even the ones from the twenties when he was a bit actor.

I took a college class on film critiques and appreciation, just so I could understand a little more about the Duke's brilliance. I scanned my collection for any possible selections. Nothing looked promising today, and I wasn't up for surfing the Internet.

A heavy bag hung from the ceiling between the kitchen and the hallway to my bedroom, not that I've hit it with any force since getting out of the hospital. I gave it a courtesy bump with my shoulder. Although I'd never be able to kick it again, I considered attempting some punches. My right arm had finally healed from the round that broke it just above my elbow. It might be strong enough now to take the workout, but I just didn't have the will to try. Maybe someday I'd give it a shot, but not today.

My good friend Jim was about to show up.

I retrieved a can of Coke from the fridge, then reached underneath the sink and removed the pint of Jim Beam. I hadn't taken a pain med since earlier last night. I'm not up for mixing meds and booze, lest I become the newest client for my old unit to investigate. Pampas would probably post a picture of my dead body on the Internet or something. Didn't want to give him that pleasure.

I filled the glass with three fingers of whiskey, then dropped in a teaspoon of Coke to add a little color. Didn't want to put in too much soda or I'd lose my girlish figure. The first swig was always the hardest. My eyes watered a bit as Jim's fierce punch made its way down my gullet. This one had a bite to it. But it would help with the pain, and maybe the leg too.

The night's events rolled through my mind like a runaway freight train without brakes. Why did it have to be my old unit? Couldn't they have found the scene on day shift when I wouldn't have to deal with it?

I tipped another swig down as my body started to loosen up. I hurried to chase the first drink with another, going even lighter on the Coke. If I wanted to get any sleep at all this morning, I'd have to dance a lot with Jim.

It wasn't the crime scene that unnerved me, although it's never fun to see mangled people. Nor was it the victim's poor sister getting traumatized. It was the looks on everyone's faces and what wasn't said.

No one mentioned the shooting—or Trisha.

That kinda surprised me. Like she just up and vanished for no reason. Or worse, never existed at all. She hadn't vanished to me. Quite the contrary.

Trisha is forever etched on my brain . . . and my heart.

Pampas's eyes had mocked me, like everyone else's, but they showed the good sense not to speak it. Since the shooting I'd stayed away from the station to avoid this very thing. The chief gave me the same look that first day at the hospital after my surgery; and the union guys who helped with my medical retirement; and Oscar, despite his words; and every other cop I'd seen since that day. They all had the same convicting stare, filled with unspoken accusations aimed right at my heart.

I was the idiot who messed up and got himself crippled . . . and his partner killed.

I slugged another jolt of Jim down, but even he couldn't numb everything.

5

One Month Later

IN ANY CONFRONTATION, the first punch always hurts the worst.

I developed this little truism during my kick-boxing years when I'd leave the relative comfort of my corner and take that first juicy shot in the chops. After that, my body would be mostly numb for the rest of the fight and could take the abuse the sport required.

This crossed my mind as I pulled into the parking lot of my apartment because I was formulating a similar theory regarding my visits with precious Helga. When she first digs her tender meat hooks into my hip, the rest of the world goes fuzzy and I yearn to lose consciousness for a while. But then I loosen up and adjust to her brutality and somehow survive her sadistic sessions.

This morning she had run me through a series of stretching exercises that any civilized nation would deem cruel and unusual. Then she had me do some pool work, which wasn't quite as bad and provided some distance between my minder and me. But I often wonder, as I'm frog swimming laps and dear Helga keeps a watchful eye from the side of the pool, if I slip under the water, would she rescue me? I don't think she likes me very much. I can't imagine why.

I eased out of my pickup, my legs in full rebellion as I planted them on terra firma. I took my time getting to the gate. Between Helga pushing me too hard and just a couple hours of tortured, fitful sleep, my mind and body were spent. Jim and I would have to wrestle later, to be sure. I didn't have to work tonight and might do a John Wayne marathon. Just John, Jim, and me. Not a bad group of guys. No one in Hollywood now was like the Duke. Clint Eastwood came close, maybe like a stepfather, but John Wayne was the man.

As I approached my apartment, a woman was perched on the bar stool next to my front door. I can lean against it for support and still stretch my leg out when the pain is at its worst. Sometimes I like to sit out there and work a puzzle, when I'm in the mood to get a nostril full of Eau de Toxic Pool.

She stood and clasped her hands over a large manila folder. I recognized her from the murders at the condos a month or so before. She feigned a smile as I got closer, but the grief was still evident. Maybe it was my years as a cop, but after a while you can just read the emotions on people's faces, even when they're trying to fake it.

"Mr. Quinn." She extended her hand. "I don't know if you remember me. I'm Pam Winters. My brother was killed at Coral Bay Condos last month."

"I remember." I didn't tell her that I read the newspaper accounts. Her brother wasn't "killed," he'd murdered his exotic-dancer lover and then turned the gun on himself. Over several days, the *Orlando Sentinel* had plastered the story about David Hendricks, his ministry, and his fall—the salacious details that sell lots of papers—on the front page. I shook her hand, then placed both of mine on the cane. What in the world was she doing at my place?

"Can we talk for a minute?" She glanced at my front door.

I should have been ecstatic to have a pretty young woman show up at my door and invite herself in, but this didn't have a warm, cuddly feel to it. And I have a tendency to suspect the worst in people. I'd feel like something was wrong with me except for the fact that I'm right most of the time.

I nodded and unlocked my door. I keep a pretty clean place, all things considered. I've always been that way, not much for clutter or dirt, a minimalist at heart. A room should have a sense of order. But it's still not the slickest abode around; the management hadn't given me much to work with. I hadn't had any visitors since I moved here, and after just having Helga belt me around a little, I wasn't in the greatest mood.

I grabbed last month's copy of *Black Belt* magazine off the coffee table and stashed it on the television, like that would soften the man-appeal of my living room. She studied my portrait of the Duke, as if it were a precious work of art in the Louvre (it was to me), and my DVD shrine below it.

"You have a nice place here." She moved around the room in the roach motel. She lied well. I made a mental note of that.

"I'm sorry about your brother." I figured that was why she was here. No use dancing around it, or we might be here all afternoon making pleasantries.

"You were very nice to me that night." She flashed a genuine smile. "I wanted to thank you for that."

I shrugged. If I were ever on trial for being a nice guy, I didn't think there'd be enough evidence to convict me. But under the circumstances, it seemed right. So her brother was a dirt-bag murderer. She couldn't be held responsible for his life of lies, and he wasn't the first preacher to be caught in some tawdry tryst. Like the Shadow used to say, "Who knows what evil lurks in the hearts of men?"

"So you came by to thank me?" I sensed there was more and wanted to get to it. I wasn't psychic or anything. I just happened to read the label on the file she was carrying: Hendricks Murder-Suicide. I opened the door under the sink and reached in, locating Jim by Braille. "Would you like a drink?"

She shook her head. Maybe she was a teetotaler and religious zealot like her brother.

I retrieved a can of soda from the fridge and poured more in my glass than I normally would. Didn't want to give a poor impression of myself. Jim was an unrecognizable dark black, and it was a bit unnerving to see him emasculated like that. I would make it up to him as soon as she left, and return him to his light brown color and more potent sting.

"I need your help," she said, as if it hurt her to speak the words.

My eyebrows rose along with my glass.

"My brother didn't kill anyone." She held out the file like a piece of rotting meat. "And he certainly didn't do what this report says he did."

"It's a closed case," I said and then coughed, nearly spewing Jim and Coke out my nostrils like a soda fountain. I wiped my lip with a paper towel from the counter. "According to the paper, Pampas closed it out as a murder-suicide. Seems pretty clear cut. Besides, what's that have to do with me?"

"There's nothing clear cut about it." She stepped forward, her eyes gleaming, her voice strong, confident. She aimed a finger at me. "My brother was murdered. They were both murdered, him and that girl. Someone set him up, and I'm going to find out who."

I hissed; my filter was working overtime with her. I'd lost count of how many suicides I'd investigated where the family refused to believe their loved ones could have done such a thing. Add murder, religion, and exotic lovers to that equation, and her reaction wasn't surprising. I couldn't blame her, but she was diving headfirst into denial big-time. "Back to my question: what does any of that have to do with me?"

"I want you to look at the case. Sergeant Yancey told me you were a great homicide detective."

"Whoa, lady. If you think I'm going to have anything to do with this, you must be drunker than I'm going to be." I tossed one back for dramatic effect. The next one would be straight alcohol. I hate when I'm wrong about people, and I regretted letting this lady into my apartment.

"Nobody else will talk with me about this. I've contacted the governor's office, the FBI, the Florida Department of Law Enforcement. They all say it's a closed case, and they won't do anything."

"Look . . . Pam, is it?" I rested my glass on the counter. "I'm sure you don't want to hear this, but maybe no one will reopen it for a reason—like it's an obvious, no-questions-asked murder-suicide. End of story."

"That's impossible."

"Why's that?"

"Because David didn't do it."

"What makes you so sure?"

"Because he could never . . . do something like that. He loved the Lord and served Him with all his heart. It was his passion."

"And . . . what else?" I rolled my hand like a director stretching out a scene. "This is the part where you fill in that you found some evidence or something to clear his name. Something to back up your suspicions."

Her eyes pierced mine. "I know my brother, Mr. Quinn, and he didn't do it."

"You know your brother? With such compelling evidence as that, I'm surprised the governor didn't fly down here and settle this thing himself."

"Make fun of me if you want, but it's true."

"There are a hundred private investigators in this city," I said. "I suggest you find one."

"I've tried, but they all wanted lots of money for a case like this. Besides, none of them were right to take this on."

"So not only do you want me, a rent-a-cop night watchman, to take your case, but you want me to do it for free?"

"I can pay you at some point. I'm a teacher and am off for the summer. I'll get another job or something. I have a little money saved and credit cards I can use. I'll do whatever it takes to get to the truth."

"Wow. You drive a pretty hard bargain, lady." I emptied my glass. I'd need a good buzz to keep this conversation going. The filter was slipping with each word. "I don't think you seem to grasp a very simple truth: I'm not a detective anymore."

I stepped from behind my kitchen counter. I lifted my cane and held both arms out, teetering in front of her, my broken body on full display. "I can barely take myself to the toilet, and you want me to chase down leads in a non case? Look at me! Those days are long behind me, and the last thing I need is some grieving schoolmarm to come in here and stir my world back up."

She tapped her hand on the folder and glared at me. "Sergeant Yancey said you once believed in the truth. You were driven by right and wrong, and you'd stop at nothing to solve a case."

"Nothing . . . but three nine-millimeter rounds." Two for me, one for Trisha, but Pam didn't need to know the details. "That's all it took to stop me for good. So unless you're gonna have a few drinks with me and maybe take in a flick, I suggest you show yourself out."

"I know you're the right one to bring out the truth and restore my brother's honor and ministry. I've been praying about this every day."

Okay, we just went into loony land. "Time for you to go."

"Just look at the case file," she said as she backed toward the door. "See if you can find anything wrong. I'll do the rest myself if I have to."

I hobbled toward her, sensing she needed some assistance opening the door and scooting her fanny out of here. "I don't need to read a file about a preacher who was living a lie and murdered his mistress."

My first-punch theory proved correct again as the schoolmarm's right hand careened off my cheek with a smack so hard it made my teeth chatter and my leg feel good for a moment.

"Don't you *ever* say that again," she said, jaw clenched and tears moistening her now scarlet cheeks. "The only lie is in this report." She tossed it on my coffee table. "Read it and see for yourself."

"You have a real strange way of asking people for help." I rubbed my face. "Now get out of my apartment before I have you arrested."

She stormed out of the room, then slammed the door, but I opened it right back up. She power walked along the pool deck toward the gate. "Take this thing with you"—I pointed back to the report with my cane—"or I'm gonna toss it in the trash where it belongs."

"It's staying right there. Maybe you can find some time between drunkenness and self-pity to read it and help me."

"I'm the night watchman!" My voice thundered through the pool area as she scurried around the corner. "I watch everyone else's life go by. I don't catch killers anymore. I'm lucky if I can even catch a cold now."

The maintenance man, Hector something-or-other, stood on the other side of the pool, staring at me. "Women troubles, no?" he said with a stupid grin.

I didn't trust anyone who smiled all the time, and I didn't answer him as I hustled back to my kitchen. I had to walk past the file, which was taking up space on my coffee table.

I grabbed Jim by the neck and decided to eliminate the middleman, leaving the glass on the counter. Her audacity stunned me. What did she think I would do, jump at the chance to take the case?

I went over and sat on the couch, stretching out some. Any chance for a John Wayne marathon was now ruined. The whole foray back into the law enforcement world only elicited thoughts and feelings I wanted nothing to do with.

6

THE BIGGEST PROBLEM in living with Jim as a roommate was waking up. I didn't do too well after a late night with him.

I'd had worse hangovers, but at least I got some sleep, so all was not lost. The dreams, though, were another matter—like some psychedelic montage of Jimi Hendrix music, colliding colorful images, and alcohol-induced plot lines that were like watching a foreign film without subtitles. Weird stuff, but it still beat most of the places my brain went at night without booze.

All too often my dreams, when they weren't of Trisha, would be of me running, kicking, and doing all the things my body used to be able to do. Then I'd wake up, still trapped in this altered reality, like some awful prison sentence with no chance of parole.

I sat at the edge of my bed and massaged the carpet with my toes, debating how long I could reasonably stay here without getting up. Since all day was out of the question, I forced the issue and stood, wobbling more from my hangover than my leg. My bedroom was cave dark so I could sleep during the day. As much as sleep was possible.

My mouth was dry and nasty. I checked out my frame in the full-length mirror on my closet door. My right leg—wrinkled and emaciated—looked like someone crept in during the night and switched it with an old man's.

I grabbed my pants off the hook on my closet door and laid them on the floor. I slipped both feet in and sat back on the bed. I used my left foot to hook the waistband and lift up about eight inches so I didn't have to bend more at the hip. My left hand cinched them up and just over my knees. As I stood, I worked them up the rest of the way, a technique Helga developed for me. I learned it quickly because she said if I didn't, I'd get more table time to stretch those muscles to make it work. It's amazing what a little negative reinforcement could accomplish.

After the production, I caned my way down the hall to the kitchen. The angry chick's folder lay where she tossed it earlier. I didn't dare touch it and left it a good twenty feet away from me as I switched on the coffeepot.

I grabbed cereal with a cheery captain on it—peanut butter crunch, my favorite—off the counter and dug in. Like making Pavlov's dog salivate, the aroma of coffee coaxed me into a semiconscious state, even before I hoisted my first cup. I'm not a coffee connoisseur by any stretch, and I wouldn't be caught dead in one of those expensive java shops, forking out five bucks for a cup. Coffee is merely my caffeine delivery system, and I prefer it hot, black, and strong enough to chip a tooth. If they ever made a caffeine IV drip, I'd be the first in line for it.

I downed my first cup and hiked out to get the paper—the file maybe ten feet from me as I passed. It looked thick, but since I didn't really care what the stupid thing contained, I picked up the *Orlando Sentinel* and would peruse the mayhem in Mickey land before I got moving for the day.

I sat at the kitchen table and turned to the Local section. A young man from the Parramore district was gunned downed in the street around 2:00 a.m. yesterday. No witnesses, or none coming forward. Police think it's drug related, according to Sergeant Yancey. I turned to the Sports page. The Magic lost . . . again. Perusing the Entertainment section, I scanned for any decent movies. Nothing of interest.

I glanced behind me toward the living room, the file still resting comfortably on the table. I bet they established a time line from David Hendricks's phone records and other statements. Did Hank Karpinski see anything odd that day during his shift? I shook my head. What did I care? The thing needed to go to the Dumpster.

I folded the paper and ambled over to the coffee table. I scooped up the file, then started toward the door when a packet of pictures tumbled out onto the floor. As I turned back to pick it up, the entire contents spilled out. A heavy sigh escaped. The day wasn't starting out in my favor.

I settled onto the arm of the couch and spiked my cane between my feet, resting my hands on the handle. The sum of Pampas's case lay scattered in front of me: police narratives, crime scene logs, inventory sheets, photos, diagrams, witness statements, and the medical examiner's report.

Once, my life revolved around investigations like this, drawing me deep into the intimate and often chaotic lives of others. Murders were complicated. The acts themselves were explained easily enough—somebody shot someone for some reason. A then B then C. But probing the victims' personal lives and the suspects' motives was where homicide cops really earned their keep. Sifting through the complex, entangled, and often convoluted schemes of intersecting lives proved to be more art than science. I stabbed at the mess with my cane, the metal tip shuffling the papers around.

Using the arm of the couch, I lowered myself to my good knee, then to a sitting position with my legs outstretched among the clutter. I gathered the papers, photo envelopes, and computer printouts, then returned them to the file. I struggled back up to the couch.

What would it hurt to just give the material a glance? Better yet, who would know? I checked with the Duke's portrait, and he didn't seem to mind.

I slipped Pampas's narrative labeled Murder-Suicide from the file. I scanned the eight pages. No immediate surprises. Everything appeared as it should if David Hendricks murdered his girl-friend, but the read whetted my appetite for more. As I pulled the two photo envelopes from the packet, I felt like some hopeless cop junkie. I'd forgotten how much I enjoyed perusing cases.

The first series of pictures were of the kitchen, living room, and bathroom. Nothing outstanding there. Typical stuff like the thermostat showing the temperature, the windows in the locked position, the medicine cabinet open.

The next set were of Hendricks's bedroom. One was from the doorway into the room, the same view I had in my brief time at the scene. The next was a closeup of David. I studied the photo and moved on slowly to the others.

"Why would that be there?" I flipped back through the photos again, just to make sure I wasn't seeing things. "Now that's really odd."

7

CREVIS SKULKED ALONG the condos' exterior rear doors, searching intently for a phantom white male I had convinced him passed by the cameras twice. I even added the detail of a red skullcap for a little creativity in the story. That should keep him off my back for a while.

I pulled the Hendricks file from my satchel and opened it at the desk. I waited until 2:00 a.m. because almost nothing happened at that time, and it would provide me privacy to review the pictures. Thumbing through the photos, I couldn't shake the nagging feeling that something was really wrong. I didn't like or respect Pampas, but I couldn't let that taint my observations.

I placed the large-scale photo of the entire bedroom on the desk. The female victim, one Jamie DeAngelo, was lying on her back on the bed on top of the covers; the bed was made. She was fully clothed. One gunshot wound to the head.

According to the report, the bullet traveled through the mattress and lodged in the wall molding. A pillow with powder burns on it lay on the floor next to the bed, probably used to silence the shots.

David's body was on the floor, crumpled in almost a fetal position. Pampas speculated that Hendricks shot himself while standing at the foot of the bed, then fell into that position. Maybe. The gun was next to his hand, and he had a wound on the right side of his head. The wound had a blue hue to it, marked by gunpowder burns and stippling consistent with a contact or near-contact shooting.

A small white dot appeared on the wound, possibly matter from the pillow. Pampas determined that pillow remnants must have hung in the air after Hendricks shot Jamie and then landed in the wound after he died. To be fair, small flecks of down dotted other areas of the crime scene. But the particle on his wound looked embedded. An abrasion or carpet burn covered the top of David's right knee. That injury had bled some, indicating that it occurred pre-mortem.

I drew another photo and laid it next to the first. This one troubled me the most. The CSI documented blood from the exit wound on the floor next to Hendricks. The round that killed him was dug out of the wall about two and a half feet above the floor. A little low for a standing contact shot. The hands naturally tilt the weapon high for a self-inflicted wound, not low or downward. If Hendricks was standing, the trajectory of the shot was off. Even if he was on his knees when he pulled the trigger.

Two shell casings were found on the floor to the right of both victims. I wished I'd spent a little more time in the scene that night. But my instincts screamed at me to get Pam and me out of there so we didn't destroy any evidence. The horror on Pam's face wasn't a pleasant memory.

My chair groaned as I worked it back and forth. I glanced at the monitors to make sure the ever-vigilant ghost chaser was waging his war against midnight monotony. Crevis passed by the rear camera for the umpteenth time. He was still good for a while longer.

If Hendricks killed Jamie and himself, why did he use the pillow to silence the shot? Maybe there was a good reason, but only David, or someone else, would know.

Why was the round impact so low on the wall? They just didn't seem to fit.

Why did David have an unaccounted-for abrasion on his right knee? Maybe he and Jamie fought beforehand, but she didn't have any defensive wounds, so it wasn't likely.

Why in the world was I thinking about this at all? I surveyed the lobby and felt the cheap plastic security badge pinned to my shirt. It was so light I hardly noticed it. Not like the thick tin badge I wore before, with a weight that never let me forget it was there.

I closed the file. So many months had passed since I considered investigative procedures that my instincts probably suffered from bedsores and atrophy. Yet with every review of the photos and supplements, I felt more and more drawn to the case. But I was a night watchman now. How far would I take this with Pam?

I checked the monitors again. Crevis hid behind a bush by the back door, scanning the entrance and street for evildoers. I decided to check out David's condo to get a stronger feel for the scene. Maybe I was just being weird about all this; a walk-through would put these nutty notions to rest.

In short order, I was at his door and used the passkey to let myself in. I flipped on the light switch to a barren room. They hadn't sold this unit yet, but all of David's things had been cleared out. I eased down the hall and turned on the light in the bedroom. My second visit to this room was a bit more pleasant. The carpet had been ripped out, probably to be replaced soon. The bullet holes had been patched but not yet painted over. My cane thumped on the wooden floor as I paced along the room.

I didn't believe in psychic energy or karma or dead spirits yearning to communicate with our world. But I did believe in going back through a crime scene to get a feel for the crime, to put myself in the killer's mind, and to understand everything that happened. I held up Jamie's picture where the bed used to be and David's photo where he had been. How did this go down? Did David Hendricks murder Jamie DeAngelo here? Or was something else in play?

The front door jiggled, and I turned off the light and returned the pictures to the file. My heart throbbed, and I reached back and drew my pistol from my waistband. The front door creaked open, and heavy steps approached the room. I stepped back and raised the sights to the middle of the doorway, waiting for whoever was coming my way.

A man walked into the room, the backlight from the hallway silhouetting him. I wasn't sure if he could see me in the darkened room or not. His hand moved to the side. He flipped on the light.

"Don't move," I told him, my sights trained on his mug.

Crevis's hands rose. "I give up." His shock quickly transformed into a grin. "I knew you kept a gun on you. Let me hold it."

"You might get a better look at it if you sneak up on me like that again." I slipped the pistol back in my holster and tucked my shirt around it to conceal it. "How did you know I was here?"

"I looked for you in the lobby, and I saw the elevator just went to the fourth floor. I figured you were coming here to poke around."

Not a bad deduction for Crevis. His attention beaded in on the file. "What are you doing with that stuff? Are you like a secret cop plant or something?"

"Yes, and I flew in on my government helicopter to keep an eye on the Coral Bay Condos." I started toward the door. "You need to get a life, Crevis."

"Really, Ray." He trailed me. "What are you doing here?"

"Let's go back downstairs. We shouldn't be up here in the first place." I'd messed up big-time. Crevis would be bouncing around like a carnival monkey until I told him what was going on.

As I hurried from the room, my foot caught the lip of the carpet in the hallway, and I crashed my crippled carcass against the wall, face first, and then fell to the floor. I rolled onto my back, and Crevis hovered over me.

"Are you okay?" He grabbed my arm and attempted to slip his hands under my armpits.

"Don't touch me!" I slapped his hands away. "Don't ever put your hands on me again."

Crevis stepped back. "Sorry, Ray. I was just trying to help."

"If you really want to help, stay away from me. Now get going. Move!"

Crevis's shoulders lowered, and he walked around me and hustled out of the condo, slamming the door behind him.

Horizontal in the hallway, I stared at an

uncovered light bulb. The sum of my life had come to this—flopping on the floor like a wounded turtle on its back, waiting for someone to right him again.

I hated my life. And I loathed the fact that I secretly hoped Crevis would return and insist on helping me off the floor because I wasn't sure if I could do it myself. But I'd rather have a second set of crime scene tape put up on this condo to mark my death than to pull out my radio and call Crevis back.

My cane was next to me, so I clutched it in my hand. I drew my left leg up and planted it on the ground. I stabbed my cane onto the carpet on my left side and braced my right hand on the wall. With an awkward and ugly push, I twisted myself off the floor.

I paused to catch my breath. How in the world would I chase down leads in this case, and maybe pursue a killer, when a stiff breeze could put me on my keister for the count?

8

AS USUAL, I WAS about fifteen minutes early to the Clubhouse on Pine Street downtown. In the old days whenever I was meeting an informant, I'd always set the time and place and would arrive early—to scout it out beforehand. I wanted to see if anyone wanted to see me. It's a cop thing. The marm was unlikely to ambush me, but some habits were harder to break than others. Another casualty of the job.

I sat in the outdoor pavilion and ordered iced tea. The patio didn't have the closed-in feel the inside did. The Clubhouse had a decent sports bar inside with several televisions playing various games. I gave half attention through the glass to a soccer match. I've never been a team-sports guy and much preferred individual competition: boxing, kickboxing, wrestling (Greco-Roman, not the cheesy television stuff), and mixed martial arts. You had to rely only on yourself, and you had no one else to blame if something went wrong. Now the only sport I'd be competing in was shuffleboard.

Pam Winters scurried up the sidewalk and rushed through the door without seeing me in the patio area. It seemed she liked to be early too, or was just overly curious as to why I called her. She talked with the hostess. I held up my hand when she turned in my direction. She serpentined her way through the patrons and tables and emerged into the patio area.

Her face revealed the conflicting emotions she must be experiencing—apprehension at seeing me again after our last meeting, and nagging curiosity about my phone call. After a pregnant pause long enough to give birth to triplets, I pointed to the chair next to me.

She sat with her purse clutched on her lap. Pam was an attractive woman. She wore blue jeans and a red button-up shirt; her blond hair was tied back in a ponytail. We didn't exchange pleasantries, only awkward stares until she broke the silence.

"I'm glad you called. I've wanted to talk with you since . . . the other day."

"Yeah, I wanted to talk too, but I thought we should meet in a public place, just in case you were going to beat me up again." I twisted the handle of my cane, digging the tip into a crack in the concrete.

Her shoulders lowered. "I'm so sorry. I've never hit anyone before in my life."

"Well, you're pretty good at it." The nicest part about religious people is you can use guilt against them like a carefully crafted blade, slicing at will with surgical precision. She'd be easier than expected. "If you kick like you punch, you could make a good bantamweight kickboxer. You'd probably rule the division, maybe even be a world champion."

She didn't look at me, her eyes fixed on the pavement. I detest any man who would strike a woman, but I had no problem with a little psychological payback for her smacking me.

"Well, you'll be happy to know I've decided not to have you arrested. But I think you loosened a crown." I rubbed my jaw. "We'll have to work out the dental bills later."

"Is that the only reason you called? You could have done this on the phone." She sighed. "I'm sorry I lost it. My emotions are a wreck right now, and I'm on edge about everything. Please forgive me, Mr. Quinn. He's my brother, my only family. If you want to poke more fun at me, that's fine, but did you review the file? That's all I care about."

I took a protracted drink of my tea. What should I tell her? I figured she'd paid enough for the slap, so now it was time for the real reason I called her. My hesitation drew her eyes to mine as sure as a magnet would snatch up a tack. They were penetrating and vibrant, yet sad. Maybe it was time to flip my filter back on.

"You did look at it." She scooted her chair closer to the table.

"Did your brother have any enemies?"

She shook her head. "No one would have wanted to hurt him. You saw something in the case?"

"Did he owe anyone any money? Have any outstanding debts, any gambling or other habits?"

"No. What did you *see*?" She leaned forward, as if ready to crawl across the table at me. I kept my distance.

"Who is this Jamie DeAngelo, and how does she know your brother?"

"Stop playing games with me, Ray Quinn. Is there something wrong with the case?"

I spun my glass on the tabletop, the condensation making it twirl with relative ease. "I have questions about the investigation."

"So you believe David was murdered too?"

"I'm not going that far. But some things about the scene and the motive don't add up."

"Praise God, someone finally believes me." An exhausted rush of air pumped from her lungs as if it were her last breath. "I knew he didn't do it."

I lifted a hand and pointed it at her. "You need to slow down. I said I have questions, nothing else. Maybe there are simple answers that I'm unaware of, so don't start acquitting anyone and dancing around praising God."

She pursed her lips and nodded, but I didn't think she really listened to what I said. A gleam of something very dangerous sparked on her face—hope. Someone in her situation would hear what she wanted to hear, then block everything else out.

I didn't know what to think of this woman. Not just her smacking me; I could live with that. I wasn't sure if I trusted her and her motivations. But even worse, I didn't trust myself. My instincts had failed me once before—with catastrophic results. Could I trust them again with something so serious?

"What questions do you have?" she said.

I struggled for the right words. I needed to move cautiously to keep her from getting the wrong impression. "I looked at the crime scene photos, and I noticed a couple of things. But before we go any further, you need to decide how much you want to hear. This is ugly business, and we're talking about your brother. Some of these things can be brutal. So tell me how much you can tolerate."

"I want to know everything. Let me worry about the consequences."

A spunky woman for sure. I'd give her that. "Okay, it looks like whoever did this used a pillow over the muzzle of the barrel to silence the shots. There are several holes in David's pillow, and it was found on the floor next to him."

She nodded. "Sergeant Yancey said the condos are so close together that he . . . David . . . didn't want anyone to hear the shots."

"True. But if he's distraught about their relationship, as the report concluded, why does he try to muffle the sounds? If he's going to take his own life, would he really care? That bothers me."

"Sergeant Yancey also said they found gunshot residue on David's hands, proving that he fired the shots. How can that be?"

"They test the skin and hairs of the hand for barium and antimony, gunpowder components that embed in your hand when you fire a gun. There could be a number of reasons why there's residue on David's hands, but that's a tough one to overcome. Between that and the fact that the door was locked and there were no signs of forced entry, I'm not sure what to make of all this yet."

"What else?" she said.

"The phone records. Your brother was the last person to call her cell phone. That's significant, but I didn't see a list of the other calls she received that day."

"What does that mean?"

"It means Pampas is lazy." I tried not to let my disdain for him show in my voice. Okay, I didn't try that hard.

"If he's not smart or competent, why do they keep him as a homicide detective? Shouldn't he be fired or something?"

"I didn't say he wasn't smart. He's very intelligent. That's what aggravates me to no end. He's capable of good, solid investigation, but he's notorious for cutting corners. And he's smart enough to cover his rear end and look good while doing it."

Not so surprisingly, Pampas was investigating Trisha's and my shooting, which was still unsolved.

She fell back against her chair and sighed. "So where does that leave us? What can we do?"

"I'm not sure if there is a 'we' in this conversation. I just gave you my observations. I don't think all the questions of this case were answered. It's like a puzzle without all the pieces. It might be exactly what the report says it is, but without those pieces, you can't know for sure."

"But you think it's possible my brother didn't do this?"

"There's more that could be done."

"Will they reopen the case with what you told me? I mean, it makes sense. Sergeant Yancey is your friend; can't you get him to assign another detective to run with this?"

I shook my head. "Oscar's a good cop, but he's sitting on a stack of fresh homicides right now. He can't afford to put them on hold to revisit this. We don't have enough to reopen anything. Only questions."

"You said *we,*" she said with a small smile. "Maybe you could just investigate a few things. If you find irrefutable proof, the sergeant might consider it."

Pam was minimizing things to draw me in. Shrewd little woman as well, especially since it was working. But could I really get involved, then turn the investigation over to Oscar? My psyche was at war with itself. Reviewing the file and talking about the case with Pam teased from me emotions I thought were long dead—like the thrill of delving back into a world that had chewed me up and spit me out a year ago. But the thrill would only get me so far, because my fear and apprehension were just as intense and palpable.

I tapped my finger on the folder. What really happened at Coral Bay Condos a month ago? Did Hendricks shoot that woman in cold blood and then take his own life? Or did someone go to elaborate means to make it look that way?

"I need to see your brother's office." I succumbed to the thrill, for however long it might last. What could a little inquiry hurt? It wasn't like I had a busy social schedule or anything.

Pam nodded with a silly grin on her face.

"But before you start celebrating, you need to be sure you're ready for the answers we uncover. They might not be the ones you hope for."

"The truth will come out." She rested her elbows on the table. "And I won't be surprised by it. David didn't do this."

"I wish I shared your certainty."

9

THIS AREA OF ORLANDO had been wounded and all but left for dead. Outreach Orlando Ministries was remarkably ordinary and easy to pass without a second thought. It was tucked away in a warehouse at the corner of Concord Street and North Orange Avenue, which was set for a revitalization program in the near future. I hadn't been to many churches in my life, but I expected something a little different: a cathedral-type building, large arches, or something ornate.

Pam paced along the sidewalk in the front of the ministry. It was sort of refreshing to have a young lady smile at my approach. But the acid churning in my stomach made me think her joy could be short lived. I hoped I was wrong, but optimism is a luxury most cops can't afford.

"Thanks for coming." She stepped forward like she was going to hug me but stopped and shook my hand. "I'll take you in and show you around, then we can get started."

Two men were talking on the front step; the unkempt clothing and poor grooming indicated they were probably homeless and seeking refuge. The front double doors had suffered abuse from years of use and squeaked as we pushed through. A reception window with a sign-in board was to my left, and straight ahead down the hallway, a larger room opened up with a row of beds.

"Mario, it's good to see you," Pam said to the man in the office.

Well tanned and slightly taller than Pam, Mario rose from his desk and walked around it to the window. He wore blue jeans, a white T-shirt, and black work boots. Deep lines creased a face with a crooked nose that appeared to have seen its fair share of punches. With a shaved head and bulging biceps, the guy bore a tapestry of tattoos that would be the envy of any Hell's Angel. I'd seen the artwork before. Mario had done time.

He hugged Pam. "How are you holding up?"

"Better. This is a friend of mine, Ray Quinn."

"Ray." Mario extended his hand. His accent was from the Northeast, possibly Boston. He sized me up, scanning up and down like a fighter. He was checking for weaknesses, which explained why he focused on my cane and legs. Cops, fighters, and ex-cons greet people this way. I did the same thing to him.

Any chance of subtlety or a cold read on Mario was destroyed when Pam broadcast, "Ray used to work as a homicide detective and is helping me with David's case."

I'd have to talk to her about that. Sometimes it's best for people not to know the whole story. People talk to you differently when they know you're a cop—or, in my case, used to be.

"Ah, good." Mario stepped back. His mouth said "good," but his eyes didn't seem so sure. "We can use all the help we can get. Where did you work?"

"OPD," I said, not offering any more. "Can we see David's office?"

"Sure. Follow me." Mario ushered us behind the reception window into the office area. David's office split off to the right and displayed the same prosaic décor as the rest of the building. It contained a simple wooden desk with a computer; a bookshelf was behind the desk, mostly theology stuff with a few novels slipped in.

"We've left everything as it was," Mario said. "Figured the cops would want to go through his things. We don't know if anyone will replace David yet or not."

"Thank you, Mario." She squeezed his shoulder. "David would be proud of what you've done. You've had a lot thrown at you all at once."

Mario's head lowered. "Pam, I gotta be honest. I

feel like I'm failing him. Since . . . since this happened, our donations have dropped to almost nothing. We have a little in savings. David managed the money well, but I don't know how long we can hold out. We're still housing about eighty clients a night, more when it's colder, and no one wants to support us with something like this hanging over our head. David built this ministry from nothing, and now it's dying. I just don't know what to do."

"I don't understand it either." She took his hand. "But we either believe God is in control or we go crazy. We'll find a way to make this work. We can't let David's dream die."

He nodded but didn't make eye contact with her. "I know. But it's still hard."

"Mario," a voice called from the window. "There's a delivery in the back."

"On my way." Mario wiped his eyes and headed out of the room. "I've got to clear this, then I'll be back."

Pam gazed my way. "Mario's been broken up about all of this. He was one of David's best friends and a real blessing to the ministry."

"I'd bet he's done a bit of prison time."

Pam cocked her head. "You think you're telling me something I don't know? He served five years for armed robbery. He'd been involved in crime since he was young, in and out of juvenile hall, then finally prison."

"And you have him here working with the money and everything? Not the best idea I've ever heard."

"He gave his life to Jesus Christ in prison and has been faithful to that call ever since. Mario has done amazing things here, and can relate to a lot of the people who walk through these doors in ways few people can."

"I gave you an observation, that's all. I don't trust ex-cons, and I'm not sure it's the wisest move to put them in charge of anything. But that's the ministry's business, not mine. I'm just looking around."

"You don't believe people can change?"

"Very rarely. And even then, I'm not inclined to trust them. Human beings are predictable—past behavior is the best indicator of future behavior." I sat in David's chair. "Since we're on the subject of trust, could you please not announce to everyone who I am and what I'm doing? I need to be a little more subtle, if you know what I mean."

"I'm sorry I'm not very good at this." She picked up a picture from the bookshelf of her, David, and an older couple I assumed were their parents.

Pam and David appeared to be in their mid-teens; she favored her mother, with the same high cheekbones and fair skin.

"Nice picture." I still wasn't sure what I could share with Pam—and what I couldn't. She had jumped to Mario's defense awfully quick. "You and David seemed close."

"We were. We grew up on the mission field. Our parents served in Papua New Guinea, so we had to rely on each other. We spent a lot of time boarding at the mission school. Sometimes I felt more like David's mother than his sister."

"Sounds interesting," was about all I could muster. I didn't understand the whole traveling to other countries and living in squalor just to tell a few Bible stories. Didn't seem like much of a life.

"Don't you have any brothers or sisters?"

"I'm an only child." Which was technically true, as far as I knew. Having been raised in the Florida foster care system, I never knew my parents or siblings if I had any.

I pulled my digital camera from my pocket and snapped a few photos of the bookshelf and the rest of the office. You never knew what you might miss while looking around. Once the scene was gone or tampered with, you could never re-create it.

She brushed some dust from the frame. "Seems like a lifetime ago. David was so excited. He was ready to tackle the world." She sighed and set the photo on the shelf.

"I need to take a look at his computer." I turned on the power. The background popped up, a picture of Jesus holding some guy who had a mallet and nail in his hand. Nice. I half expected a comment from Pam, but none came.

David's computer wasn't password protected. Trusting guy—or foolish. I attached my external hard drive to the USB port and started copying his hard drive. When I had time, I'd go through his last e-mails and contacts. He had QuickBooks loaded as well as Excel, so I'd review his financial records too.

There are a few reasons why people kill other people—most of the time it revolves around money or sex. Sometimes there's a deranged killer who does things beyond explanation. Or there's revenge. But if you dig deeper into the revenge motive, you'll almost always find money or sex at the root. If cops follow those angles, they'll almost always find their suspects. *So much for just asking a few questions.* My old instincts were kicking in, albeit a little slowly.

Mario walked back in. "Hey, what do you think you're doing?"

"Looking," I said, not inclined to explain myself to the ex-con.

"What exactly are you looking for?" Mario said. "And don't you need a warrant for that?"

"Information." I swiveled the chair around and faced him as the hard-drive copying continued. "Any problem with that?"

He clenched his fists and took a deep breath. Pam flashed him a stand-down stare. "There's just a lot of ministry business on there, so you should've at least asked."

"David's business is on there as well, which means it's my business now." I pushed back in the chair and steepled my fingers. It was his move next, and that would tell me volumes about him. "But you decide if I can take this or not. If there's something on here you don't want me to see, just let me know. Your call."

"Pam?" He opened his arms, palms up. "I don't like this. I want to help, but we can't have someone digging through our stuff. There's sensitive financial records and donor information we have a responsibility to protect."

"Ray knows what he's doing. It could help find David's killer."

Mario's demeanor softened, with Pam anyway. He glared at me with his fiery felon eyes. "Fine. Take what you need."

I checked the screen. Two more minutes before the copying was complete. Mario made a good decision, but regardless of what he would have said, I was leaving with that hard drive. I just wanted to hear his objections before I took it. That could point me in a valuable direction.

"Do you know the girl, Jamie DeAngelo, who was found dead with David?" I said.

"Never heard the name," Mario said.

"Did David ever mention that he was dating anyone?"

"He would have told me if he was." Pam glanced at me. I preached to her with my eyes. Mario needed to answer his own questions.

"No. And I think I would've known if he was,"

Mario said. "Most people tend to keep their lives private. Not David. He was a pretty open book."

"Did David seem worried about anything?" I said. "Do you know of anyone who would want to harm him?"

"Look, we run a street ministry." Mario tossed his inked arms in the air. "We give meals to those in need. We help people get jobs, give 'em a place to stay for a while if they need it, and help get them into rehab. We preach the gospel. The streets can be tough at times, but no one wanted to kill David for helping people."

"What do you think happened to him?" I said.

Mario paused and glanced sideways at Pam. "I don't know. I just don't know."

"Well, there are only two possible explanations." I stood and faced them. "David either did what the detectives claim, or someone murdered him and Jamie DeAngelo."

10

WHEN I TOLD PAM I was going to talk with Jamie's best friend, Ashley Vargas, she begged me to tag along. I filed several cogent and passionate objections to her coming with me—none of them being the true reason. She finally agreed it would be best for me to do the legwork alone, even if one of my legs was hobbled.

Since Ashley worked as a dancer or "entertainer" with Jamie at Club Venus on Orange Blossom Trail, I knew all too well the world I was entering. The fundamentalist schoolmarm had no clue who or what I might have to deal with. We might get into some sensitive areas regarding David's relationship with Jamie, and that could be a bit dicey. Pam would hamper any serious discussions. She said she was ready to hear everything, but I wasn't convinced.

David was less of a mystery now, although I hadn't exonerated him yet. I definitely wanted to know more about Mario, but that would come in due time. I needed to know who Jamie DeAngelo was, how she was linked to David, and what—exactly—was the nature of their relationship.

Pampas's report stated they were involved in a sexual relationship, but he didn't have much corroborating evidence, other than Jamie's history as a dancer, one arrest for prostitution two years before, and her being on David's bed when she was murdered. While that theory was probably correct, I needed something more tangible before I'd say that with conviction, especially since she was fully clothed and lying on top of the covers at the time of death.

I arrived at Ashley's complex, the Fox Croft Apartments, just off State Road 528 at Narcoossee Road near Orlando International Airport. I grabbed the file and checked her picture again. Blond, young, and attractive, Ashley was around the same age as Jamie, twenty-three. She drove a green Honda Civic, which I spotted in the parking lot, so odds were good she was home.

The day after the bodies were found, Pampas got a brief one-page statement from Ashley. Nothing revealing in it, just that she and Jamie had worked together and Jamie had known David for a few months. Since Ashley was the only friend listed in the report, I hoped she could enlighten me about Jamie DeAngelo.

Ashley lived in apartment 311, and there was no elevator. Lovely. I scaled the first set of steps and took a break on the landing to the second floor. I was as winded as if I'd just hiked Everest. The same round that broke my arm also ripped into the right side of my chest, collapsing both lungs. The other took out my hip and pelvis.

They said I was lucky to survive. I didn't feel so lucky. Recently I had been able to increase my aerobic endurance by the pool workouts dear Helga developed for me, but this little jaunt revealed how out of shape I really was. I made it to the top; Helga would have been proud of me. Maybe I should have planted a flag up here in her honor.

I took a left from the stairs and found Ashley's apartment. The television blared so loud I had to pound twice before she came to the door.

"What do you want now?" She swung the door wide and stood with one hand on her hip, the other on the edge of the door.

"My name is Ray Quinn." I flipped out my wallet with my badge and ID. "I'd like to talk with you about Jamie DeAngelo."

She glanced at the badge and opened the door wider. If she'd taken the time to actually read the ID, it clearly stated I was a *retired* Orlando cop. I had several stories prepared about why I was here asking questions, but since she didn't ask, I didn't offer.

"I'm sorry." She rubbed her eyes. "I thought you were the manager again. He's been on my case since I moved here."

"No problem. Do you mind if I come in?"

She waved me in as she sauntered toward the television and turned it off. It looked like Springer had another lively show going on. Too bad we had to miss it.

Ashley directed me to a small kitchen table next to a freestanding birdcage containing an animal I was loath to correctly identify. (I'm not a big nature guy.) I think it was in the parrot family, and the thing had a huge hooked beak that could remove a finger with ease. As I sat next to it, it squawked and waddled across its little perch to the edge of the cage in an attempt to stare me down. If Ashley weren't watching, I would have pacified it with my cane.

She pulled up the chair next to mine. She wore a pink muscle T-shirt, and I use the term *wore* in the loosest sense of the word, as it just barely

77

covered her, depending on how she shifted in the chair. The well-maintained chemical-blond hair from her driver's license picture had been replaced with a bed-head mess I suspected she used to house the bird at night. She didn't seem concerned about her appearance. Maybe working all night trying to attract men to make a buck numbs a girl to prettying up in the off-hours. She pulled a cigarette from her purse.

"What did you do to your leg?" Her raspy voice seemed too old for her.

"Long story. I wanted to talk with you about Jamie. Tie up some loose ends and all."

"I already told you guys about Jamie." The cigarette smoke mixed with an overpowering odor from my feathered friend to the point that I wanted to cut the interview short. "I'm still pretty upset. She was a good girl and didn't deserve that."

"I'm doing some follow-up on the case and wanted to make sure I have everything." I turned on my thin digital recorder and placed it on the table. I explained the formalities of the statement, then asked her name and date of birth for the record. She raised her right hand as she answered. Since I was looking into this, I might as well do it right. I like having details on tape, so there's no arguing later about who said what. Memory can be imprecise.

"You were friends with Jamie DeAngelo when this murder happened, correct?"

"Yeah. We worked together at Club Venus. I still work there." She glanced at the clock. "I had a shift last night and didn't get off until early this morning, so I'm still a little outta sorts."

"Did you ever see this guy there?" I held out a photo of David Hendricks.

"No. Like I told the other cop, he never came to the club."

"But you do know him?"

"Jamie and I met him at Starbucks one morning. He was in line behind us and started up a conversation. He and Jamie chatted away, but I thought he was hitting on us, so I didn't say much. Then he started with the God and Jesus stuff. I just let her do the talking, if you know what I mean."

"How long was this before the murder?"

"Maybe two or three months." Ashley extinguished the butt of the cancer stick while reaching for another. A veil of tobacco residue hovered around me; my eyes watered.

"What was their relationship like after that?" I coughed. "Were they seeing each other?"

"I guess so. Why else would he hang around her?"

Big Bird shrieked in my ear, and I jerked in my chair.

"Oh, pipe down, you big bundle of feathers. We have a guest." She smiled at me. "He's harmless."

I squeezed the brass handle of my cane and waged a valiant fight not to play an inning of birdie baseball with my noisy friend. Between Big Bird and Puff the Magic Dancer, my filter was facing its greatest challenge in some time. I needed to get back on track.

"Was there anyone who'd want to hurt her?"

"Jamie was sweet but a real bum magnet. She loved the losers. She was seeing a guy about a year ago, a bad drug-dealer type. He'd knock her around quite a bit. One night, he beat her so bad she had to go to the hospital."

"Who is this guy?"

"Tay or something like that," Ashley said. "She stopped hanging out with him shortly after she came to the club."

"Is Tay his street name, real name, last name, or what?"

She shrugged. "I only know Tay. Never saw or met the guy."

I pulled a notepad from my pocket and jotted down some names. I'd try to catch up with this Tay later. "Was she dating anyone else?"

"She mentioned a couple of guys. I think one was rich because she kept showing me presents he gave her, like clothes and jewelry. She didn't say much about the other one, except that he was very demanding. She didn't look happy when she said that. I figured he was another one of her deadbeat boyfriends."

"Any names, descriptions?"

"No. Jamie wasn't like that. She kept her business close to her." Ashley smooched her cigarette like a lover, puffing a plume of smoke over the table. Silence engulfed the room for the first time since I entered; even the bird hushed. Ashley glanced at the recorder. "Can you turn that thing off for a minute?"

I picked up the recorder and flipped it off. It was clear that something was bothering her, and I didn't want to let anything stand in the way of her telling me.

She scanned the room, as if expecting to see someone other than Big Bird and me. "I don't want this part on the record or however that works."

"Fair enough." I laid my pen on the table and leaned back in the chair.

"Do you think someone other than the preacher guy killed her?" She hit the cigarette hard again and exhaled dramatically. "It seems that way from what you're asking."

"I don't know for sure." I shrugged. "Maybe." I'd revealed a little more than I wanted, but I hoped my answer would prompt her to tell me what was really on her mind.

Ashley brushed some dust off the table for several seconds before engaging me again. "Jamie's life was . . . complicated. She had people coming down on her. I don't think she wanted to do this anymore. You know . . . entertain and dance and stuff. I think she was just done with it all."

"Who was coming down on her?"

81

"Chance Thompson, the manager at Club Venus, for one. He put her under a lot of pressure. He always wanted more and more from *his* girls."

"I imagine he puts all the girls there under pressure," I said. "That's what guys who run those clubs do. They try to keep the girls down so they can rake in the cash. I'm sure you know that better than I do."

"You don't understand. Jamie was different. She was . . ." Ashley toyed with an errant lock of hair hanging down across her eyes. "I don't know if I should say this."

The tinglies swam down my spine, and I did everything I could not to telegraph to her that we'd just hit a hot spot. I was so giggly I almost reached in and tickled the bird. The foreboding beak kept me from doing that. I'd forgotten how much I loved a good interview, extracting information out of reluctant souls.

"She was what, Ashley? What's so important that it's bothering you so much?"

"She was one of Chance's special girls. Jamie was part of the Lion's Den."

"What's that?"

"It's a spin-off of Club Venus," she said. "Only a few of the hottest girls worked there. Jamie was gorgeous and made a ton of money when she danced. Chance's girls entertain for some powerful and very private groups. Men who like a little more discretion and attention with their entertainment. No one outside of the Lion's Den is supposed to know it even exists . . . but I do."

"How did you find out about it?"

"Jamie got high one night and spouted off some things about Chance and the Lion's Den and important, powerful people. Then the next day she came over and begged me not to tell anyone. If anyone found out she talked, she could be in serious trouble. Jamie was crying and seemed pretty upset."

"Did you tell the other detective about this?"

"No," she said. "It seemed like you guys already thought the preacher killed her. Why would I bring up all this other stuff?"

"Do you know any of the players with the Lion's Den?"

"Bigwigs. Connected and rich people. City officials, power brokers, judges, lawyers . . . and cops."

Her smirk told me she knew she'd scored a hit. For the first time in the interview, I didn't quite know what to say, and she had me flatfooted and against the ropes. I let the peculiar pause pass and regained my bearings.

"How sure are you about this? The cop part?"

"Only what Jamie told me, and she had no reason to lie. She said she wouldn't tell me any names of the Lion's Den, but if she did, I'd recognize some of them. I've been around dancers for a couple of years now. A lot of them talk trash and can't be trusted. Jamie had her problems, but she was honest. She shared all this with me a couple of weeks before she died, just before she started acting really weird."

"What do you mean *weird?*" I was sure her definition and mine would differ significantly.

"Jamie didn't want to party with me anymore. She stopped . . . you know, using and all. She'd ask me stupid questions about life, God, her purpose, and stuff like that. I think the preacher guy was getting into her head."

"Did she ever say she was afraid of the preacher?"

"No. She just said he was really nice and listened to her. That's why I have a hard time believing he murdered her. But I guess you never really know people."

She was starting to sound like me, which creeped me out a bit.

"Detective Quinn, I only told you this in case the preacher man didn't kill her. I want whoever did it to pay. But if what Jamie said about the Lion's Den is true, then these people can make a girl like me disappear. Don't tell anyone you talked to me, especially any of your cop friends. I can't afford for any of this to get out."

No one had called me Detective Quinn in a very long time. I probably should have corrected her right then and explained myself. But I didn't. For a moment, I felt like my old self. I was so into the interview, I mostly dismissed the ache in my leg.

"I give you my word. No one will know we talked." I stood and thanked her for her help. I stuffed my recorder in my pants pocket and loaded up the notebook.

"One more thing, Detective. If you're going to take on Chance, be very careful. He acts all nice to everyone's face, but he's got a mean streak. You seem like a nice guy, and I'd hate to see you get hurt."

That was the second time in recent history that someone called me nice. Maybe it was the cane.

"Don't worry, Ashley. I'll be fine. And just for the record—I'm not that nice."

I headed out the door and mentally prepared for the perilous descent to the parking lot from Mount Birdbreath. I slipped my second recorder out of my top pocket and shut it off. Her comment made me feel a twinge of guilt for keeping it on when she spilled her story. But it faded quickly. That information was much too juicy to lose. I took the stairs carefully and hoped the breeze would brush off some of the stench from my clothes; I smelled like the backseat of a taxi.

Ashley turned my little fact-finding mission upside down and made me question Pampas's conclusions even more. If he'd taken the time to actually talk with Ashley, perhaps he would have discovered this information too.

I'd check out this Tay guy, see if he was around and still interested in Jamie. Then I'd track down her dating schedule, which sounded like it would be voluminous and time consuming.

Ashley's revelations about the Lion's Den were disconcerting, especially the possibility of tainted cops in the mix. I wasn't so naive to think that officers couldn't be corrupted; I'd seen more than a few fall and crash hard. But a dirty cop is the worst kind of criminal—he knows the system, knows our tactics, and isn't afraid to take people out if necessary. My list of tasks in this case had just grown considerably.

But the first order of business was to chase down Chance Thompson.

11

HELGA ONCE TOLD ME, just before tweaking my hip in that special way of hers, that sometimes she'd have to hurt me to help me.

This statement came barreling back to me as I checked David's Internet history on his computer. Some sites he'd visited were inappropriate at best, bizarre at worst—especially for a so-called pastor. They'd been deleted from the history, but I had software on my laptop that could retrieve deleted pictures and Web site info. It had come in handy more than once on homicide investigations. Just when I thought this David character might be the real deal, I discovered he had a couple of predilections that bordered on the very disturbed.

The all-too-quick knock came at my apartment door. Pam was early . . . again. I printed the list of porn sites, then turned it facedown on the table before I opened the door.

Refreshed and in a much better place than I'd ever seen her before, Pam looked almost giddy. Her hair wasn't tied up in the usual ponytail, and her blond locks bounced around her shoulders. It was a good look for her. She'd wanted an update, and I promised I'd tell her about my visit with Ashley earlier today. I just wished I had more time between my discovery of his Internet viewing habits and her visit to formulate how and what to tell her.

"Ray"—she extended her hand—"how'd it go?"

I shrugged. "Learned a little."

"Is everything all right? You seem down."

"I'm fine," I lied. If I didn't plan to visit Club Venus later tonight, I'd have already been talking with Jim. He'd help me wash down the bitter taste of this finding. But I needed to be somewhat sober for my upcoming visit.

I told Pam about my talk with Ashley, how she'd told me things she didn't reveal to Pampas. I told her about the Lion's Den, but not about the types of people they served—especially the cop angle, which turned my stomach. No use going there until I had something more concrete.

"This is fantastic," she said. "I knew you'd come up with something."

"Well, I've come up with a little bit more." I didn't know quite what to say, which was really unusual for me. So I limped over to the table, grabbed the sheet, and handed it to her. "I found these sites on your brother's Internet history. They'd been deleted in an attempt to hide them. There could be more. I haven't been able to check everything yet."

She read a few lines, then glanced back at me like someone had just given her a death notice. "This can't be."

"I'm sorry, Pam. I've checked out a couple of the sites and would recommend that you do not. The names will tell you everything you need to know. It seems there were things in your brother's life nobody knew about, not even you."

Her eyes scrolled down the list, and the room was eerie quiet for a while.

Just because Hendricks surfed porn sites didn't mean he was a killer. But it did chip away at the facade of his being a super Christian and practically perfect in every way. He had issues and definitely dabbled with a double life, if only in his head. But that's where murder starts—as a thought, a passing rumination of the possible that morphs into something monstrous and ugly. Maybe Pampas had this whole thing right to begin with, which irked me to consider.

"This isn't right," she said, more asking than telling. "David . . . There's got to be some other explanation."

"It's pretty clear. He had stuff going on in his life—weird stuff."

"But even if that were true, it doesn't mean he killed anyone. He could have been struggling with this and still not murdered that girl."

"I know that," I said. "But it doesn't help his case either. He's at least hanging out with strippers and looking up porn on his computer. And, Pam, haven't you asked yourself why your brother was carrying on a relationship with Jamie and neither you nor Mario, the closest people in his life, knew anything about it? Doesn't that strike you as odd, especially for a pastor?"

She poured herself down onto the couch, her shoulders rolling forward, the incriminating writ still clutched in her hand. "Of course I've thought about that—every single day since this happened. I can't explain any of this. But the David I knew couldn't have done what we saw that night. That wasn't my brother."

"We don't know what other things he could have been into, so I can't take him off the table at this point."

"So now you think this trash proves he's a murderer?" She waved the paper in the air.

"I don't know what to think. My interview with Ashley opened up a whole new direction to pursue. I need to find out more about the Lion's Den and what was really going on with Jamie. But I can't and won't ignore the facts. If David did do this, I won't lie to you."

Pam stared at my blank television screen awhile. "Are all men driven by their lusts and desires? Is that the only thing that motivates you? Just grab as much pleasure as you can and then move on?"

Not the line of questioning I expected from her. How in the world did I answer that?

"My husband left me," she blurted out. "Out of the blue, he just walked out of my life."

I gave a sympathetic nod, not tipping my hand that I already knew this. The indentation on her ring finger was a good indicator of a failed marriage, but so was the divorce decree on the Orange County Clerk of Courts Web site. I dug up her marriage certificate, the divorce decree, and the final sale of their home.

Some days I feel like a snoop, nosing around in everyone else's business, but after Pam showed up and made her bizarre request to clear her brother's name, I needed to know who and what I was dealing with. I don't like surprises. I may have stopped being a cop in title a year ago, but I don't know if I can ever pry the cop from my psyche—even with good therapy, strong medication, and a crowbar.

"He left me eight months ago for another woman, a teacher I used to work with who I thought was my friend. I came home one day thinking everything was fine, and he was gone. He said they'd fallen in love and it was over between us. We'd been married barely two years. We were looking to start a family . . ."

"I didn't think religious people believed in divorce."

"I could love God and forgive my husband, but even that wasn't enough to make him stay. He ruined our marriage just to satisfy his lust. Now this with David. I just don't understand what's happening, what God can be doing in all of this."

At least we agreed on that. But if we kept this gloomy conversation going, we'd both soon be drinking poisoned Kool-Aid and waiting for the mother ship to come take us away. *Time for a new direction.*

"Look, there's still a lot for us to investigate. I'm going to talk with Jamie's ex-boss and see what info I can glean. I want to go through more of David's finances as well and see what's up on the ministry's side."

"I need to go." She stood, oblivious to me, then ambled to the door with the printout still in her hand. "I don't feel so well."

I took hold of the list. She wouldn't let it go.

"Why don't you let me keep this?" If she walked out the door with that list, she'd be on the Internet looking up Web addresses. Her tenacity reminded me a lot of my former partner Trisha,

which made the conversation all the more difficult. Trisha would have done that, to be sure.

Pam finally turned my way and surrendered the
list. I walked her out to her car. She was pleasant
and said good-bye, but her vacant eyes told a different story: her heart was broken . . . again.

After she drove away, I caned my way back
through the gate, then stopped alongside the pool,
its stench repulsive in the humid night air. As the
algae breathed, little air pockets snapped and
popped like crispy rice cereal with milk poured on
it. The polluted creature was alive and growing.

I wished that I could take back a hundred things
in my life—mostly the day I was shot and the day
I ever thought about helping Pam. *The only thing
I've been able to accomplish so far is to inflict
more pain on her and myself. Maybe I should
just shut up, stop asking questions, and send
Pam on her pleasantly ignorant way.*

I probed the pool with the end of my cane and
swirled it around like Jell-O. The green goo clung
to the tip, so I scraped it along the concrete. I
took a nickel from my pocket, then flipped it out
about a yard; it smacked the surface and
remained for a moment before the bubbling beast
drew the coin into its murky depths. I probably
had ten bucks on the bottom of that pool.

I inched precariously to the edge. What would
happen if I lost my balance and plunged into the
slimy mix? Or even better, if I spread my arms

and belly-flopped into the noxious creature only to be sucked into the abyss? I could just slip away, probably unnoticed for months.

Most important, I could experience the preciousness of rest again—the kind of sleep I could only fantasize about now but yearned for daily.

I eyed the green goo again. Maybe a final sleep awaited me there, a rest beyond all imagination. Or maybe something else. Heaven? Hell? Nothing? I knew what Pam would say.

"Fools rush in where angels fear to tread," someone once said. Don't know if I believe in angels, but I've seen enough fools to know this statement is at least true on its face. If there is a God—and that's a very big *if* in my book—I believe He does punish people for their sins.

And for mine, He let me live.

12

THE BLINDING PURPLE NEON of Club Venus pulsed in the night like some beacon to the lonely and depraved. It had to be clearly visible from the space station.

The gaudy sign hung out practically across International Drive. And to add to the odd décor, the place had valet parking. I decided to park myself in the back. This wasn't going to be an all-nighter.

I had headed out to Club Venus to scope out the

93

place and get some face time with Chance Thompson, get a feel for him. The revelations about David weren't sitting well with me, and I couldn't dismiss what I'd uncovered so far. I couldn't think of any reason why Ashley would lie to me about Chance, the Lion's Den, and Jamie, but you never know with people. I had to check it out. Besides, after my conversation with Pam, I needed to get out of the cave for a while.

Ashley's advice to watch myself with Chance seemed wise. I checked my accoutrements before I got going, especially my Glock and the backup Kel-Tec .380 in my pocket. I used to carry my backup on my ankle, but if I needed it in a hurry now, I'd have rigor mortis before I could ever bend down and get it out of that holster. The pocket gun worked fine for what I needed.

I adjusted the recorder in my other pocket, then grabbed a smaller envelope I could carry in with me.

I paid the cover: ten bucks. Prices had gone up since I used to club hop. I walked past two bouncers dressed in black long-sleeve dress shirts with red bowties—in a vain attempt to add some respectability to the bar. One guy was a solid six-six with a moon head that could eclipse the sun. The second guy was a little shorter, but what he didn't have in height, he made up for in girth. His shirt sleeves stretched tight over swollen arms. He could give my dear Helga a difficult rumble. My money would still be on Helga, though, for sheer meanness, if nothing else. Club Venus took its security seriously.

Strip bars were never my thing, a waste of time and money, and I couldn't in my wildest dreams imagine John Wayne standing at the edge of a stage, jumping up and down like an idiot with a wad of cash in his hands. He had more class than that, and whatever else was going on in my life, I'd like to think that I did too.

As I entered the main bar area, a large disco ball splashed light around the room like a cluster bomb, and the music thumped with enough force to make my ears hemorrhage. The inside was much larger than I thought, with dozens of circular tables covering the open floor area and a stage that was more a runway platform in the middle of the room. A long bar was set off along the far wall. More than a dozen dancers worked the floor, moving from one group to another. The men ranged from Crevis's age to old enough to know better.

For a Thursday night, the crowd was thick and energetic. Ashley was at a table in the corner, dancing for a guy old enough to be her father. She glanced my way but quickly returned her attention to her "client." I scanned the rest of the club for the manager. I didn't want anyone to even suspect that Ashley and I knew each other.

"Can I get you something to drink," a lady said as she tugged on my shirt. A bit older than the dancer onstage, the woman was quite tan, or at least looked that way in the chaotic lighting of the club. She carried a tray with a couple of beers already on it.

"No." I noticed she had something reflecting off her face—glitter. I checked the room, and glitter was everywhere: on the floor, on the stage, on the walls, and on the dancers. The entire room sparkled like a giant, lascivious snow globe. I pulled out my wallet, then waved my badge and ID at her. "I need to speak with Chance."

She checked out the ID, then gave my leg a casual glance. "He's in back. Can I tell him what this is about?"

"Jamie DeAngelo."

"I'll let him know you're here." She stepped through the maze of mesmerized men, then hurried behind the bar. She spoke with the bartender, and they both gawked at me for a moment before she disappeared through a doorway at the far end of the room.

The bartender eyed me as he filled another customer's drink. I kept my distance from the bar and the doorway she went into and remained in the middle of the crowded club on purpose. I wanted Chance to come to me. Less than thirty seconds later, I wasn't disappointed.

A black goliath and an older white male emerged from the doorway's shadow, and they both locked in on me. The older white guy must be Chance; he carried himself like he was in charge. His hulking physique drew his shirt taut, and he looked like someone had cut and pasted an old guy's head on a herculean body. The twin titans pushed through the crowd toward me as the pulse of the music quickened. I smiled but didn't budge.

Chance stopped just in front of me. He and I were about eye to eye; I was eye to sternum with his partner.

"Who's asking questions about Jamie?" Chance said.

"Detective Ray Quinn."

"Former detective Ray Quinn," he said, smiling. "I know who you are."

"Great, now that we're all chummy, what do you know about Jamie DeAngelo?" I yelled it loud enough that most everyone standing around us heard, even over the music.

Chance scowled. "Let's talk in my office, Mr. Quinn."

Chance and his massive minion led the way to the edge of the bar and then into an office. He held the door for me, then closed it behind us. Chance lumbered over to his chair. Pictures of him in bodybuilding competitions lined the office—one showed him in a power pose as Mr. Florida 1981. I'd have to check that out.

Chance's chair groaned as he leaned back. His mane was peroxide blond and meticulously primped with a mullet two decades out of style. He probably had enough steroids in him that he could whinny at any moment and pull a salt lick from his desk drawer.

"Glad to see you're back on your feet, so to speak, Quinn," Chance said, not very enthusiastically. "I heard they never caught the person who shot you and your partner. What was her name?"

"Detective Trisha Willis." I knew full well he was trying to rattle my chain, like I was his. Chance had a little more on the ball than I first thought.

"Very tragic when someone guns down two public servants in cold blood like that." He rested his chin on his hand. "And now this with Jamie. What's the world coming to?"

"Insanity, I guess."

"After you were shot, we sent a donation to the police fund, to help out with your recovery and all. I see our money was well spent. We've always had a great relationship with the city and appreciate the work of the police department to keep everyone safe."

"My Tupperware hip thanks you." Did he really believe I was buying his line of garbage? I wasn't about to let him direct me off course. "So, how long did Jamie DeAngelo work here?"

"What business is that of yours, Quinn? You've been off the force for several months now."

Chance's aide was so close to my left side that if he flexed his chest, he'd smack me in the ear with one of his pecs. He was breathing deep and hard in a childish attempt to intimidate me. He needed a reason to back off a bit. I lifted my cane and stabbed the brass end onto his toe and ground my weight on it.

"Ouch!" He slipped his foot out and hopped back two steps as he growled. He leaned forward like he was ready to rip my head off.

I flashed him a glare that dared him to try. My body was broken and he'd tear me to pieces, but I was still not inclined to take a large amount of crap from anyone, especially him. Besides, my right hand was tickling the .380 in my pocket, should he be so dumb.

"Carl." Chance pacified him with a look. "Let me handle this."

The big man gave me my space but wasn't happy about it.

"Why are you here about Jamie?" Chance said. "I thought that was a police matter and it was closed. The guy who murdered her is dead, and we can all move on now from this terrible tragedy."

"I'm looking into the case for a friend. Just to make sure everything is how it should be, if you know what I mean."

"Must be a good friend."

"The best," I said, not giving him an inch. "So, how long did she work here?"

He tapped a meaty digit on his desk while giving me the once-over. "Fine, I'll play. She worked here a little over a year. She was a good employee. Never had any problems with her. We were all very saddened by what happened. Several of the girls even put up her picture in the dressing room. Made a shrine of sorts."

"Do you know if she had any drug problems or major debt?"

"I terminate any of the girls who are caught doing drugs, no questions asked," he said. "I make too much legitimate money here to put this club in jeopardy for someone else's bad habits. All the girls know this, so there are no surprises if they violate that rule. I can't control them when they're not here. So, no, I never knew of any drug problems with Jamie. Never heard anything bad about her from the other girls either."

I pulled David's picture from the file. "You ever see this guy at the club?" I shook the paper for Carl to come and fetch it.

He paused before finally walking back over and snatching it from my hand. He didn't seem to appreciate my putting him to work. He gave it to his boss anyway.

"No. I did see his picture in the *Sentinel* when all this happened, but he's not been in here," Chance said.

"You sure?"

"I know my club, Quinn. I'm very sure."

"Do you know of anyone who would want to hurt Jamie?"

"Nobody would want to hurt her," he said. "She was a nice kid."

"At least one person did."

"And that person is burning in hell right now for what he's done." Chance dropped his heavy arms on his desk. "You're asking questions that have already been answered. You're a smart guy. All this seems like a waste of your time."

"Maybe it is, maybe it isn't." I was pleased to hear that Chance the Flesh Peddler drew his moral line somewhere, with all his talk of hell and such. Somehow I doubted that he and Pam attended the same church though.

"We've come across some new information that makes me question the earlier findings." I like casting out bait at times to see what gets hooked and reeled in.

"Like what?"

"Just things," I said. "Ever heard of a guy named Tay? He used to date Jamie."

Chance shook his head. "Doesn't ring any bells. Are you doing this PI thing full-time now?"

"I've got a couple things going." I wondered when he would tire of my double-talk, but when I conduct an interview, I want to be the one gaining the information, not giving it.

"I might be opening a new club in a few months. I could use a good manager to run the place. You interested in the job? You'd make more in one year working for me than in five with just your police pension. It could certainly be a lot more lucrative than a PI job. You have no idea what a new club like that in the right location could pull down between the entertainment and liquor sales. It would be a good gig for a guy like you. The pretty ladies and the perks alone would be reason enough to take the job."

"Why me?" I glanced at Carl, whose jaw dropped as he gawked at Chance. "Looks like you've got plenty of staff here that could fill that spot."

"I like cops," Chance said. "They know how to weed through the garbage and get a job done. I bet a guy like you could run a tight ship over there. And that's what I need. Besides, you take me up on my offer, and you won't have to be poking around in other people's business all the time."

"Wow, I didn't expect a job offer tonight, but I'm afraid I'll have to turn you down. I kinda enjoy poking around in other people's business. And I haven't had all my shots this year, and who knows what a guy could catch in a place like this." I wiped my palm on my pants.

He grimaced, and I figured our conversation had just ended. "Have it your way, Quinn."

"I always do. I'll let you know if I come up with anything on Jamie."

"I don't expect to hear from you again," Chance said. "I think everyone already knows what happened."

"We'll see." I caned my way toward his office door; Carl blocked my exit. I wasn't about to walk around him, so I waited until he moved. After a few seconds, he stepped aside. Just as I exited the office, I stuck my head back in. "I'm sorry, I forgot something. Have either of you ever heard of something called the Lion's Den?"

The timing of that missile was near perfect as Carl and Chance traded stunned stares; their pauses told me more than the coming lie. Chance finally sputtered, "Never heard of it."

"Just thought I'd check." I couldn't hold back a smug grin. "Well, as much fun as this has been, I need to get going. Thanks for the chat, fellas. Catch you later."

I pushed through the crowd and out the door, pausing for a few seconds so Carl could catch up with me. I figured he'd tail me to the parking lot, to ensure my safety, of course. I was right. He trailed me about fifty feet back.

On the way out I turned off my recorder. I got in my truck and waited there for a moment. Carl and another bouncer came around the corner and then stopped. They kept watch on me as I drove out of the parking lot.

As I headed down I-Drive, several questions vied for equal time in my head. Why was Chance Thompson trying to buy me off this case with a job offer? And why the crazy looks when I mentioned the Lion's Den? Maybe Ashley knew her stuff.

But how could I prove it, and what did it really mean to the case? Even if Jamie "entertained" at the Lion's Den, did that necessarily mean that David didn't shoot her? Both could still be true.

My visit with Chance at Club Venus had done little to alleviate my suspicions. If anything, I was more convinced that I was missing something huge here and that everything wasn't quite as it appeared.

13

THEY SAY TIME FLIES when you're having fun. I can say with passion that it's not true, because the past year had sailed by, and I was by no means having fun.

In my previous life, June 2 had no major significance, and I've never made a big deal about holidays or anniversaries. Those things never mattered much to me. But today as I woke up on June 2—one year later to the day that I was shot and left for dead while Trisha lay dying next to me—anniversaries suddenly had a new and quite melancholy meaning.

I considered calling in sick for my shift and settling in with Jim for the rest of the night in a vain attempt to pickle my own brain, but that would end poorly. And I did have some questions to mull through at work—which was a good thing.

I pulled a picture of Trisha from one of the boxes in my closet, one I hadn't opened since the shooting. Trisha and I were walking along Cocoa Beach. We got a tourist to take our picture. She was smiling and so was I. I could smell her hair and the coconut-oil lotion she was wearing that day. As soon as I laid eyes on her, I regretted getting the photo out. I returned it to its spot, buried deep underneath the refuse of my former life.

I spent the majority of my drive to work alternating between my thoughts of Trisha and my meeting the night before with Chance.

"Hey, Hank," I said, as I was about fifteen minutes early to my shift, not that I was vying for employee of the month. I just needed to talk with Hank before he took off.

Judging from the medical examiner's report and my personal observations that night, David and Jamie had been dead for about twelve hours before Pam and I discovered the bodies. Hank would have been on shift then.

It's unlikely someone scaled the outer balconies for four floors in broad daylight to enter the apartment. The report's Crime Scene section indicated that the patio door was locked and there were no pry marks indicating forced entry. If David didn't kill Jamie, then whoever did had to have passed through the lobby at some point.

"Ray," Hank said. "You're a bit early."

"I guess I am. I was thinking the other day about

the preacher guy who was killed up in 419. You were working that day, weren't you?"

"I remember that day pretty well. We've never had a murder here before. I talked to the police officers the next day and gave them my statement."

"Do you remember anyone unusual coming in here that day?"

Hank rested his weak chin in his gnarled hand and gave a fair impression of *The Thinker*, although a more wrinkled version. I considered it fitting since Hank was old enough to have been around when Rodin was forging the statue. Just as I was about to pass my hand over his face to see if he was still awake, Hank said, "There were lots of people in and out that day. Like any other. Nothing stands out."

"Are you sure? You need to think back. Anyone come through those doors who didn't belong here?"

Hank's face contorted and strained to come up with any answer other than the obvious—he couldn't remember who came in an hour ago, much less a month ago. Pushing him wouldn't help anything.

"It's okay, Hank." I rested my hand on his shoulder. "I was just curious."

Since Mr. Savastio had decided to save a few bucks by not recording the security cameras, whoever came in and out of the condo that day would remain an unknown.

* * *

Crevis had been steering clear of me since I snapped at him a couple of days ago—my good fortune. I hadn't seen much of him since I'd been at work. When he came in earlier, he was acting weird, or weirder, depending on how you looked at it. He said hello and then disappeared. No quizzing me about police stuff or droning on about his physical prowess and finely honed warrior skills.

Most of the shift was uneventful. I answered a couple of calls early and let two people in, but it slowed down and died about ten. I attached my external hard drive to the computer at the front desk and opened up David's copied hard drive. I'd been going through his Word documents, mostly ministry stuff. I made some notes, but nothing caught my eye. I really needed to review his e-mails.

I opened his Outlook and clicked his in-box. Nothing noteworthy jumped out at me. A couple of advertisements from a news source. One message from Mario about the ministry's budget process.

A folder on the side was labeled Personal. I opened it and found hundreds of e-mails stored there. Many from winters79. I opened one, and it was from Pam. They seemed to correspond a lot.

Then there was 2hot4u, which was out of place from all the other e-mails. I opened it and struck gold. An e-mail from Jamie to David about a month before the murder.

David

i had fun talking with u last night. i still can't believe u waste your time with me. Things are crazy right now and i feel like my head is going to explode. The things u said make sense and i want to believe them, but everything isn't always as easy as u make it sound. i feel like i'm way too deep in this ocean to swim my way out now. i'm tangled in things u couldn't possibly understand. Several people are tugging at me, pulling in all different directions. Now u have come into my life and are shaking things up. i think Club Venus is all i'm able to do in life, just trying to survive the best i can. Maybe this is all god has for me.

Jamie

I checked the Sent folder for his reply.

Jamie,

I enjoyed talking with you as well. You sell yourself so short. You're intelligent, caring, and, yes, beautiful, but not just in the way men see you. You have inner beauty that shines because that's the way God made you. He created you special, and I have no doubt He allowed our paths to cross for a reason. You've been through a lot in your life, and I know things don't seem fair or right. But

I truly believe God has created you for a greater purpose than what you're doing now. I'm not trying to condemn or judge you, but I want you to know that God has so much more for you. I hope you'll consider what we've talked about. I'm here if you need anything, and I'm praying for you.

David

Crevis's police gear rattled down the corridor toward me, giving me enough time to close out of the program before he made it to the lobby. I picked up my Sudoku book just as he rounded the corner. His shoulders slumped forward as he dragged his feet along the carpet; he exhaled in an overly dramatic manner and plopped onto the chair next to me.

I peered over my book, gave him the eye, then returned to my puzzle. I'd been working this one for some time, and I couldn't seem to get the rhythm. It wasn't especially hard, but for some reason, I was lost in this thing.

Crevis released another deep moan and spun the chair just enough for his baton to knock against the arm of my chair, much like a puppy scratching at my leg for attention.

I tried to focus on my puzzle. It was frustrating me, and I considered going to the back of the book for the answers, but I've never done that in my adult life on any puzzle, and I wasn't about to start now. It was like admitting full-on defeat.

The third and loudest sigh caused me to close my book and ask the dreaded question, "What's up, Crevis?"

"I got this in the mail today." He handed me a letter.

It was from the City of Orlando Human Resources Department—a well-written rejection letter for the position of police officer. He had failed his written exam and was no longer in consideration. Glad to see the city still held to some kind of standard.

"I failed it again."

"Again?"

"This was my second turn," Crevis said. "At this rate, I'm never gonna be a cop."

"How could you fail this test . . . twice? A baboon with a Magic Marker could pass that thing."

"You're not helping, Ray."

I wasn't trying to. No need to tell him that.

"I have a hard time writin'. My teachers said I'm learning disabled, dyslexic. My dad says I'm an idiot. He doesn't want me to be some stinkin' cop anyway. Some Orange County deputies beat him up a couple of years ago, so he hates the idea of me being a cop. But I don't care what he thinks. I'm gonna do it anyway."

His dad sounded like a sweet guy. "Why do you want to be a cop? Be a fireman. Everybody loves firemen. People are happy to see them show up at a scene. Nobody likes the police. Do anything else but law enforcement, Crevis. I'm telling you that for your own good."

"Don't want to be a fireman. That's no fun. I wanna catch bad guys. I wanna be there when people need help . . . and make a difference. I just don't want to sit back and do nothin'. I've seen what that looks like."

Maybe Crevis had some free thought pinging around in that ugly melon of his after all. I took out my wallet and lifted my badge to eye level. "It's just a piece of tin. After fifteen years and my mental and physical health spent, I have a piece of tin and a ton of bad memories. That's all that's left. TV glamorizes it, but it's the kind of life I wouldn't wish on an enemy."

Maybe the kid would make the decision on his own and try something else. Because if he couldn't even pass the written test, he had no business being on the streets in the first place. He'd be eaten alive.

Crevis stared in hypnotic fascination at the badge. "Can I hold it?"

I slid the tin out of my wallet; it was my flat investigator badge I used to clip to my belt when I was in Homicide.

He snatched it from my hand and rubbed it between his long bony fingers, as if memorizing every detail by Braille.

What kind of life must he have had? Maybe he wasn't the sharpest kid around, but at least he wasn't smoking crack and knocking off convenience stores. I guess he had a sense of decency to him.

"You can keep that one. I've got a couple more like it at home."

Crevis's mouth dropped. "Really? You're not messing with me, are you?"

I considered answering yes and taking it back. But I couldn't. My third incident of niceness lately—I seemed to be on a run.

"No. It's yours, if you want it." My moment of pity might come back to haunt me at some point, but I'd been known to do some not-so-smart things.

"Thanks!" He jumped to his feet and held the badge up to his shirt. "I'll be back." He sprinted down the hallway, to the bathroom, I presumed.

Less than a minute later, on his way back, his hoofs trampled the carpet like a bison stampede —his snaggle-toothed grin wide like I'd never seen it before. My old badge was pinned to his chest. I hoped it would forgive me for the indignities it would suffer in that position. Crevis slapped his hands on his hips.

The world would never be the same: Crevis Creighton had been deputized.

14

HAVING DONE MY OBLIGATORY good deed for the year, I took the elevator down to the parking garage. I'd finally convinced Mr. Savastio to let me park there. He wasn't going to go for it until I mentioned something about the Americans with Disabilities Act and a potential lawsuit. He seemed to get my point then.

The echo from the brass tip of my cane's stabbing the concrete reverberated throughout the garage. I made it to my pickup and jiggled my key ring as I searched for my door key. Something moved to my left.

A large man in a ski mask stepped from behind a van, pistol at the ready. "Don't move, Quinn," the guy said in a deep, graveled voice.

I could see the skin on his neck and around his eyes; he was African American and big. He stood in a Weaver stance, the one most cops use to shoot, and I could see right down the barrel. He had the drop on me, and if I went for the Glock in my waistband, I would be dead before I touched it. I raised my right hand, keys still in it.

Feet shuffled behind me as I turned just in time to catch an elbow to the side of my head. The second guy slammed my body against the side of my truck and tossed me to the ground on my back; the pistol in my waistband stabbed into my spine.

I shook my head to clear the cobwebs and drew my fists to the sides of my head, instinctively covering up like I used to in the ring.

The man with the pistol loomed over me, aiming it at my head. "You need to mind your own business, Quinn, if you want to stay alive." He mashed his foot on my hip and pressed down, jamming it into the concrete.

I was going to puke. A guttural cry, not much louder than a whimper, escaped me.

He smirked through his little mouth hole; he was enjoying himself. His partner was a white guy, shorter than him but well muscled too.

"Hey, what are you doing?" a voice echoed through the garage. "Let him go." Crevis marched toward us.

"He's not armed," Bigfoot said to his crony. "Take him out."

"Crevis, run!" I managed. "Get outta here!"

He ignored me and picked up speed. The second hulk hurried to intercept Crevis, who had my big, shiny investigator badge dangling boldly on his chest.

"Leave him alone," I bellowed, helpless. "He doesn't have anything to do with this. He's just a stupid kid." I couldn't bear to watch someone else get killed for me.

With his right hand tucked in his pocket and his left at his side, Crevis sprinted toward the assailant.

The huge guy took a swipe at Crevis, who ducked at the last second. The guy's arm sailed over Crevis's head, leaving him off balance.

Crevis sidestepped and raised his left hand, pepper spraying the guy.

"Aaah!" The goon's gloved hands covered his eyes.

Crevis pulled his hand from his pocket and fired a punch to his face so hard I heard it connect. The guy's legs wobbled, and he staggered back.

Crevis crashed two more rights to his opponent's face and then followed up with a beauty front kick to the man-spot. The thug released a primal scream as he collapsed to his knees.

Bigfoot crushed down harder on me. "What are you doing? Take him out!"

His focus shifted off me for a second as he watched Crevis draw his baton and whack his buddy about the face and neck like he was beating a piñata. My cane lay just underneath my truck. I reached out with my right hand, caught the tip, and held it tight.

As Bigfoot's accomplice fell sideways on the floor, clutching his groin and moaning, Crevis stepped over his writhing body and pointed to my attacker. "You're next!"

He raised his pistol at Crevis. I whipped my cane from underneath the truck and caught his thick wrist hard. He yelped and dropped the gun, which discharged when it hit the ground. Crevis scurried behind a couple of cars.

I loaded the cane over my head and thumped the brass handle down hard on Bigfoot's chest, knocking him back into the truck. I squared up again and gave him two more whacks for good measure.

He slid down the quarter panel of the truck, catching himself before he fell to the ground. He crawled behind the van next to me.

I rolled to my left and snatched my pistol out of my waistband, pumping out three rounds his way. Plastic exploded from the taillight. I searched underneath the van, and he sprinted between the vehicles.

I fired a couple more times at his feet, sparks flaring up from the concrete. I didn't know if he was going to get another weapon. I wasn't taking any chances.

"Ray, are you okay?"

"Stay down, Crevis!" I pushed with my left leg and scooted forward like an inchworm to see more of the garage.

The big man crossed between two cars toward his cohort. Another salvo of rounds thundered from my Glock, and glass shattered as I tracked his movement. A car alarm erupted, echoing through the garage. His battered buddy managed to make it to his feet and stumbled toward the cars, still crumpled over and limping.

A door slammed shut and tires squealed. I pumped a few shots at them as they sped out of the garage in a blue Lincoln Town Car. I didn't know if I hit either of them or the car. I needed to get over and look for a blood trail.

Crevis ran to me. He removed a set of bloody brass knuckles from his right hand, then jammed it back in his pocket as he knelt beside me. "What do you want me to do?"

"Give me a second," I said, catching my breath. I fell back against the deck, my pistol still in my hand, smoke pouring from the barrel. The acrid smell of scorched gunpowder permeated the air around me, and my ears rang from the concussions of the shots. A car alarm warbled around us.

Bigfoot had stomped me good, and I think I finally found a decent date for Helga. My right leg twitched uncontrollably, and I hoped I wouldn't need another surgery. I needed to try to stand up.

"Take my hand," I said to Crevis. He looked reluctant, especially after the last time he tried to help me and I nearly bit his head off. I rolled up onto my left hip and slipped my pistol back in the holster. "It's okay. Just take my hand and help me up."

He took my right hand and pulled hard. I stiffened my left leg and kept all the weight on it as he lifted. I was unsteady and swayed like a palm tree in a hurricane. Crevis wrapped his arm underneath mine and kept me balanced.

This case just leapt from professional to personal.

"You did good, Crevis." I rubbed my forehead. Between the knock to my head and the Texas Two-Step on my hip, I fought to stay conscious. "You really put it to that guy. But you should have listened to me and run for help."

"I wasn't going to leave you, Ray. You're my best friend."

"I'm your *only* friend."

"Same thing."

Crevis propped me against my truck as he scurried underneath the van to get a look at the big man's gun. I had him jot down the make, model, and serial number, but told him to leave it alone. It would be some good evidence.

I looked up at the camera just over the door to the garage. Had the day-shift guy seen anything (unlikely) or called the police? I punched in the number to Dispatch and reported the incident.

"Officers are on their way," I said after I hung up. I was woozy and gripped the truck bed.

Crevis slid his arm underneath mine again. As the sirens approached Coral Bay Condos, my legs gave out, and Crevis was supporting my full body weight.

The kid was a whole lot stronger than he looked.

15

AFTER EXPLAINING to the rookie officer for a third time what had happened, my patience was wearing thin. I rested on my truck bumper and declined any medical attention, thinking Sasquatch hadn't botched up any of the doctor's work.

I did, however, leave out a couple key points in my statement, mainly that my attacker knew my name, asked me to back off, and that he'd assumed a police stance while holding his firearm. Not that others don't use the same tactics as the police, but when you're on the other end of the gun, you tend to notice things in a little more detail.

The guy seemed at ease with the weapon and wasn't holding it like a novice or gang member. Those details mattered, especially since I'd been told that a cop could be mixed up in this mess. I didn't need that kind of information on the official report for just anyone to read.

CSI Dean Yarborough responded to the scene and took the suspect's weapon, a Colt .45 semi-automatic pistol, into evidence. They'd probably run an ATF check to see who purchased it last, at least the last legal purchase. The rest of the owners might be tracked down from there. He took some pictures of the garage and the damage to the cars, as well as collecting the shell casings, mine included.

"We'll process the gun for fingerprints and run it through the system to see if it's stolen," Dean said. "When I can get to it, anyway. I don't have much time for just a minor robbery attempt. We've got some major cases going right now, so this one will have to wait."

"Thanks for extending yourself for the cause of justice, Dean. I really appreciate that."

He grimaced as he grabbed his evidence bags and loaded them into his van. Everything was a fight with him.

The rookie, who appeared young enough to be dressing for PE class in junior high, gave me his business card with a case number on it, and returned my pistol to me.

The watch commander, Lieutenant Bernard White, had shown up at the scene to oversee the incident. A thirty-year veteran with frosted hair and a lean frame for a guy over fifty, Lieutenant White was a good cop who ran a tight patrol crew. We knew each other in passing through the years.

He made some small talk with me, asking the usual questions of how I was doing and such. He wasn't going to put my gun in evidence because, in his opinion, it was a justifiable use of force. And since it was my old department gun, they had the ballistics already on file. He'd been around long enough to know how to take care of another cop. I appreciated that. He put out a

BOLO—Be On the Look Out—for the suspects and for any vehicle matching the description.

My cell phone rang. "Ray Quinn."

"Are you okay?" Oscar said.

"I'm fine. A little sore, but I'll survive. I've been worse. How'd you find out about this so quickly?"

"Bad news still travels fast in the city," he said. "Any idea who did this?"

"Probably just a couple of crackheads looking to make a fast score."

"I heard you got a couple of shots off," Oscar said. "Do you think you hit 'em?"

"Doesn't look like it. The patrol officers couldn't find any blood."

"We'll check the hospitals just to be certain. I'm coming down there now to see you. I'll make sure the case is taken from Robbery, and I'll have some of our guys take a look at it."

"No need to show up, Oscar. I got jumped. No big deal. Let the Robbery guys work it. I'm fine, really."

Oscar paused. He didn't take well to people attacking cops—or ex-cops. Even though he agreed not to have his people look at the case, I knew he'd pull a copy of the report and follow up himself. He was that type of guy, which was why I found it necessary to leave out some of the particulars of the attack. I just didn't think he would be on top of it so soon.

"Keep me updated if anything changes," he said.

"I will."

"Let me talk to White."

I handed Lieutenant White the phone. Oscar's heavy voice carried from the phone as he Q&A'd White on all the particulars.

He hung up and handed me the phone. "I'm clearing out all my guys. We'll let you know if we find anything."

Mr. Savastio was talking with one of the other officers. He tossed his hands into the air and yelled at the officer in broken English. He locked eyes with me and headed my way.

"Vay, you and Crevis talk now."

Crevis sprinted next to me and stood at attention. I balanced myself with two hands on my cane, my rump still firmly planted on the bumper. I was too sore and too tired to stand for one of his rants.

"You two think this is like the O. K. Collow or something?" He spun in a circle with his hands out. "Bullets everywhere. I do not understand. You are supposed not to have a gun? No shooting here!"

"Retired cops can carry concealed firearms," I said. "It's a federal law."

"I do not care whose law it is. No more guns. You not allowed to have gun on duty here. Understand?"

I nodded. "I understand." I didn't really and had no inclination whatsoever to follow his orders, but for argument's sake, I allowed him to vent. I didn't mention Crevis's brass knuckles and other accessories of war either. That might have pushed the man over the edge.

"Crevis," Mr. Savastio said. "I expected better from you."

"Sir, yes, sir!" Crevis barked with military precision, still locked at attention.

"First, we have murder here, now this. It is bad for business. People will want to move. If I was not friends with your Sergeant Yancey, you would be looking for another job right now, Vay. Understand?"

"Yes sir," I said, without nearly the enthusiasm of Crevis. "No more guns, no more shootouts. Got it. I just hope the bad guys get it too."

16

IN POLICE WORK, you never paid attention to the rookies when they first joined the squad. They're ignored, for the most part, until they get into their first conflict and prove themselves worthy of the badge—and your trust. After that, the other officers treated them with a little respect, talked with them, and showed them the ropes. Not that it's right; it's just the way it is, a rite of passage.

This morning Crevis and I needed to have a serious talk. The crime scene photos on my living room wall caught his attention; he eased closer and inspected them. I had a time line of events underneath them in storyboard fashion. It helped keep things in order in my mind. Since Jim was my only roommate, I hadn't had any complaints about the décor.

"Please stop smiling at me, Creighton. You're freaking me out."

"I can't help it." Crevis's animated expression had been pasted on his face since we left the Coral Bay; the rush from the fight still surged in his system. That kind of stress affects everyone in different ways. Unfortunately for everyone on the planet, with Crevis, he smiled.

I removed Jim from his resting place and poured myself a quick one. My hand trembled as he slipped into the glass. I was no stranger to shootings. I'd been in four as a cop.

My first was a drug dealer who ran from me when I was a rookie on patrol. We volleyed shots at each other down the street like something out of the Old West. I finally nailed him in the leg. The emergency room doctor stitched him up, and he went to jail.

The second guy tried to ambush me in a bar bathroom when I worked undercover in Narcotics. I shot him twice. He survived too and went to jail. The third guy murdered his girl-friend's child and was on the run. Oscar and I tracked him down and cornered him at an apartment complex on the east side. It was a pretty ugly gunfight—not that there are pretty ones. He didn't survive. It was one of my first cases in Homicide.

My last was with Trisha. I didn't even get a shot off.

Even though I'd seen a lot in my career, it was still rough coming down from the extremes of the fights and shootings. I was on my refill of Jim before I spoke to Crevis.

"You want a drink?" I held up my glass like a peace offering.

He shook his head. "I don't drink."

"Are you even old enough? I'd hate to contribute to the delinquency of a minor."

"It's not that." He touched every picture on the wall and ran his hands along the length of my mural. I didn't think he was capable of sitting still or not touching things. He must have been a treat for his teachers in school. "My dad's a big drinker. I'll never drink."

After our little wrestling match with the thugs-of-the-month club, I was tempted to finish the bottle, but I had a therapy session later this afternoon. So I'd drink enough to help me sleep and take the edge off the pain. When the adrenaline and Jim wore off, I'd be in some serious hurt later.

"Where'd you learn to fight like that?" I said. "It was pretty impressive."

"You don't grow up looking like me without gettin' in a few fights," he said, still examining the murder wall. "I told you I could throw down, but you didn't believe me."

I shrugged. The kid had me there. He'd had some pretty solid moves with better-than-average tenacity, and he showed that he wasn't above devious tactics with the brass knuckles and baton. Cheating in most life situations is unacceptable, except when it comes to a good street fight. Even the Duke would've agreed. Then, it's not only acceptable, it's necessary.

But most important, when Crevis had a chance to run and leave me, he didn't. Whatever else could be said about the kid, he had guts. And that was enough for me.

I owed my own martial-arts skills, or former skills, to Tommy Mason, another foster kid at the sixth house I lived in—the Stricklands'. One day for no reason, Tommy held me down and pummeled me bloody. He was a little older and a lot larger than me; I was defenseless against his assault. I took my licks and walked away when he was done . . . or so he thought. Two hours later, I nailed him with a two-by-four to the face when he walked out the back door. Tommy got twenty stitches; I was moved to my seventh house.

As soon as I got settled, I found a karate studio and started my training. I'd clean the dojo and do what I had to do to pay for my training. Even though I was nine years old, I promised myself that no one would ever hurt me again.

"Who do you think those guys were?" Crevis said.

"I'm not sure." I really wasn't, but I had my ideas.

"It didn't seem like those guys were trying to rob you. It looked like they were just out to get you. Maybe it was some mafia guy you put in jail years ago who's out now and wants revenge."

"You watch a lot of TV, don't you?" I said.

He gave me his best bobblehead-doll impression. While he'd gone a little overboard, his observations weren't terrible for a kid not privy to the conversation before he arrived. And he certainly didn't know I had lately been pushing buttons on some very irritable people.

"I think you're right. Robbery wasn't the motive. They were definitely out to get me."

"I was right?" He raised his eyebrows.

I didn't just invite Crevis to my house to thank him for saving my behind. He needed to know what was going on. Because by helping me, he'd just put himself in the line of fire. While in the past I'd had a tremendous amount of fun at his expense, I wasn't so callous that I'd let him be in danger and not tell him. He deserved to know the truth. He'd earned the truth. And, as this incident proved, I wasn't sure if I could continue this investigation without help.

"What happened this morning was no accident, Crevis. I've been looking into the murder at the condo and asking questions that are making some people nervous."

"I knew you were getting into that the night I caught you in David Hendricks's apartment. So who's the killer? Is that who jumped you?"

"I'm not quite sure yet. If I share my observations with you, you can't talk about this with anyone."

"I can keep a secret." He rubbed his hands together, as if warming them over a fire.

I didn't believe him, but then again, my opinion of him from three hours before had altered a bit, so I was willing to take a chance.

"The pastor's not completely off the suspect list yet. He's a strange fellow for sure, and I have my doubts about him, but I'd be a fool to ignore the fact that somebody is willing to attack me to stop me from asking questions about this case. I don't take kindly to threats and intimidation. So this is my business now."

"Our business," Crevis said. "The guy was gonna shoot me too."

A knock on the door interrupted us.

"Who is it?" I said.

"Pam. Open up, Ray."

Crevis opened the door. I'd called her right after our little donnybrook in the parking garage. She needed to be in on this conversation.

Pam gave him a casual glance, then blew past him and met me in the kitchen.

"Are you all right?" She reached out to touch my forehead, which I was sure had a bruise from a well-placed elbow shot.

"I'm fine." I pulled away. "I'm like a roach— easy to hit but hard to kill."

She frowned. "That's not funny."

"It's a little funny." I pointed to the kid. "This is my . . . friend Crevis. He's the only reason I'm able to stand here right now."

Pam shook his hand. "Thank you, Crevis. You did a brave thing."

"It's nothin'." He blushed and puffed out his chest with my old badge still dangling there. "Ray and I whooped 'em pretty good."

"I was telling Crevis about how I think the attack was linked to my investigation."

Pam looked worried. "Are you sure, Ray?"

"Yeah. The big guy called me by name and told me to mind my own business."

"You didn't tell the cops that," Crevis said.

I had to inform poor Crevis of what Ashley had told me about the Lion's Den and the possible police connection. Then with trepidation I told them of my attacker's firearm skills. I'm not big on sharing my suspicions with other cops, much less a woman scorned and a . . . Crevis. But my options were limited at this point.

"If some police officers are involved, how can we do anything against that?" Pam said.

"They're not likely to do anything to draw

attention to themselves," I said. "So first, we need to take a deeper look at Club Venus and the Lion's Den. I'll get to know Chance Thompson a little better too. He's a snake if I've ever met one."

"How do we do that?" Pam said.

"I'll make some nocturnal visits to his neighborhood." I struggled to get the next words out, but I was desperate. "I could really use your help, Crevis, chasing down some of these leads. I can't pay you, but I can teach you about police work." I shuffled into the living room and sat on the arm of the couch. "But this isn't a game. This is real life . . . and death, if we're not careful. Can you help us?"

"I was born for this, Ray."

His ecstatic grin made me question my sanity . . . again.

17

THAT AFTERNOON, I CALLED Helga's office and rescheduled our session. If she got her mitts on me after the beating I'd taken earlier, I wouldn't be able to get out of bed for a week. I got a few hours of sleep and then reviewed more of the case notes.

At around 3:00 a.m., I rolled up to Crevis's house in Bithlo—home of the Bithlo Speedway, where they have smash-up derbies every Friday night. Crevis was doing jumping jacks on the sidewalk, like I couldn't see him standing there. Wearing camo pants and a dark Molly Hatchet concert T-shirt, he was nearly unrecognizable without his uniform on, looking even more like a goofy kid.

His navy blue house was an old Florida block home, small with a flat roof, probably built fifty or sixty years ago. The yard was unkempt; an old Buick was parked in front of the house. Grass grew up, around, and through it, as if the rusted-out jalopy had burst forth from the earth right there. A faint glow shone out the living room window. Someone pulled the curtains back as my truck idled there. I could only see the shadows.

"Let's go." Crevis got in my truck, then slammed the door shut. He checked the window and slapped the dashboard twice. "We need to get moving. My dad's really lit tonight and being a jerk." Crevis didn't seem like he wanted me to see his house or his father.

When I was young, I imagined that my father and mother were spies who had placed me in the foster-care system to protect me from their dastardly enemies, a selfless act of familial love. Unfortunately, at some point I had to grow up and face the probable truth—they simply didn't want me. Nothing noble or romantic about that.

As Crevis stared straight ahead, I wondered which was better—not knowing for sure what my parents' reasons were for abandoning me, or living with a father who apparently wanted nothing to do with his son. At least with my situation, I could make up stories and excuses for my folks, remaining in a purgatory of ignorance. Crevis, on the other hand, had to live in an unpleasant and unappealing reality. He didn't look back as we sped away.

"Are you sure you're up for this? As you saw yesterday, the bad guys are not playing around."

"I'm in, Ray. Nothing you say can talk me out of it."

It would take about twenty-five minutes to reach our destination—the Sanctuary, a gated community on the north side of Orlando. The farther from Bithlo we got, the more Crevis relaxed and took on his normal persona. Then he started chattering away, making me wish we were still somewhere near his home. He treated me to several of his cartoon impressions and strange animal voices. He did a fair Barney Rubble and a frighteningly good Elmer Fudd.

I nodded at the appropriate times in the conversation and would even add an uh-huh on occasion. But my mind was elsewhere and restless, working through all the possibilities in the case. It didn't take a brilliant deduction to figure out that my buddies from the parking garage were connected in some way to Chance Thompson and Club Venus. What exactly were they afraid I would discover? And how was it all connected to David and Jamie? I needed more information about Chance. Our little midnight run might help with that.

I glanced at Crevis, who was carrying on a one-sided conversation, not stopping to even breathe, while drumming a schizophrenic beat on my dashboard.

As we arrived at the Sanctuary, I stopped on the road just outside of Chance's neighborhood. A car pulled up to the call box in front of the gate. The driver lifted the phone and dialed some numbers. A few seconds later, the gate rolled open. I flicked my lights back on and followed the car, but not too close, so the driver couldn't get a good description of me, Crevis, or my truck.

"What's Chance's address?" Crevis said.

"Fourteen twenty-two Freeman Lane." My GPS unit mounted on my windshield diagramed our way to the house. We were to follow the road as it curved around to the right, and Chance's house would be just on our left.

"I'm going to pass by his house. Then we'll get an idea of what we're dealing with."

Chance's abode came into view: a two-story brick home with a three-car garage that could fit Crevis's whole house in it. Faux shutters bordered every window. The yard was manicured and magnificent; landscape lights lined the driveway at perfect intervals. An ample oak tree stood watch in the front yard.

The kid slunk down in his seat as we passed.

"Sit up, Crevis. You look like you're up to no good."

"Well, aren't we?"

"Yeah, but you don't have to announce it to anyone who sees us. If you act like you're supposed to belong somewhere, nine times out of ten you won't draw any attention to yourself. Act natural."

Crevis scooted back up, and I continued down the road, turning around well past Thompson's residence and stopping in front of another that was for sale and appeared to be abandoned. I shut off the lights and raised my binoculars. We were a good seven houses away, and I had a clear view of Chance's front door and driveway. I zoomed in on the door. A small motion sensor hung above the porch entrance. It was connected to a light and something else . . . a camera. Chance did like his security. The three corners of the house I could see had motion lights but no cameras. We'd have to be very careful.

Then I got a good eyeball on our target— Chance's trash at the curb. One man's trash is another man's treasure, so the saying goes. I prefer to say that one man's trash is another man's felony indictment. Not nearly as poetic but certainly more fun—and accurate.

I'd garnered some good info and evidence on many past cases just by garbage-picking the suspect. Personal letters, cell phone bills with call logs, drug residue, credit card and banking information—it all finds its way into the trash at one point or another. And according to the law, once it hits the curb, it's open season for the cops or whomever.

The street was well lit though. That could be a problem. I had checked Chance's address on the Orange County property appraiser's Web site. He'd built it about two years ago when development was booming. The assessed value was around three-quarters of a million dollars. Judging from Chance's posh accommodations, the adult entertainment industry certainly wasn't in a recession.

"What do we do now, Ray?"

"I want you to grab two white trash bags from someone else's garbage." I pointed to a neighbor's can. "Then head up to Chance's house and replace his white trash bags with the two you get. I'll drive up when you're done."

Crevis's tortured expression begged for more explanation.

"I don't want him to notice before the pick-up time that some of his trash bags are missing. Otherwise, he'll know someone is investigating him. Criminals talk, and they know the techniques cops use, so we don't want to do anything to give Chance a heads-up."

"Got it." Crevis thrust his bony thumb in the air.

"It looks all clear right now. If I honk the horn, run or get ready for me to pick you up because something has gone wrong. Keep your cell phone on vibrate."

Crevis nodded, then slipped out of the truck. He almost had the door closed when he opened it again. "I really think I need your gun for this."

"Not on your life, Creighton."

"What if something happens to me?"

"Die with dignity."

He scowled.

"You'll be fine. Just do as I said. I'll watch your back."

He closed the door quietly and skulked to one house away from where my truck was parked. He opened the lid on the can and reached in. He glared at me, shook his head, and frowned.

"Welcome to the wonderful world of investigations, Crevis." He could probably see me snickering. Trash searches were a cornucopia of information, but also one of the nastiest jobs in police work.

He lifted a white trash bag out and then another. He ambled down the sidewalk toward our target, a colonnade of streetlights illuminating his path.

I zeroed in on Chance's house again. I wasn't sure if he was home or not. Lights were on inside the house, but that didn't mean much. As Crevis was nearly to the curb at Chance's house, a set of car lights turned and headed down the street—directly toward Crevis.

18

"HIDE, CREVIS," I SAID ALOUD, as if he could actually hear me.

With a white trash bag in each hand, Crevis spun in a circle, looking for a place to hide. He dropped the bags next to Chance's cans and sprinted to a hedge next to his garage. He slid into the bushes like he'd stolen home plate just as the car—a black Hummer with a set of running lights that would be the envy of any 747—touched down onto Chance's driveway.

Crevis disappeared into the thicket's shadows. Chance's poofy pelt was visible in my binos and a female accompanied him, although I couldn't get a good look at her face. The garage door opened, and Chance coasted his man-vessel in, the door closing behind it.

A few seconds later, Crevis poked his head out from behind the hedge. An upstairs light flipped on. I called Crevis's phone.

"Where is he?" Crevis answered, huffing and out of breath.

"He's in the upstairs bedroom as best I can tell. Do this quick and let's get out of here."

Crevis hung up and replaced two of Chance's trash bags with the two from the neighbor. He jogged toward my truck, a bag in each hand.

A porch light turned on one house away from

me, and a white male in his early fifties walked outside with a German shepherd on a leash. I thought I was the only person on the planet who kept these insane hours. Who walks his dog at three thirty in the morning? Didn't anyone sleep in this neighborhood? The man headed down the walkway to the sidewalk, the meaty mongrel dragging him along. I couldn't tell who was walking whom.

The dog barked at Crevis, halting him in his tracks with the trash bags at his side—busted big-time. The canine stretched its lead as the man confronted Crevis, barely able to restrain the dog. The man raised his voice, but I couldn't hear exactly what he was saying. I put my right hand on the ignition key and speed dialed Crevis with the left.

Crevis looked down at the phone on his waist as the man continued to yell at him, asking him what he was doing and saying something about the neighborhood watch.

Crevis eased the bag onto the sidewalk.

"I'm calling the police!" the man said.

Crevis slipped the phone off his belt. "Help me here, Ray."

"Run back toward Chance's house now, and I'll drive up to you."

Crevis hung up, slipped his phone into its pouch, smiled at the man, grabbed the second bag from the ground, then sprinted up the street away from the man.

I turned the ignition over and floored it, the tires spinning until they caught on the pavement. I kept my lights off as I sped toward Crevis. His lanky legs churned up grass as he fled, his arms flapping with the trash bags like an ostrich trying to take flight.

The man unclipped the dog's leash, and the mutt was in full sprint toward Crevis. I pulled up alongside him, and he tossed the first bag into the back, then the second. The hound from hell was gaining on him. I slowed up enough for Crevis to grab the side and jump, straddling the side of the truck bed. The dog leapt, seized his pant leg, and jerked, yanking him back.

"Drive, Ray, drive!" Crevis clung to the side of the truck—one leg in the bed, the other being shaken by the beast.

I floored it, and Crevis's camos ripped. The dog gained a souvenir of Crevis's tattered pants as it veered off to the sidewalk.

Crevis rolled into the bed with the trash. I took a corner fast, and he thumped around with the bottles and refuse. I drove to the gate to leave the Sanctuary, and it creaked open.

"Get in," I said.

Crevis hopped out of the bed and joined me in the front seat.

"Wahoo!" Crevis punched the roof twice. "That was great."

I hung a right on North Mills. An OPD unit

passed us and turned into the Sanctuary. We got out of there just in time; I don't think the guy got my tag number.

I smacked the steering wheel. "That was easily the worst trash pull I've ever seen."

"Yeah, but it was fun. Can we steal someone else's garbage?"

I parked behind my complex near the Dumpster and opened the truck bed. I dragged one of the plastic bags onto the tailgate and ripped it open. I didn't think Hacienda del Sol could smell any worse, and I could toss the stuff in the Dumpster when we were done.

Crevis fiddled with the torn bottom of his pant leg. I tossed him a pair of rubber gloves. "Dig in."

I located three envelopes and sifted through them—junk mail. But if Chance responded quickly, Ed McMahon could visit him. I tossed them aside. I found his Bright House telephone bill, which included his Internet information as well. I set that in the pile we'd keep.

"What exactly are we looking for?" Crevis pinched a soiled piece of paper between his fingers and held it as far away from himself as possible.

"Papers, letters, credit card and banking information, personal items—anything that can tell us more about our good buddy Chance. Read every piece of paper. You never know what could be in here. Look for notes and phone numbers too."

Crevis hoisted up some multicolored mystery meat in a clear plastic bag that didn't even begin to contain the rancid stench. His body convulsed and his carroty complexion turned pale, but with a great deal of strength he didn't puke on my truck. With a dull thud, Crevis dropped the bag into the trash pile.

"It would be just like this on TV," I said, "if only they had smell-o-vision, of course."

"This is disgusting." Crevis braced himself on the side of the truck.

I picked up a crushed McDonald's cup and felt something rattle inside it. I ripped it open and emptied two glass cylinders into my hand. I held up the small vials.

" 'Testosterone enanthate.' Steroids." Chance must have tried to hide them in the cup—like he was the first person to ever think of that. I placed them to the side. What a surprise, Chance was hitting the juice. I think his Cro-Magnon forehead and not-so-cheery disposition had already given that away.

"What's this?" Crevis held a piece of paper as he shone his flashlight on it.

"A receipt for the J & M Corporation." The wrinkled and stained paper was for a title search for property in east Orlando. I laid it to the side to be dealt with later.

I found a one-inch-by-one-inch plastic bag containing white powder residue. "Chance has a few more drug habits than he'd like to admit."

"What is it?"

"Probably cocaine. Looks like Chance's drug-free-workplace speech was a crock. But I don't have a test kit to confirm it."

"Can't you just lick it or something and see if it's cocaine?" Crevis said.

"Do *you* want to lick it?" I held the bag close to his face.

"No way." He stepped back.

"Well, neither do I. From this point forward, you are no longer allowed to watch any TV police dramas or comedies. They're ruining you for police work. Understand?"

Crevis nodded but looked sad.

"Law enforcement is a lot like kindergarten," I said. "To start with, you never, ever put anything in your mouth."

19

MY CELL PHONE RATTLED and vibrated on my nightstand as I pawed around to find it. I finally located the nuisance and flipped it open.

"What?" I said, more like I was talking into the pillow than the phone.

"Ray," Pam said in a hurried tone. "I found something at the ministry you need to see. Please meet me there as soon as you can."

"Fine." I didn't even say good-bye as I dropped

the phone back on the nightstand.

I can't say that I sprinted to my truck, squealed the tires, and violated every traffic law as I raced to Outreach Orlando Ministries. Truth was, I woke up with cotton mouth, fuzzy vision, and a wicked whiskey-inspired headache along with a battered and bruised body that punished me with every movement.

After trash-picking with Crevis into the wee hours of the morning, I hit it pretty hard with Jim, so my midafternoon waking routine was much slower than normal. I slugged down several aspirin and made a second pot of coffee to take some with me as I headed out to meet Pam.

I parked in front of the ministry and caned my way in, my plastic coffee cup in tow. As I walked in the door, Pam and Mario were in the office. Mario was sitting in a chair like a schoolboy preparing to see the principal.

"Ray." Pam crossed her arms. "I think Mario has something to tell you."

I sipped at my now-cooling-but-still-potent java and nodded to him, seriously wondering what in the world she was up to.

"I have a problem," he whispered.

By my estimation he had several, but I let him continue.

"I used David's computer to look up sites I knew I shouldn't be looking at. I thought I erased them, but I guess I didn't."

"What kind of sites?" I just wanted to be sure we were talking about the same thing.

He shook his shiny head and lowered his face into his hands. "I'm so ashamed. I've been fighting this wicked battle in my soul for a couple of years now. I'm addicted to porn, and I need help. After Pam and I talked yesterday and she told me what you found, I went to my church elders and confessed my sin. Then I called Pam. No way was my problem going to be attached to David. It falls on me and me alone. I'm sick that his name as well as Christ's has been associated with my sins and weakness. May God forgive me for the damage I've done to both of them."

"You could have told me this sooner," Pam said. "Do you have any idea how I've agonized over this?"

"I'm so sorry, Pam," Mario said as he wept. "I never meant to hurt you or David. That's the last thing on earth I'd ever want to do."

"Is that why you didn't want me to look at the computer?" I said.

"Yes." Tears flowed faster now. "I didn't know if you would find out or not, and I was afraid. Now I'm glad you did so I can start dealing with this demon. I owe you an apology too."

"That's nice." I didn't float my forgiveness so fast, and I was still concerned about how Mario played out in all this. Being an ex-con, he'd have to do a bit more than drop a few tears and burp out a couple penitent words to lift himself off my list.

"I guess that sometimes things aren't always as they seem," she said.

I can't say I was totally surprised by Mario's confession. Although I'd only been able to read a couple of David and Jamie's e-mails, I didn't get the feeling that David was hitting on her or that there was some sort of tawdry relationship between them. They referenced several prior conversations, all of which were about life, God, and Jamie's search for a deeper meaning to her existence.

I'd been having difficulty reconciling the David of those correspondences to the Web sites or the dead young woman in the condo. Mario's confession made a bit more sense of things. And Pam knew it because her face shone with a hopeful expression again.

"I'll be praying for you, Mario. But if there's anything else Ray needs to know—and I mean anything—you need to tell us now."

"That's it." He wiped his eyes. "There's nothing else."

"We're definitely going to talk more later." Pam still looked a little miffed with Mario. "We've got a lot of things to deal with."

I didn't say anything to him as we left. Pam and I hoofed it to my pickup. The ministry was in a rough section of town, but since she possessed a strong overhand right, I felt comfortable with Pam as my bodyguard. She remained strategically quiet for our walk and let me eat a whole lot of humble pie for those silent few moments.

"Nice work, Detective Winters. I might have to put you in for a commendation for that one."

"I just knew David wasn't visiting those sites, just like I know he didn't kill that girl. And I'm going to find the truth, Ray Quinn, with or without you."

As a wry smile crossed her face, Pam looked more determined than ever. Whatever else I believed about this case, I now knew one thing for sure—Pam would stop at nothing until we had all the answers. And I pitied anyone who got in her way.

20

AFTER OUR OPRAH-LIKE emotive session with Mario the Weeping Felon, my stomach beckoned me to fill it with something that would clog my arteries and shut down my heart on the spot. I was hankering for a huge sloppy burger and fries.

I wanted to run some things by Pam, so I asked her to join me over a late lunch, early dinner, or something. She agreed, so we drove to the Wildside BBQ & Grill on Summerlin Avenue, east of downtown.

I ordered a double burger and cheese fries, and she ordered a chicken salad. She ate like she lived, no frills or fluff. I didn't see her as a chili-and-hot-wings kind of gal. Sometimes it bothers me that I'm always analyzing every aspect of a person, but I do enjoy making the connections between one personality trait and another, how one aspect or pattern of a life feeds directly into others. I wish I could turn it off, but I am a ruined soul.

I was glad to hear Mario's confession. It helped me focus on other areas that needed to be fleshed out. I slugged down my first iced tea in record time. My sparring session with Jim last night was just about wearing off, but I was still a little dehydrated.

"I checked Jamie's cell phone records," I said. "The subpoena for the records is in the report, but the records themselves are missing. I don't know if they were just never followed up on, or if they were removed."

"Why are the phone records important anyway? And why wouldn't they be in the report?"

"I'm not sure what to make of that. They should be in the report with everything else. I like checking phone records. They tell patterns about people—when they're up and moving around, who's their favorite person to call, then the second, and so on. If Jamie and David were killed by someone else, then it's very possible one of them knew and had contact with that person. The phone records should provide more people to interview. I need to get ahold of Pampas's investigative notes and see if the phone records were mentioned, or if there's anything in the report I don't have."

"So can we get that information now?"

"Maybe," I said as the waitress arrived with my refill. "We have a couple of options. Plan A, and my least favorite, is I ask Oscar if he knows what happened to the records and if he can give me full access to all the case notes and let me conduct a review. But then I have to explain why I want them and what I'm doing. It won't play well with my old unit that I'm going back over their work. If we start making progress on this case, they'll find out anyway, but the longer I can delay that, the better. I might be able to glean a lot of information without their knowing it, before we have to go public. And with a possible dirty cop involved, I need to be very careful. I don't know who I can trust at OPD."

"Any other options?"

"Yes," I said. "But I don't think you want to know what I have in mind for plans B through Z."

She raised an eyebrow. "But I . . . never mind." She held up the palm of her hand.

"When I tell you that you don't want to know something, trust me, you really don't want to know. It's for your own good."

Pam rolled her eyes. "Is there anything else going on?"

She nibbled on her salad, and I eased back in my chair. The chaotic sounds of waitresses hurrying past and glasses and silverware clanking carried with them a fresh realization that I had not been out to a restaurant for a relaxing meal with anyone in many months. But with Pam it just seemed to flow naturally.

As much as I searched and parsed her every word, I had yet to see a false motive in what she was doing or who she was. She loved her brother and wanted to find his killer. She was sincere and honest, something I wasn't used to, and it was throwing me a bit off kilter. I breathed in the atmosphere.

"We're entering a time in this investigation that I'm not quite sure how to deal with," I said. "I'll need more records and subpoena powers for others. I can't go through the state attorney's office because I'm not a sworn cop anymore, and I'm not a certified private investigator. But we've got to dig deeper. I need access to the police data banks and files and such. We'll have to be creative from here on out."

"I need to pray about this," she said. "God has brought us this far. I believe He's going to lead us to the killer."

Just when I started to warm up to Pam, the God-talk flowed from her mouth like some holy water spigot forever stuck in the "on" position.

"I'll leave the praying to you, while I do the work."

"You don't believe in the power of prayer? You

think it was an accident that we met and now you're working on a case you didn't really want to take?"

"I don't believe in a lot of things you believe in. It's just dumb luck that you and I met and this whole thing happened. I think we're all just clinging to a giant boulder hurtling through space, and it's up to us to make the best out of what we have."

"There's not much hope with your beliefs," she said.

"Maybe not, but it's realistic. We don't have a greater purpose for being here. We're just here. That's all."

"Didn't you ever go to Sunday school or church when you were younger?" she said.

"Yeah. At some of the homes I was at, they'd force religion down my throat."

"Some of the homes?" Her eyes filled with tenderness. "You were adopted?"

I bit my lip and felt like a fool. Pam played dumb with me and had used the techniques of a good interviewer to draw information out of me. Not bad for a rookie.

"Not exactly. I grew up in the Florida foster-care system. I never knew my parents and was never adopted, so I bounced from foster home to foster home."

"That had to be tough," she said.

"Well, life is tough. I was told the police found

me when I was about three years old, walking on the side of I-75 with a note pinned to my shirt that said 'Ray.' That's all I know. So I don't see a whole lot of God's purpose in leaving a little boy abandoned on the side of the road for just anyone to find. Doesn't sound like a loving God to me."

I hadn't shared this much about myself with anyone except Trisha; not even Oscar knew. But Pam caught me hung over and weak, seduced me with iced tea and greasy burgers, then extracted the information like a pro.

"I guess I can understand why you'd think that," she said. "I struggle with a lot of questions too. David really loved God, and sharing that love was his passion. Ever since he was a boy, he knew he wanted to be a pastor and to serve God and others. That mission was his dream. Why would God let something like that happen to him? It's so unfair. I can't explain any of it."

"And yet you still believe? Even after all this?"

Pam nodded. "God is still God, even if I don't understand everything. Even when it hurts. I trust that He has a plan."

"Sound's like a cop-out."

"It's not a cop-out, Ray. He's God. Where else am I going to go?"

The waitress showed up again, and I accepted my third glass of tea. I'd need it to chug this conversation down. I'd let enough about me slip. It's not that I was paranoid or anything, but information is power. And I didn't like handing others that kind of power over me.

"Getting back to the case, I'm going to find out about the cell phone records, and Jamie had an ex-boyfriend named Tay. I need to find him as well. If nothing else, he could provide some insight into Jamie as a person. Or he could be our suspect. I'll get back to Chance and Club Venus as soon as I can, but right now I should follow up on these leads. I could use another three or four investigators to run down some of this stuff, but it looks like it's just you, Crevis, and me."

Pam dabbed her mouth with a napkin and agreed. I could tell she wanted to talk more about God, life, and personal stuff. I was done with that.

"So what's our next move?" she said.

"I don't think I have any choice now." I removed my wallet from my back pocket. "I've got to do something I haven't done in a year."

"What's that?"

"I'm going to the police station."

21

INCOMPETENCE RULED THE DAY when it came to getting rid of employees in bureaucracies as large as Orlando's.

I kept that in mind as I punched in the old security code on the keypad, then the gate rolled open. They hadn't changed the code in a year, which made me hopeful about other things. The homicide unit was on the second floor of police headquarters on Hughey Avenue.

I'd waited until almost five o'clock to clear out as many cops as I could. No one was in the parking lot, although a few cars were still there. Oscar's dark blue Buick Century was parked near the front door.

Just as they hadn't changed the gate code, I'd bet my old passkey hadn't been taken out of the system. I swiped my keyless entry card, and the small light went from red to green. No turning back now.

I headed up the stairs that led to the back door of Homicide that allowed investigators to come and go without walking through the main lobby. The bull pen was pretty much as I remembered. Cubicles lined the walls, and individual offices dotted the hallway.

But now a picture of Trisha hung against the wall in the middle of the room, a black ribbon strung across it.

Her fire red hair was tied back, and she stood in her dress uniform, smiling. A small narrative and a proclamation from the governor were below. The Medal of Valor was underneath that for gallantry under fire. That meant she died well, as if that really mattered now.

The checkout board still hung on the wall with the names of everyone in the unit listed. Oscar was a freak about detectives signing out when they left the office. You had to record where you were going and when you expected to return.

"Ray," Oscar's bellowing voice called. "Is that you?" He hurried toward me with his larger-than-life smile. Much of my fear melted with his approach. It was great to see him.

"Yeah. I thought I'd take you up on your offer to see what's going on."

Oscar shook my hand and wrapped a big wing around my shoulder. "Doesn't look like the muggers did too much damage. Lieutenant White said you gave 'em a good fight."

"Well, I had some help. Looks like you replaced me pretty fast." I pointed to my old desk, which was crammed full of someone else's stuff. A picture of a young guy with a wife and three kids occupied the upper shelf.

"That's Bowden. I brought him over from Narcotics. Pretty sharp kid. I think he's gonna make some good cases. He reminds me a lot of you."

"Troublemaker, huh?"

"A little." Oscar smiled. "Come on down to my office so we can talk. You look great."

Oscar was good with greasing people and building them up. I didn't mind so much. As we walked toward his office, I saw a familiar back of the head at one of the cubicles and hoped he wouldn't see us. No such luck.

"Ray-Ray." Steve Stockton rolled his chair out and hurried over to me, meaty arms out.

I punched my hand out quickly so he couldn't give me an awkward hug. He was a little too touchy-feely for me.

"Good to see you." Steve shook my hand like he meant it. But his eyes were at work again. I questioned my sanity when I heard the back door open then slam shut as more detectives approached us.

"Night Watchman Quinn," Pampas said. "I heard you got your butt kicked the other day by some homeless guy."

I didn't answer Pampas but considered the benefits he could receive from a good cane lobotomy. I should have been able to smell him before his approach. Pampas swaggered up to me and almost extended his hand but didn't. What a guy. The detective from the picture on my old desk was with him.

"Greg Bowden." He gave me his hand. He was a bit taller than me with a thick build, like a football lineman, and receding brown hair. "Good to see you up and around."

"Thanks."

"Tell Bowden where you're working now, Quinn." Pampas posted his hands on his hips.

"Is he training you?" I pointed at Pampas with my chin.

Bowden nodded.

"Don't listen to what he tells you," I said. "You

really can solve cases and actually arrest people in this unit. And if you want to help Pampas, clean his handcuffs for him and knock some of the rust off. I don't think they've been on anyone since Reagan was president."

"The rent-a-cop perspective is always a treat to have," Pampas sneered.

"Well, it really does feel like the old days," Oscar said. "Give it a rest, guys. Ray and I have some business in my office."

I shook hands again with everyone but Pampas, who deliberately turned away from me and went to his work station. The department's pistol-shooting award was above his desk. After three years in a row of coming in second—to me—he finally pulled it off. I didn't mention it. Didn't want to give him the satisfaction.

We made it to Oscar's office, and he closed the door. I never used to like it before when we'd have our closed-door sessions. It generally meant I had enraged someone or pushed the envelope too far.

His desk was ordered, much like the man himself. The in-box was empty, as he was efficient as well. Most of the reports these days were automated. When a detective finished with a case, he'd e-mail it to Oscar to be reviewed then forwarded to Records. I remembered the days of reams of paper on his desk, as the reports were booklike. Times had certainly changed.

A picture of Oscar's wife, Mimi, and his two daughters hung on the wall behind him. He was a family guy, to be sure. If I had a dad (other than the Duke, of course), I'd want him to be like Oscar. He took breaks from homicide scenes to drive across town just to cheer at his daughter's basketball games for a few minutes. Then he'd head back to work. He once told me that he could mess up anything else in his life but not them. I respected that.

"I'm glad you came around," Oscar said. "It's long past due."

"Thanks for steering me to the Coral Bay gig. It's been good to get out of the apartment."

"Not a problem." Oscar rested his elbows on his desk. "I knew you couldn't sit in there forever. It's not healthy. You're makin' good steps, Ray. Mimi really does want to have you over for dinner."

"You married well, Oscar. We'll get together sometime."

"How's the therapy going? You making any progress?"

I shrugged. "It's okay. I'm in a lot of pain and horribly out of shape. Just walking in here wore me out." I released a deep, drawn-out sigh and feigned my most pathetic face.

"We'll just sit here awhile until you catch your breath. No need to hurry anywhere."

"I appreciate it." I slumped in the chair, but not too much, trying not to overplay my hand. "I was just hoping I could make it to Personnel and pick up some of my retirement statements before they closed. But I don't think I have the energy right now. I'll have to come back another day."

"I'll take care of it, Ray." He hurried to his feet. "No problem at all. I'll go see if they'll release them to me. Just sit tight and rest."

I nodded. "Thanks, Oscar. That's a big help."

He hustled out the door. After my Oscar-winning performance, I had maybe ten minutes.

As soon as I couldn't hear him anymore, I maneuvered around his desk and took his seat. I wiggled the mouse, and his computer came to life from sleep mode. I found the Case Management icon and clicked on it. The hourglass spun for what seemed like forever. Oscar needed a computer upgrade so I could hack into what I needed a little more efficiently.

I typed in the Hendricks murder-suicide case number. The hourglass spun again. I watched the doorway to the hallway. As Stockton's bellowing voice laughed at his own lame joke, my heart spun like the icon, waiting for the stupid machine to finish.

The file finally uploaded, and I had access to the whole thing. I copied it and e-mailed it to my home address. I'd read it later. It would be more detailed than the report issued to Pam and should have all of Pampas's notes as well as a complete list of the items in the report.

I pulled up Oscar's e-mail account and found the IT's address. The door to Homicide swung open and smacked the wall. Footsteps echoed down the hallway . . . right toward Oscar's office.

22

I FUMBLED WITH MY CANE and stood, wobbling. A secretary with her arms loaded with notepads passed by and gazed at me next to Oscar's desk. As soon as she left, I sat back down. I typed a quick e-mail to the IT supervisor, Doug Farnham.

Doug,

Could you reinstate Ray Quinn's username and password to the department uplink as well as his e-mail account? He'll be doing follow-up work for some of his old cases coming up for trial in the next few months. Could you also send your response to this request on my personal e-mail at SgtYancey@yahoo.com? I'll be working from home a lot this week.

Thanks,

Sergeant Yancey

No going back now. I deleted the e-mail from his Sent folder as well as the record of the file I sent myself. That would provide me at least some cover, but it was still a big risk. If Doug courtesy copied Oscar's work e-mail as well as the one I had set up, I was toast. I'd think of an excuse later, maybe a medication switch that made me a little loopy.

The hallway door opened again. I made my way back to my seat and parked my rear in the chair just as Oscar entered the room.

"Here you go, Ray." He handed me the folder. "They had the paperwork waiting right there."

His sympathetic smile elicited a flicker of guilt that faded quickly. I could have approached Oscar with everything going on and asked him to help. But knowing the bad blood between Pampas and me and that the case had been closed, it would be next to impossible to get the access I needed. And I still had no idea about the cop connection to this case. If I divulged any of that to Oscar, he'd be obligated to tell Internal Affairs and everyone in the chain of command. He might as well broadcast it in the department newsletter. I'd make it up to him, though, maybe with dinner or something.

"Well, I need to get going. I really appreciate your help, and it was good seeing you again."

"Whatever you need, Ray. When you have more time, let's do lunch. I've still got more things we need to kick around."

"Yeah, we'll do that."

Oscar escorted me to the back door. Steve, Greg, and Pampas huddled in the hallway as we walked out.

Everyone said their good-byes, but just before I

turned and walked away, I asked Pampas, "Rick, whatever happened with that case at the Coral Bay?"

"I would've thought with all the free time you have now you would read the papers more. Murder-suicide."

"So they were having an affair, the pastor and his girlfriend?"

"She was a dancer at a strip club and had a history of prostitution," Rick said. "What do you care?"

"Just curious, I suppose. I find it interesting that I'd never seen her at the condo before, and neither had anyone else in Security. If she was his girlfriend and he was so crazy over her that he'd kill her, it's just a little odd that he didn't have her over to his place often enough to be noticed."

Pampas's eyes narrowed at me, knowing full well I had some knowledge of the case and was probing for more. "They could have met anywhere. He was a pastor. Not real likely he'd take her home to mother, if you know what I mean."

"So you say."

Pampas eyed me hard as Oscar walked me out the door. I'd hit a nerve, but I didn't feel bad about it.

"Why are you always messing with Rick?" Oscar said as we made it to my truck. "You need to let bygones be bygones. It's not good to let these things fester. It'll only tear you apart."

"Has he solved Trisha's murder yet?" I didn't care about the attempted murder on me, but Trish deserved better.

Oscar hissed, removed his glasses, and pinched the bridge of his nose. "You know the leads have run out and the case has gone cold. That's not Rick's fault. Whatever you might think of Pampas, he busted his tail like everybody else when that went down. We probably put a hundred people in jail for any charge we could find, including that scumbag Dante Hill. Rick and I worked him over good, but he wouldn't confess to nothing. Nobody's talking about this. You can't make evidence appear from the air. You need to let that go."

"I'll let it go when Pampas finds her killer." I eased into the truck but kept the door open. I didn't need to hear his excuses for Pampas.

He did arrest Dante Hill, the guy whose house Trisha and I were shot at, but Dante was only arrested for possessing two firearms as a convicted felon and a load of cocaine. He denied any involvement in the shooting, and no evidence linked him to it, other than that it happened in his front yard.

"If all the other leads have dried up, maybe Rick could start by finding that witness," I said. I really didn't want to get into the shooting with Oscar or anyone else, but when I'd decided to come to the station, I knew it would inevitably come up.

Oscar rested his hand on the roof and leaned in. "We all scoured that neighborhood. Some people heard the shots, but no one saw what you said you saw."

"Didn't you read my statement? Someone knelt between us and stayed there until the first officers arrived. That person had to have been there the whole time. As soon as I hit the ground, he was right there. He put a hand on my shoulder. I know what I saw, what I felt."

"I've been over your statement a hundred times," Oscar said. "And we've done everything we can to find that person, but you know how that neighborhood is. People don't often come forward to help us out. And—Never mind."

"What?" I said, not liking his tone.

"You'd lost a lot of blood. You should have died too."

"What are you saying, Oscar? That I don't know what I saw? I can't be relied on as a witness because of that?"

"Are you still seeing the psychologist?"

"Does it matter?"

"Look, Ray, posttraumatic stress disorder is nothing to play with. It kills more cops than any bad guys out there. The department pays for the visits, so use them."

"What does that have to do with Pampas not following up on the witness?"

"You went through hell that day. Trisha was

murdered right in front of you, and you were nearly killed yourself. I'm just saying that maybe as you were going unconscious, you thought you saw someone who wasn't really there. With everything else going on, that's not impossible."

"I know what happened that day. I know it so well I can't get it out of my head. Someone else was there. There's a witness who saw the whole thing and can solve this. Pampas just needs to get off his keister and find him."

"Okay. I'll make sure Rick and our guys go door to door and canvass the neighborhood again. I promise."

I didn't like it when Oscar patronized me, but I suppose after I just used him to get into the system, I couldn't be too put out. "That's all I ask."

"So is that why you took Pampas to task on the condo murder?"

"It happened in my building. I'm just curious about it. Pampas might have overlooked things there too. You never know."

Oscar cocked his head toward me and slapped the top of my truck twice. "Nice seeing you, Ray. Let's get together next week and I'll let you know about the progress with the witness."

"Sounds good," I said as I backed out of my spot. Oscar stayed put and didn't take his eyes off me as I pulled away.

It really didn't sound good. A witness to Trisha's murder was out there. Now Pampas had fumbled the Hendricks case as well. I'd avoided the station for a reason. I knew I couldn't show up without someone dragging me back to that day.

Sometimes I do hate it when I'm right.

23

MY CHARADE WITH OSCAR proved fruitful as I checked my e-mail when I got back to my apartment. I received the confirmation from Doug Farnham on the Yahoo! account I set up for that purpose, and it hadn't been cc'd to Oscar's work e-mail. So far, so good.

I tried my remote password entry on the system, and it worked perfectly. I had full access to all the police databases and information galore. I ran a check for the name and alias of Tay, which would search through all the reports and records for a match. I spelled it several different ways and came up with about a hundred possibilities. I saved them on my external hard drive and would get to them later.

I searched the Internet for several items I would need soon. As I made several pricey purchases, I came to the painful conclusion that at some point, financial debt was a little like treading water in the middle of the ocean—it doesn't matter if you're in a hundred feet of water or a thousand, you're still going to drown. So I clicked the Finish icon for my last round of online buys and sent them through, as the tide of my latest excesses surged well above my head.

I still had some of my cop gear with me from when I retired, or was retired. My digital recorders, a camera, binoculars, and bunches of little things. But the investigation would need more in-depth equipment if we were going to be successful. My new toys—a digital scanner for cell phones, several minicameras, audio surveillance equipment, a cell phone cloning unit, and some software to enhance my laptop—would be shipped to me within three days with a money-back guarantee.

My credit card should be just about ready to melt in my wallet.

I had a little time before my shift, so I rifled through the file and removed the subpoena for Jamie's phone records. I really needed to review them, but with only the subpoena for the records available, I would have to get a little . . . creative. I called Jamie's service provider's subpoena compliance center, a division that helps with law enforcement issues twenty-four hours a day. After an infuriating series of computer-generated options, I finally found a human to speak with.

"Subpoena compliance center, this is Derek. How can I help you?"

"Yes, this is Detective Ray Quinn with the Orlando Police Department. I was hoping you could help me with a problem."

"I'll try."

"I'm putting the finishing touches on a homicide case, and I see that we subpoenaed some phone records. I have the subpoena but not the records. Well, I'm looking to close this case out, and I really need the records as part of the packet. Is there any way you can resend them without a new subpoena? I can't afford to wait a couple more months to get this done."

"Hmm," Derek said. "I'm not sure. Can you give me your case number and the subpoena number?"

I gave them to him, even adding Jamie's name and date of birth for more credibility. I'd made calls like this a hundred times as a cop and never paid much attention. Now, I parsed every word and voice inflection from Derek to see if he suspected anything.

"I'll have to run this by my supervisor to see."

"I understand. I can wait."

Derek put me on hold, and I was treated to a Barry Manilow medley for several minutes. As Barry crooned about writing the songs the whole world sings, my spirit wasn't much in the mood for song and merriment. I wouldn't characterize myself as a liar, though my skills seemed to be improving daily.

As a police officer, I always used the term *bluff,* which was a euphemism for a lie. I made excuses for it, though it was for a legitimate investigation to do the greater good by catching bad guys. But as I held on the line, preparing my next round of stories for Derek, I wondered if at some point I would venture so far away from the truth that it would become unrecognizable. How many "bluffs" would I have to pull off to make this case? My flash of self-reflection was interrupted by Derek.

"Detective Quinn, I show that this information was sent out a month ago."

"Yeah, I know. I had a junior detective taking care of that, and he lost the information. You know how it goes. It's government work—you can't fire anyone these days."

"Believe me, I understand," he said. "My supervisor advised that I can release the information again, but only the subscriber information and phone tolls that were covered in the original subpoena."

"That would work great. You're a lifesaver."

"I can mail them out today."

"Derek, I hate to ask this, but is there any way I could get that in an electronic format, maybe by e-mail? I think that would be easier for both of us."

"Not a problem. I'll send it out shortly."

I gave him my newly reinstated OPD e-mail address. "Derek, you have a great day."

"You too."

Glad I could brighten Derek's day a little.

I wanted Jim to join me at my laptop in the living room, but I had to pull a shift at the condo in a couple of hours. Raising my arm over my head, I stretched out my ribs. My body still bore the aches and bruises from the beating. I didn't know if I would tell Helga about the fight. She might get jealous that someone else got to knock me around instead of her. Speaking of my fragile flower, since I missed my session with her yesterday, I hoped she didn't take it personally, or I'd feel her wrath at my next visit.

Settling back in my chair, I caught the ever-watchful eye of the Duke mounted on his steed. His stare confused me today. He didn't seem to know what to think of me now. We have that kind of relationship, going back to when I was very young.

The Duke and I first bonded when I lived with the Pearlmans. I stayed with them for about five months, and Mr. Pearlman remained in his chair in front of the television for most of the time I was there, John Wayne movies rolling along the screen. I don't remember Mr. Pearlman ever uttering a polysyllabic word. He communicated with Mrs. Pearlman through a series of grunts and hand gestures she understood without question, most of which revolved around bringing him another beer. He did, though, tolerate me in the room with him while he immersed himself into every single John Wayne movie ever made.

Before too long, I was captivated by the Duke. It didn't matter what character he played—from Davy Crockett to Sergeant Stryker to Rooster Cogburn—the Duke was always heroic and funny, and he had a sense of right and wrong, black and white, that was unequaled. After my seventeen foster and group homes in fifteen years, the Duke was the one person in my life who remained consistent. He and I were traveling partners after that.

The bell chimed on my laptop. I clicked into my department e-mail. Jamie DeAngelo's phone records had arrived.

I had a lot to do before I headed into work. I needed to get through more of David and Jamie's e-mails, work through the list of Tays I downloaded, and review Jamie's cell phone calls. I hoped it would be a slow night at the condos.

I got dressed and prepared to load up the laptop to take with me. I couldn't wait any longer, so I opened the e-mail from Derek and saved Jamie's file to my hard drive: two months of her cell phone records, calls to and from, times and dates. The subscriber information—the person whom the phone was registered to—was at the top of the page. I blinked. Was I seeing things? Jamie's cell phone number was listed to a J & M Corporation.

I went to my room and checked the receipt I'd found in Chance's trash—J & M Corporation, one in the same. What was this J & M Corporation, and why was it paying for Jamie's phone?

24

"CAN WE STEAL more trash tonight?" Crevis ambushed me as I entered the lobby. "We could leave when we're sure Mr. Savastio is asleep."

"No trash tonight," I said. "Our last search paid off already."

"What did you find?"

I explained that J & M Corporation was paying for Jamie's cell phone and was somehow connected to Chance, however tenuously. Finding out how J & M was related to Jamie and Chance would now be critical. I gave Crevis his most important task to date—stay out of my hair all night so I could do some Internet research. He reluctantly agreed.

I logged on to the Orlando PD system and ran a nationwide records check on J & M Corporation. The report compiled quickly. J & M was a subsidiary of the Relk Corporation, which was a subsidiary of Dorchester Distributing, which meant absolutely nothing to me. J & M was so layered with different corporations and affiliations, the confusion had to be on purpose. The address was listed as a PO box out of Nassau in the Bahamas. No officers of the corporation were listed, and since it was an offshore deal, it would make it nearly impossible to find any.

After typing out some notes until our shift ended, I treated Crevis to breakfast at Denny's and thanked him for letting me get some work done. I told him I might need his help later in the day. He agreed, in between the steam shovels of food to his face. The kid could pack it away. He wolfed down a breakfast special with a three-egg omelet, bacon, and a side of hash browns, and he washed that down with a stack of pancakes and maple syrup. How he stayed so lean I'll never know.

We parted ways. As I drove home, my cop tingles were out big-time, the little voice that warns of impending danger. I kept an eye on the traffic behind and around me and pulled into two parking lots on the way home to see if anyone was following me. Nothing . . . that I could see, anyway.

I finally made it home. You're only considered paranoid if people aren't really out to get you. I'd already been jumped once, so I wasn't being paranoid, just prepared. If my adversary knew where I worked, there was a good chance he knew where I lived.

Once at the apartment, I went straight for Jim, but I had a dilemma. I had too much to do in the afternoon to get very plowed under. If I didn't drink any alcohol, I wouldn't get anything resembling sleep. And I really needed some rest. I decided on a happy medium of a single glass of Jim. I stretched it out to three.

I had a lot to do when I got up, so I was on my feet quickly, chugging down coffee. I was scheduled to meet with the most significant woman in my life—Helga—in the afternoon. That would have to wait—again. I'd call her later and come up with some excuse.

After printing out a copy of the last two months of Jamie's cell phone calls, I grabbed my highlighter and another cup of coffee, then settled on the living room couch. I conducted a quick review of the times and noted that Jamie, like me, worked and lived in the midnight hours. Most of her calls didn't start until around 2:00 or 3:00 p.m., going well into the early morning, stopping around 5:00 a.m., for her to sleep, I figured. It was amazing the information about a person you could garner through their phone records.

I highlighted David's number in red—a few calls. Then I singled out Ashley's in yellow—fewer than David's but still a noticeable amount. I checked the phone book for the number to Club Venus and matched it against the records, marking it several times. My process of elimination rainbowed most of the page.

Two unknown numbers showed regular contact with Jamie: one appeared about once a day. The other, two or three times a day in some fashion—even more contact than with David. More significant than that, that same number called Jamie's phone no less than six times the day she was murdered. Jamie's last two calls were to David, though.

I chose to find out about the lesser of the two. I dialed the number with my cell phone. After a couple of rings, someone picked up. "Chance," he said.

"Yes, may I speak with Marion Morrison please?" I disguised my voice enough for my buddy not to recognize me.

"Wrong number." He hung up and was a little rude, I might add.

I laughed as I scribbled Chance's name next to that number. My little call told me a number of things about my buddy Chance, mainly that he had more contact with Jamie than he initially led me to believe. And he knew nothing about John Wayne, or he would have picked up on the fact that Marion Morrison was the Duke's real name. Another good reason not to like or trust Chance.

Most of the records were accounted for now. Only sporadic, random numbers were left with no discernable pattern—with the exception of her most frequent caller. I yearned to press my luck with another cold call to that number, but I wasn't sure if that was the right move. I considered the pros and cons for a moment, then a better idea presented itself. And if I was right, it could reap a harvest of pertinent information.

Instead of calling the number, I dialed Pam's and told her I had a mission for her.

25

AS I WAITED FOR PAM to arrive, I logged on to the OPD system again. I ran the mystery phone number through the database, but nothing came up. I checked through several of the reports with different Tays, wondering if this thug had made another appearance in Jamie's life and was calling her a lot. Nothing jumped out at me. It was invigorating to have a couple different avenues going on the case; it felt like the old days.

Pam knocked on my door in less than fifteen minutes. I closed out what I was doing and let her in. She leaned forward like she wanted to hug me, then pulled back; I just shook her hand. I don't know what it is about church people, but they do seem to hug a lot.

I filled Pam in on the phone number that called Jamie the most often. "I can't just whip out a subpoena and find out who it is. Even if I could, it might be listed in someone else's name. I'd like you to call the number and try to find out who it belongs to."

"What do you want me to say? I doubt this person will just blurt out who he is and why he called Jamie."

"True," I said. "So I want you to tell whoever answers that you're a friend of Jamie's. I think coming from a female caller this would be more believable."

Pam raised an eyebrow at me.

"Trust me. I'll brief you on the way."

"On the way to where?"

"I don't want to do this with my cell or home numbers," I said. "We need to find a pay phone. I took a real risk calling Chance's number, but I wasn't trying to get information from him, so I don't think he suspected anything. With this next call, we'll have to be a little shrewder."

"I'll do whatever I have to for the case. I just want to be sure I don't mess it up."

"We just need to hone your bluffing skills a bit."

"And just how do you plan to do that?" She folded her arms and scowled at me.

"Okay, try this line for practice: 'Ray Quinn is a supernice guy.' If you can say that with a straight face, you'll be ready to make that call."

"Robert De Niro couldn't even pull that line off," she said. "I'd rather make the call than attempt that." She smirked. "I think I'm ready."

We got in my truck, and it took us nearly half an hour to find a working pay phone at a gas station on John Young Parkway. I wasn't even sure there were any around anymore, since almost everyone on the planet owned a cell phone. We discussed the strategy along the way. Pam was sharp, but I hoped her religiosity wouldn't get in the way.

"Whoever used that number to call Jamie has a

major connection to her, so much so that he had to talk with her several times a day," I said. "I'm betting that person bites big-time. But you have to remember everything we talked about. If I want you to say something different, I'll write it on the pad."

I had a two-way earpiece plugged into the microphone of my digital recorder. Pam would have one earpiece in her ear and place the phone up to it, so I could record both sides of the conversation. I had the other to listen to the call.

I didn't inform Pam that this was mildly illegal. I suppose it's like being kind of pregnant. You either are or you're not. Recording this conversation was illegal, but I would erase it as soon as I could. I'd just hate to miss some good information. If we could come up with something solid, I'd take the fall to get the information to solve this homicide.

She put the earphone in and nodded to me. I punched in the numbers. The midafternoon traffic would make hearing a bit difficult.

"Hello," the man on the other end said.

"Ah . . . yes." Pam glared at me. "I'm a friend of Jamie's."

Her statement was met by silence.

"She told me that if something ever happened to her, I . . . I was supposed to drop a package off to you."

"What kind of package?"

I nodded to Pam and rolled my hands. He was talking. That was good. The more he chatted, the better.

"I don't know what's in it," Pam said. "She just told me it was imperative that I get it to you. She said this package would be important to you too. I just found out about her death. I'm sorry I'm so late getting in touch with you."

Pam improvised that last part. Not bad for a woman not inclined to lying, bluffing, or whatever.

"I . . . I'm not sure about this," he said. "How do I know you're on the level?"

"I had your number, didn't I? Jamie gave it to me with strict instructions. I'm just trying to follow them. Evidently, this was very important to her, so I want to make sure it's done right. I'm supposed to give it to you personally."

"I understand," he said. "How do you want to do this?"

She'd reeled him in; now it was time to net him.

"Meet me in an hour in the Burger King parking lot on International Drive near Municipal Drive. I'll be driving a blue Mercedes. What will you be driving?"

"I'll find you," he said.

I scribbled my knockout punch on the pad and showed it to Pam.

She nodded. "I really miss Jamie."

"So do I." He choked up and then disconnected.

"That went well, Detective Winters. You're earning your keep."

Pam smiled. "Maybe I'm a better actress than I thought. But even though that went well, I'm still not ready to try your line yet."

"I can live with that . . . for now," I said, giving her the deadeye. "But we're not nearly finished yet."

26

I PULLED INTO A STRIP MALL across from the Burger King, which was on the outskirts of a much larger shopping center. The parking lot was open, and I could keep a good eye on the entire area and ease back into traffic without too much difficulty.

Pam adjusted herself in her seat. "What do we do now?"

"Wait." I scanned the Burger King parking lot with my binoculars. A fair number of cars flowed in and out, making me question my decision to lead him here. I was still a little rusty with the surveillance stuff, but it was too late to change things, so we'd have to make it work. I checked a couple of parked cars. All of them seemed empty.

"What if he doesn't show?"

"He'll show," I said. "Out of curiosity if nothing else. Did you hear the emotion in his voice? I think you more than piqued his interest."

Pam wrapped her arms across her stomach. "Do you really think this is the person who killed them both?"

"Don't know. But for some reason this guy lit up her cell phone constantly and called her six times on the day she died. That sounds a lot like a jealous or angry boyfriend. I still haven't identified Tay. Maybe this is him."

"I just feel so weird," she said. "Like I want it to be the person, but not really the person who did such a wicked thing. I feel like I'm going to jump out of my skin. How do you police officers deal with the stress?"

"We drink . . . a lot. But first things first. We have to identify this guy. Once we do that, we'll turn up the stress on him."

"Do you mind if I pray?"

"What would you do if I did?" I said.

She shrugged. "Do it anyway."

I chuckled. She was consistent if nothing else. "That's what I thought. Go ahead. But don't take too long; I have a live one that just pulled in."

I tracked a black Suburban that turned off International Drive into the parking lot. A lone male driver slowed down and peered at each car as he passed. He was looking for someone. He did a measured lap around Burger King, then parked toward the front. He got out and lingered at the back of his car, leaning against the back hatch doors.

If it was him, he wasn't quite what I expected. The voice on the phone seemed older and a little gruff. This guy was about thirty with thick dark hair and a stout doughy frame. He wore a blue power suit with a red tie and had a purposed look on his preppy face. He smacked of an educated professional there for business. He crossed his arms and scanned the parking lot. He checked his watch and continued searching.

"He's our guy," I said. "I'd bet money on it, except you religious folks probably don't gamble."

"How can you be so sure it's him?" She ignored my stab at humor.

"Body language. He's checked his watch a number of times, and he's only been there a couple of minutes. He's standing outside, not going in or through the drive-through, so he's not a customer. He has a business face on. He's there to meet someone. He's there to meet you."

"Do you want me to go over and meet him? I'll try to get him to talk to me." She unlocked her door and was almost out before I stopped her.

"Luckily, we're not going to do that right now," I said. Pam had chutzpa for sure. She would have hopped right out, marched across the street, and demanded answers if I would have told her to. I wasn't ready to release her on this guy yet. "Besides, I think we can get more information from him by not showing up. A lot of police work is trying to anticipate your opponent's next move.

What will he do if the person he's waiting for doesn't show up?"

"Leave?" she said.

"Not bad for a rookie." I snapped a couple of photos of him and stowed the camera on the seat. The guy alternated his attention from his watch to the parking lot. "Does this guy's looks match the voice you spoke with?"

She checked him out with the binoculars. "I would have thought he'd be older."

"Precisely. He looks quite professional as well. This kinda guy doesn't go by the name of Tay, I can tell you that much."

It was about ten minutes after one, and Doughboy paced around the car a couple of times, then hustled from one end of the parking lot to the other. He was working up a sweat.

"It's hard to just sit here and watch," Pam said. "I feel like we should be doing something."

"We are. We're being smart."

He pulled his cell phone off his belt and dialed a number. I retrieved my digital cell phone scanner from underneath my seat. Easing the knob around, I listened to a variety of calls. None of them fit. I passed a terse baritone and tuned in.

"I've been here fifteen minutes already, and nobody has showed up." Our guy's mouth matched the words. He plugged one ear with a finger as he spoke. "I think someone is playing a game with us."

"I want you to stay as long as it takes," the voice on the other end said, the caller Pam spoke to. Our guy had sent someone ahead for him, to scout things out. Very clever. He was making the hunt interesting.

"Whoever this girl is, she knows way too much. We have to find out who she is and how she knows about Jamie and me. Then we'll work on making it go away. Understand?"

"Got it, Mike," our guy said. "But I think you're a little too worried about this thing. It was probably a crank call, or someone trying to rattle you."

"We really don't have the luxury of taking that chance, now, do we? What if Jamie did have something hidden away, an insurance policy of sorts? It could take us all down. Got it?"

Our guy flipped the phone shut and passed his chubby little fingers through his hair.

"So we're looking for a Mike." I jotted down on my notepad the time of the call and what was said. I also noted the scanner's dial position for that phone, which could come in handy later. Any confusion I had on "if" Jamie was seeing someone else was obliterated by that one call.

Pam smirked at me. "You know this was all set up by prayer, don't you?"

"I'm just starting to have some fun on this case, so please don't ruin the moment for me."

"God's going to clear David's name. I've felt it since we first met."

"You mean the very first time we met?" I said, my filter slipping a bit. "I felt something entirely different at our first meeting." I rubbed my jaw.

Pam's eyes narrowed and her face brightened. "Maybe not the first time we met. But soon after that."

I still wondered about a woman who could believe so passionately in a God who would lead us to David's killer and clear his name, and yet she refused to be angry with that same God for allowing the murder to happen in the first place. Life isn't always logical, but that one didn't make much sense. At least Pam had a sense of humor and could take a little ribbing, a rarity among the religious people I've known.

Trisha used to take teasing pretty good too, but she gave it back even better. On her first day in the unit, I made some snotty comment about her shoes. She punk'd me about my hair and tie without missing a beat. She was quick and tough and didn't take anything from me. We hit it off right away and were partners after that.

Our guy grunted it out for another forty-five minutes, about fifteen minutes longer than I thought he'd stay. I took the opportunity to snap more photos of him and his car. At a little after 2:00 p.m., he tossed his hands in the air and got back into his SUV.

"Now we're getting somewhere." I started the truck and waited for him to pull into traffic. "So, rookie, I'm going to give you a little quiz on your understanding of police work thus far. Since we didn't show up to meet him, where's he going now?"

Pam shifted toward me and was silent for a moment. Then her face lit up. "He's going to see Mike."

"You're getting the hang of this." I eased into traffic several cars behind him. "We're going to let our buddy lead us to right to Mike."

He headed west on I-Drive and then north on Kirkman until he picked up I-4 north toward downtown. We kept our distance, always hanging back and using other cars for cover. I was able to get a clear view of his license plate number—an Orange County tag, which piqued my interest all the more.

He signaled to get off at the Anderson Street exit downtown. Rush-hour traffic was awful, but we locked on our target as he zigzagged through some side streets. He drove into the back parking lot of the Fairwinds Building on the corner of West Central and Garland. We passed by but turned around in time to see him power walking into the building.

"Are we going to follow him in?" Pam said.

I killed the engine and prepared to get out when I looked across the parking lot at the huge sign at the end. "I think I know exactly where he's going."

Pam gawked at me.

I pointed to the sign that read "Campaign Office of County Commissioner Michael Vitaliano." A picture of a distinguished, gray-headed gentleman graced us with his pompous politico's smile. A thousand realizations collided in my head.

I turned to Pam. "Call me psychic, but I think I might know who Mike is."

27

IF GOOGLING WERE A SPORT, I'd be on my way to the Olympic Village right now. I enjoy digging through page after page or finding that one obscure fact out in cyberspace. It's been worse since I got hurt and don't get out of my apartment as much as I should.

After I dropped Pam off at her place, I went back to my apartment and logged on to my computer right away. I navigated my way to the good com-missioner's Web site. Having worked in Orlando for over fifteen years, I'd have to have been blind and deaf to be ignorant of County Commissioner Michael Vitaliano. As election season was gear-ing up the last couple of months, his magnanimous mug had intruded on the televisions of everyone in Orange County, the flag flapping behind him. Nice. His Web site wasn't a lot better. I've never had much use for politics or politicians.

Scrolling through different areas of the site, I determined that any rational human being would have to be fairly intoxicated to enjoy this kind of stuff. I was tempted to have Jim accompany me on my tour so I could stomach the putrid political pabulum. Family values. Fair wages. Health care. Blah, blah, blah. Nothing revealing . . . until I clicked into his staff. Chief of Staff Gordon Kurfis, my Burger King guy, popped up. A smug-looking fellow, to be sure. Graduated from Princeton, top of his class too. A fine education wasted on being a political hack's do-boy. I'd have to bring my dictionary with me when I talked with him. I printed the picture and added his name to the notes.

I stabbed his photo on the wall with a pushpin next to Michael "Family Values" Vitaliano. I wrote the phone number I contacted them with underneath and drew some hasty lines connecting the others. The prefix for Vitaliano's number was the same, and the last four digits were only a few off from Jamie's. A coincidence? Not in this case. I wrote "The Lion's Den" between the two.

I absorbed the collage that was becoming this case. I had phone links from Chance to Jamie, Jamie to the Commish, and Jamie to David, all on the day of her death. If I had time, I'd print out a larger graph showing the connections more clearly, at least better than my hasty Magic Marker on the dry wall.

I had a full-fledged crime scene section set up as well. I'd covered the gruesome photos with a piece of paper I could lift, so that when Pam was here, it wouldn't freak her out. Whatever else I was struggling with, I generally didn't like being sadistic. And the little fundamentalist marm was growing on me. She did a good job reeling in the Commish. I'd have to tell her that.

I pinned the cover paper back and studied the photos of David and Jamie at the crime scene. Since the first time I saw the photos, something's always bothered me about them. Why did David have a scrape on his knee that looked like a rug burn? Why the piece of pillow embedded in his head wound? Why would a pastor even own a pistol with the serial number filed off? Why would he kill her at all?

Then there was the gunshot residue found on David's hands, verified by the Florida Department of Law Enforcement lab. That was a tough one to explain. The locked room. No one seen coming or going. I had a lot of dots, but no great connections . . . yet.

I pulled a kitchen chair into the living room and checked my notes on Gordon's call to his boss. "What if Jamie did have something hidden away, an insurance policy of sorts? It could take us all down." The "us" intrigued me. I didn't think the good public servant hung out with Jamie for her savvy political skills. The emotion in his voice was raw, palpable. He was a man in love. I'd remember that when we spoke.

With everything in this case spinning out of

control, I couldn't ignore some serious facts. I'm not the sharpest tack in the box, and I was able fairly quickly to put together the phone connection between the Commish, Jamie, and David. Why weren't those phone records in the original report—even after being subpoenaed? The stunning simplicity of that answer had been hounding me since I saw Vitaliano's campaign sign.

Ashley was a truth teller about the Lion's Den. There was no doubt now that someone inside the police department had intentionally removed the records.

I made my way over to the kitchen sink and released my good friend Jim. Since I had no shift to cover, I would consult his wisdom on this case.

28

AT ABOUT 1:30 P.M. the next day, Pam and Crevis met me at my apartment. I made attempts at being cordial, but my head hummed and throbbed. I hustled to chase my mental fog away with a potent cup of java. I offered them both some, but no one was taking, which meant more for me.

As life flowed into my veins via my caffeine push, I briefed them on the status of the investigation. I had planned to turn the investigation back over to Oscar at some point, help Rick Pampas pack up his desk and escort his incompetent butt back to patrol for his shoddy work, and be on my happy way. But the disappearance of the one piece of evidence that could transform a murder-suicide into a full-on double murder changed those plans. This case was never going back to OPD.

Crevis raised his hand. "With all this dirty-cop stuff going on, I'm going to need a gun."

"Not on your life," I said. "Any more questions?"

"What about Sergeant Yancey?" Pam said. "Surely you can trust him."

"Sort of. But a bad cop in the department or the unit somewhere could cause a lot of trouble. It wouldn't be wise to risk it by revealing anything to Oscar now. I need to find out who removed those records. And, even more important, we have to find all the players in the Lion's Den. Once we do that, most of these questions will fall into line." I needed to call Oscar and find out what was going on with the gun they took off the goon who attacked me.

Crevis jabbed my heavy bag twice, then followed up with a stinging right. The bag swung high into the kitchen then back toward him. He stopped it with a solid knee strike. He had good power for his size, but if I worked with him, it could be even better. When I got some time, I might run him through some drills and tighten up his skills.

I dialed Oscar; he picked up on the second ring. "Hey, Ray. What's going on?"

"Same, same. I was just curious if they'd tracked the .45 from the thug who attacked me."

"I made sure they sent off an ATF track on it," he said. "We should have the last legal owner by next week sometime. Maybe when it comes in, we could meet for lunch or something?"

"I'd like that."

"You're starting to sound like your old self again," Oscar said.

"Starting to feel like it too." In more ways than I could explain. "By the way, do you know anyone with the street name of Tay? Anything like that crossed your desk?"

Oscar paused. "I know a few. Are you messing with me about the Pampas thing again?"

"No. Just curious about a Tay."

"You need to get off that, Ray."

"I don't think we're talking about the same thing."

"I think we are. The last Tay I came in contact with is Dante Hill. He sometimes went by Tay, as well as Dantevious."

"That's . . . not what I meant." My body locked up, and so did my mind. "I . . . I'll call you next week."

"Take care," he said, not nearly as jolly as when he answered the phone.

I slid the phone back in the pouch on my belt and staggered back to the chair in front of my laptop.

"You okay, Ray?" Crevis said. "Looks like you're gonna hurl."

Pam called my name twice and then said, "What did he say?"

"Oscar knows a Tay. And so do I; although I didn't know that was his street name. I never got the chance to interview him."

My head swirled. I logged on to my computer and the OPD system, then ran a check on Dante Hill. Two dozen reports rolled past, which didn't surprise me, given his record. I clicked into each, hoping I'd turn up nothing.

"Ray, are you all right?" Pam rested her hand on my shoulder. I shook it off.

"I'm fine. Let me finish this."

She backed off and crossed her arms.

I found a domestic violence report about a year and a half old. I opened the file and read. Dante's neighbor called in a domestic battery in progress where Dante was beating his girlfriend in the front yard of his house. The girlfriend was gone when the police arrived. They interrogated Dante, who was less than cooperative. They were only able to ascertain Dante's girlfriend's first name— Jamie. A neighbor said he thought she was a dancer at a strip club.

I hissed and flopped back against the chair. What grievous offense had I committed to be placed in this position? "This can't be."

"Ray," Pam said. "What's going on?"

"I believe Dante Hill is the Tay who used to date Jamie."

"Well, that's a good thing, isn't it?" she said. "You found him and now you can talk with him."

"I can talk with him all right. I know exactly where he is right now. I also know he had nothing to do with David's and Jamie's murders."

"How can you be so sure?" Pam said.

"Because he's been in jail since June second of last year. The night Trish and I were ambushed."

29

FRIENDS ARE TRULY a rare commodity—rarer still for some than others.

I found that out when I was flat on my back in ICU for three weeks, staring at the ceiling tiles as the respirator breathed for me. The rhythmic beat of that machine—methodical, sterile, and relentless—haunts me still and invades my dreams at times. Each ceiling tile in that unit contained between 114 and 172 pinholes. No more, no less. Three weeks is an eternity in ICU.

About three days after my first surgery, I had been in and out of a haze as the respirator awakened me. Oscar stood next to my bed in full dress uniform, his hat tucked under his arm, his face solemn. I wondered why he was so decked out.

I tried to turn my head toward him, but the intubation tube down my throat wouldn't let me move. A black band covered his badge. He informed me—between the beats of that awful machine—that they had just buried Trisha.

Florida Department of Law Enforcement agent Tim Porter was one of the few others who came to my bedside. I don't remember anything he said that day; the medication was particularly powerful. I just remember him standing there, looking down at me.

He'd worked in our unit some years before and was shot in the stomach while busting up a bank robbery in progress. He recovered, retired, and went to work for the FDLE. I always wondered why he came to see me. Maybe he remembered what it felt to be laid up like that.

After Oscar's revelation about Dante Hill, I knew I needed law enforcement help, but I didn't know who I could trust. I called Tim out of the blue, and he agreed to meet me. Tim caught my eye as he entered the Perkins restaurant on 192 and Dwyer in Kissimmee.

Tim and I had to meet somewhere out of Orange County; he worked out of the FDLE Melbourne office, south of Kennedy Space Center. I figured this would be about halfway for us both.

"Great to see you, Ray. Still ugly as ever."

Tim was a burly African American with a chest like a bulldog and eyes to match. He was always hungry for a fight and feasted regularly. Not a bad thing for a cop. Time had tinted his hair some on the sides, but he looked like he'd been taking care of himself. The former marine had a strong rep with the department.

"Not much I can do about that. I only have so much to work with."

He shook my hand, slid into the booth, and picked up the menu. The waitress showed up with a couple glasses of water.

"You buying?" he said.

"I suppose that depends."

"I don't like the sound of that. Sounds more like business than pleasure."

"Glad to see that FDLE hasn't sucked out all your investigative skills," I said.

"I have to admit I was a little surprised to hear from you. Glad, but surprised."

"I need some help." The words didn't come out easily, because I'm not used to speaking them. Unfortunately I'd been speaking them with more frequency of late.

"What can I help you with?" He crossed his brawny arms and gave me his full attention.

I explained about the murder, the marm, and the mess I'd gotten myself entangled in. Tim nodded a lot but didn't say much. I respected his opinion, but I didn't know where his loyalties would lie. Would he tell Oscar what I was divulging to him? Would he open up an FDLE investigation? I didn't want either, not right now, anyway.

"You have a knack for the difficult," he said.

"Even when you were a young detective, you could find trouble like fleas find a dog."

I couldn't hold back a smile. "Maybe, but I'm neck deep in it now and could use some help."

"Go to Oscar." He slapped the table like he was telling me something I hadn't thought of. "He's been through everything you can imagine. He'll work with you on this."

"I can't do that."

"Why? I talked to Oscar when you were in the hospital. The man respects you, and that's not easy with him."

"I think we have a problem at the department," I said. "Potentially, a big problem."

"What kind of trouble are we talking about?"

"Someone in the department is on the take. He's wrapped up with the Lion's Den."

"You know this for sure?" Tim said.

"Yeah, I'm pretty sure. And I think this relates back to my shooting."

"Oh boy. What do you need from me?"

"A couple of favors would be good," I said. "First, I need a prison visit for two. Second, I need some subpoenas, for phone records, to be exact."

"The prison visit is easy." He rubbed his chin. "The subpoenas are a little tougher. I'm gonna need to open a case of my own for the numbers. The state attorney's office won't even look at a subpoena without a case number. And even if I *can* do this, I can only keep it quiet for so long, especially if what you're telling me is true about the dirty cop. My bosses will want to know about that right away." Tim's expression was conflicted. "This puts me in a tight spot, Ray. I've got to do something."

"All I'm asking for is a little time. If we're not careful, this thing could get out of control. I don't want this person to get away with it. If he's responsible for Trisha's murder and my shooting, I want him to pay. We can't do that until we smoke out whoever it is."

I'd heaped a pretty large request on the guy, someone who owed me nothing. Most cops in his situation would wash their hands of it and walk away. It was his move now; I'd stay quiet until he answered.

After about thirty agonizing seconds and three discernible sighs, he returned his attention to me. "I can give you one week. No more."

"Thanks, Tim. We're gonna link these cases, I promise you that."

"I hope so. Or the only link you and I will share is at the Job Link." Tim drained his water.

The waitress returned and took our orders. I got a big fat burger with fries. Tim ordered a steak, a baked potato, a side salad, and an extra order of fries, and topped it all off with lemon meringue pie for dessert. He knew I was paying now.

"I have one more thing," I said as the waitress left us.

"I figured once you got your way, you'd push

for more." Tim folded his hands on the table. "Some things never change."

"This is different. It's . . . personal."

Tim nodded. "Go ahead."

"Why did you come to see me at the hospital? I mean, I didn't know you that well before you left. That's been bugging me for a while."

"I'm glad you asked." Tim smiled like he'd been waiting for me to bring it up. "When I heard the news about you and Trisha, I was sick. Been there, done that. I got down on my knees and started praying for you."

"Don't tell me you're one of those God types." I rubbed the back of my neck to work out a kink. "I didn't know that about you."

"I wasn't when I worked in Orlando. Gave my life to the Lord about six months before your shootin'. I went through a rough time with my daughter, but God blessed me through it, and He can do it for you too."

I didn't realize Tim had been drinking the God Kool-Aid. But since he was doing me several serious favors, I was compelled to at least appear like I was listening to him. I think he knew that too, because he had the same silly expression on his face that Pam gets when she's going God on me.

I tipped him the courtesy nod. He appeared disappointed that I didn't engage him. But since I'd already bought him some pie, I wasn't sure how much further I was ready to go with him on this.

"Anyway, I prayed hard that God would spare you and bless you. I felt in my spirit that He was telling me to visit you. I came to your bedside to pray and hear God's voice."

"And what did He say?"

"That you were going to be all right," Tim said. "God's not finished with you yet, Ray Quinn."

30

I'D HAD GOD IN MY FACE every day since Pam and this case shoved its way into my life. Now the Prophet Porter?

Meeting with Tim had gone well, at least from the investigative end. I got more from him than I thought I would. His last comment stuck with me, though. In no way would Pam find out about that part of our conversation. It could whip her into a religious frenzy.

The metallic buzzer signaled, and the sliding door rolled open. Prisons don't seem to have that homey feel for me. I had to give Tim Porter credit. With just a few phone calls, he got me a two-person contact visit with Dante Hill at the Lawtey Correctional Institution near Jacksonville. Crevis and I made good time on the drive up.

This contact visit would put me in the same room with Dante Hill—quite possibly Trisha's killer and the man who crippled me.

"They're bringing Hill up now." Our minder was a burly corrections officer about my height but supersized, a good forty pounds heavier, most of it in the chest. He sported the Lex Luthor hairstyle: slick and shiny all over.

I had to wrap my head around a couple of serious facts. Dante Hill had been dating Jamie around the time Trisha and I were ambushed in his driveway. Eleven months later Jamie was murdered in David's apartment, the same condo where I work. If I were of a suspicious nature, I'd say I was a little too tangled in this mess.

Crevis was nearly unrecognizable, with his shirt tucked in and his flattop trimmed to a razor's edge. On the ride up, I filled him in about Dante. I told him he'd have to be on his best behavior when we arrived, and that under no condition could he bring any weapon into the prison—no knives, no brass knuckles, no saps, no Kubotans. If he brought any of those, he'd become a guest here, not just a visitor. I left my pistol in the truck. After carrying one for so long, I felt naked and vulnerable without it.

"This is weird." Crevis searched the walls for any escape. "I don't like it."

"I've never been big on doors locking behind me either."

Lex's boots tapped out a cadence for us as we marched down a narrow green hallway toward the interview rooms. In nearly every prison I've been in, and I've visited many, I can't figure out why they always seem to be painted green. Maybe there's some deep psychological reason for the color, like it calms people and such. It drove me nuts.

Lex drew a set of keys from his duty belt and unlocked the door, which had a frame of glass in it. Not much larger than a closet, the room had a table and three chairs. It was used by the prison system's investigations division. Crude, but good enough for what we needed. I took a seat while Crevis leaned against the wall.

A shuffle of feet outside the door announced the guest of honor's arrival. Dante Hill's chest and head filled up the window. Dante was African American and had shaved his dreadlocks since I'd seen him last. He'd beefed up too. He used to cruise at about a hundred eighty pounds; he was around two twenty now. The door jiggled open. He wore the thick-rimmed prison glasses that gave him a slight intellectual, albeit felonious, look.

Dante sauntered in, dark blue jumper and all, and locked eyes with me. His confused stare told me that he didn't recognize me. It had been awhile.

"Do you want the cuffs on or off?" Lex said.

"Off will be fine," I said.

Crevis kept his back to the wall as he stood next to me.

Lex removed the cuffs and pulled a chair up for Dante. "Sit," he said, like commanding a dog.

Dante took his time but finally eased into the chair.

"I'll be right outside if you need me." Lex winked. Maybe Lex was all right after all.

Dante exhaled dramatically and crossed his arms. "What can I do for you fellas?"

"You don't remember me?" I shook my head. "That hurts my feelings."

He scanned the cane propped against the table and leaned in. "Detective Quinn. Good to see you again. You weren't lookin' so hot the last time I saw you."

"Doing better now. No thanks to you."

"I was wondering how long it would take you to talk with me," he said. "To tell you the truth, it took longer than I thought. I'm disappointed in you, Quinn. Maybe you're losing your touch."

I toyed with the pen on the legal pad I had set out next to my folder. My pulse was surging so hard I thought I might pass out. Maybe the room was too small for a decent interview. I tunneled in on Dante and did everything I could to replay in my head that night. All I could come up with was a shadow running away from us. If I could have fingered this guy for anything, I would have. But I just didn't know.

Dante folded his hands on the table and scooted his chair forward. He smiled. "When are you going to ask me the question you came all this way for?"

"I'll get to that." I was so shaken that Dante

had to see it. Maybe this wasn't such a great idea. The room was hot. Really hot, like a sauna. Perspiration beaded on my forehead. I swallowed hard and pulled Jamie's picture from the folder. "Tell me about her."

"Jamie DeAngelo." He smiled. "Hot little girl. We hung out for a while."

One confirmation down. Many more to go. "Tell me about him." I flicked out David's driver's license photo.

He studied it for a moment. "Never seen him."

"Ever?"

"Nope. Got anything else, Quinn?"

"How long did you and Jamie 'hang out'?"

"A few months maybe," he said. "What are you looking for? You're dancing around it. Just ask the question."

"I'll get to it when I get to it." I still needed him to think I was running the interview, although at that point, I wasn't so sure myself. "Where was Jamie working then?"

He shrugged. "She did lots of things."

"Did she work at Club Venus?"

A Cheshire grin creased his face. "Been doing some homework, Quinn. I like that. Yeah, she started with Club Venus around the time we broke up. She was hard working and hot."

"A lot of people thought so." I took my photos back and placed them in the file. "Did you know Jamie was murdered?"

Dante raised an eyebrow. "I've been locked up, so I hope you didn't come here to pin that on me too."

"Did you know she was dead?"

"No. And I didn't have anything to do with it. So if that's why you're here, you are wasting your time."

Jamie and Dante must have had a beautiful relationship, evidenced by the fact that when I told him his ex-girlfriend was dead, the only thing he could think about was himself. What a guy. Not surprising, though. Dante's criminal history was long and distinguished—everything from trafficking cocaine to armed robbery. And he liked to beat his women too. I searched for some redeemable characteristic in him to share with Pam later. (She'd want to know, I was sure.) He was making me work to find any.

"I know you didn't have anything to do with her death."

"That's never stopped OPD from making up charges anyway," he said.

I haven't met a con yet who ever took responsibility for his crimes, so I let him stew for a few seconds.

"What did she do at the club?"

"Danced," he hissed. "What do you think?"

"That didn't bother you? Her dancing around half naked with other men?"

"What do I care?" His brow furrowed. "She

brought home up to two stacks a week. I didn't care what she had to do to get it. We had a good thing going for a while."

"What happened?"

"She started gettin' uppity, like she was better than me and all. I got sick of her and kicked her butt to the curb."

"There were a couple of reports that you knocked her around a bit," I said.

He waved a hand at me. "No chick is gonna get in my face about nothin', Quinn. You can bet on that. Maybe you put up with that from your women, but I don't. She knew better than that too."

"Two grand a week is a lot of money. Even for an attractive dancer. Was she doing anything on the side other than dancing?"

He shrugged. "She wasn't stupid. She knew what she was doing. Like I said, we had a good arrangement. She made good money and made some good connections."

"What kind of connections?"

Dante sat straight up and rubbed his chin. "Why haven't you read me my rights? You should have done that by now."

"Because I'm only here to talk. I'm just gathering intel for something I'm working. So even if you confessed anything to me now, I couldn't use it against you. I just need to know some things about Jamie."

Dante nodded. He was uneducated but not

stupid. He'd been in and out of the system enough that he understood the workings better than most cops. I was shooting straight with him on that and he knew it.

"Jamie had an 'in' to help me out," he said.

"What kind of 'in'?"

Dante smirked. "She was seeing someone with OPD."

"You have a name?"

"Nope, and I really didn't care. She said she'd know if the cops were looking at me for anything . . . if I needed that kinda information, of course."

"Did Jamie tell you that Detective Willis and I were going to your house that night?"

"'Bout time, Quinn." He leapt to his feet and pounded his knuckles into the table. Crevis pushed himself off the wall and was at my side in a second, fists clenched. "I was wondering when we'd get to this. I didn't shoot you, her, or anyone else. And who's this retard with you?"

"He's Crevis, and I wouldn't push him too far. He bites."

Crevis clacked his teeth together and growled. Nice touch. I'd reward him for that later.

"Tell him to back off." Dante eased back into his chair. "Dude makes me uncomfortable standing over there all quiet like he's Rain Man or something."

I nodded to Crevis, who stepped back to hold up the wall again. The kid was doing exactly what

I told him to do—stand there and look crazy but don't ever speak. Evidently, he had unnerved Dante a bit.

"We were walking up to your front door when we were ambushed," I said. "You're telling me you had nothing to do with it?"

"I heard the shots and looked out my window. As far as I could see, I had two dead cops on my front lawn. I'm the one who called 911. Why would I do that if I was responsible for shootin' you? It doesn't make any sense."

"Did you come outside to help me?"

"No way," he said. "I stayed in the house and on the line with the dispatcher. I wasn't going out there."

"So you must have seen the person who showed up to help me."

"No one helped you until the first officer came screeching up. You can ask the dispatcher. I thought you were both dead. I didn't want two dead cops in my front yard. It's bad for business."

"You didn't see *anyone* bend down next to me?"

"Are you deaf? I said no. After the first cops arrived, there was more police in my yard than I've ever seen in my life—like it was a doughnut convention or somethin'. And because of my record, they yanked me outta my own house and got a search warrant. They said they found cocaine and guns in my house, but I think they planted them there. Either way, everybody thinks I shot you two. They gave me thirty years for the guns and the drugs. Thirty years! I didn't shoot you, man. I told them that night I had nothing to do with it."

He said it with such conviction I didn't know what to think. I know someone came to me when I was down, but why would Dante lie about that? "If you didn't shoot me, who did?"

"Don't know. I woulda given them up that night if I did. I'm not doing someone else's time. You've got to believe me, Quinn."

"You gave a statement to the investigators?"

"Yeah, after they beat me like an animal." Dante aimed a finger at me. "And when you get back, tell Sergeant Yancey I owe him one. He grabbed me by the throat and shook me like a child. He had no call to do that. I was cooperating. Then they started knocking me around and charged me with resisting arrest. How can I be resisting arrest when I'm the one taking the beating? My lawyer told all this to Internal Affairs, but they just threw me away and moved on."

I could see Oscar fired up with two of his people down. With Oscar, you didn't mess with his family or his people.

"Were you and Jamie still together when I was shot?"

"No," he said. "She'd just moved out a couple of

days before you showed up. What were you coming to talk to me about, anyway?"

"The shooting on Broadview Street, Gerald Pitts. I was told you knew something about that."

Dante grinned and crossed his arms. "Well, I don't know anything about that shooting and won't talk about it without my lawyer here. But everything else I've told you is the truth. I've been straight with you. Now, get me out, Quinn, and I can work the streets for you. I'll find out who shot you and the lady cop. But I can't do nothin' from in here."

"I don't know what I can do, Dante," I said as I stood. Crevis handed me my cane. "I'll talk with the state and see what they might consider." I said this knowing full well the state would do nothing for him. He was a violent career criminal, and they had him locked up on weapons and drug charges.

Crevis opened the door, and Lex came in to take Dante back.

"Your people put me here, Quinn. Just promise me you won't forget about me."

I couldn't promise him. He probably didn't shoot me, but he needed prison like a mole needs dirt: it's where he belongs.

I was already forgetting him before Crevis and I made it to the parking lot.

31

CREVIS AND I ARRIVED back in Orlando late that afternoon, and I dropped him off at his house. The confirmations from Dante were encouraging, but like everything in this case, they only led to more questions. Since I had time, I'd seek more confirmation from another man in Jamie's life.

I arrived at Michael Vitaliano's campaign office and staked out the parking lot for about half an hour to get a feel for the place before I hobbled my way to the door. The office was in a ten-story commercial building with a credit union, several attorneys' offices, and a large CPA firm. Vitaliano took up most of the office space on the second floor.

My voter registration card was grossly expired; the brittle paper crumbled in my hand. I hoped that wouldn't impact my visit. I was still a potential voter in the county, so maybe that would count for something. I hiked my way to the lobby and rode the elevator to the second floor.

A man leaving the suite held the thick glass door open for me as I caned up to Vitaliano's office. I snarled at him. The belittling gesture took me off task for a moment. I could still open my own doors. I needed to stay focused.

"I'm Ray Quinn," I said to a kind-looking, middle-aged woman at the front desk. "I called ahead for an appointment."

"Yes. You're with the police union?"

"Yes ma'am." Which was technically true. I was still part of the union, although that wasn't what I wanted to see him about.

"He'll be with you in a moment. Can I get you something to drink?"

"I'm fine." I parked myself in a comfortable chair my county tax dollars had purchased. The secretary's desk was directly in front of the Commish's office. The lobby area was small but professional. Various magazines covered the table in front of me, but I ignored them, keeping both hands on the handle of my cane.

After several minutes, the office door opened, and my buddy Gordon Kurfis hurried over to meet me. Gordon sported the physique of a first-class pencil pusher—soft in the middle with a butt that was conforming to the shape of his cushy chair. But his eyes were deep blue and penetrating. They had a spark that spoke of his Ivy League training as much as his résumé did. Gordon might be a political hack, but he was no dummy.

"Detective Quinn." He shook my hand with a feigned enthusiasm. "Nice to meet you. The commissioner will see you now."

I swayed a little as I caned my way into the office, exaggerating my limp and hunching over a bit. I wanted them to underestimate me. When I used to fight, the first few punches and kicks I'd throw were always much slower than I was capable of. My opponents would misjudge my speed and strength. I'd lull them into a set of expectations—and then *boom*. I'd explode full strength, and the knockout punch would come from nowhere. Fighting smart, not hard, was my philosophy.

"Detective Quinn," the Commish said. "Good to finally meet you. I'm glad to see you're up and around now. I'm so sorry what you went through to protect our community."

"Thank you, sir." I rested my posterior in another posh piece of publicly funded furniture in front of the Commish's dark mahogany desk.

Gordon sat off to his side. A picture of Vitaliano with the flag as a backdrop hung on the wall behind him. The picture next to it was of him, his attractive blond wife about his age, and two sons and a daughter, all adults. One big happy family.

"So, I guess you're working for the police union now," Vitaliano said. "I've always been a strong supporter of law enforcement. One of my platforms has been to increase the police presence in the downtown area as well as several of the high-crime areas of Orange County."

I let him grease me a bit. I nodded when necessary and listened to him prattle on about his vision for the security of Orange County and the nonessential blather he thought would ingratiate himself with the Orlando police union. Gordon didn't say much, just sat there with a silly expression on his face as his boss continued to speak.

"Now, how are things going with the union this year?" he said.

"Couldn't tell ya. There must have been some mistake with your secretary. I am part of the union still, but I don't work *for* the union." It's fun to watch people's expressions when they think you're going one direction and then you hit them with a 180. Both the Commish and Gordon shared plastic smiles they must teach in politician school.

"What business, then, do you have with the commissioner, Detective?" Gordon said. "His time is quite valuable."

"I'm sure it is, so I'll get to the point. A friend asked me to investigate the murders of David Hendricks and Jamie DeAngelo."

I paused. So did they. And we all shared a moment of silent, awkward stares. But it was Commissioner Vitaliano's eyes that told the story. His pseudo smile didn't change, but he squinted and the hint of a tear formed. After listening to his phone call, I knew he was weak at heart. And I had my dagger ready.

"What does that have to do with the commissioner?" Gordon said.

Vitaliano dummied up quick and seemed quite content to have his high-paid puppet do his talking from this point out.

"It's kinda strange," I said. "Yesterday I got a call from some crazy lady. She said that

Commissioner Vitaliano knew something about the murders and that I should talk with him. She had some off-the-wall notion that he and Jamie DeAngelo were involved in an unseemly relationship, and that I should come here and check it out."

A little disinformation in the case couldn't hurt. Since Pam had contacted him for the non-meeting, my story about a female calling me would have a ring of truth with them.

"I'm not sure what kind of game you're playing, Detective"—Gordon stood and straightened his coat—"but it's time for you to go . . . before we call security."

The commissioner's smile carried on long past its usefulness. Shaking off his stupor, he finally spoke. "No, no, Gordon. It's okay. I think we need to hear what the detective has to say."

"*Ex*-detective," Gordon said, not taking his eyes from mine.

"Once a detective, always a detective." I rested both hands on my cane and grinned at Gordon, who didn't seem to share the joy I was having at that moment.

"I hate to waste your time." Vitaliano stood and waited for me to do the same. I didn't. "But it seems that someone is playing a cruel game with us both. I do have enemies in Orange County. People who don't want to see the kind of progressive change I'll bring to this community I love so much. It won't work, though. I'm used to these kinds of attacks, Detective, as you should be. I won't let hatemongers ruin what we're working for here."

"Well, then I only have two questions, and I'll be on my way," I said, still seated. He'd recovered well. He was a trial lawyer by trade, so thinking on his feet was a learned skill. "Did you know Jamie DeAngelo? And do you know anything about her murder?"

"No to both." He tipped his head to me. "Is there anything else I can do to help you?"

"I'm real happy to hear you have no connection to Ms. DeAngelo. That puts my mind at ease." The next best thing to a confession is a known lie you can blow out of the water. I'd thrown some soft punches his way, enough that he thought he had my timing down. Time to pick up my pace and knock him out.

I slipped my hand in my pocket and pushed the Send button. I had preset the number to the cell phone he used to call Jamie, the one I suspected he still used to communicate with Chance. "Because if you did, that could pretty much destroy a good political career. You know, being involved with an exotic dancer and all that messy stuff. I think voters would be a little fickle about those kinds of things."

The buzz from the silent mode of Michael's cell thundered in the office like Big Ben through the streets of London. But the buzz wasn't coming from the expensive phone on his belt. It was emanating from the top pocket of his coat, near his heart. How sweet. He wouldn't be so foolish as to call Jamie on any phone that could be traced to him. His secret little phone vibrated away. A pathetic pall washed over the Commish, and he looked as if he'd be sick.

"Please, don't let me stop you. I'll wait." I pulled my hand from my pocket and posted it on my cane. "I'm sure any call to you must be *very* important."

"I'll let it go to voice mail." He swallowed hard. "I still think someone is pulling your leg, Detective. As politicians, we're used to people playing games with us, and we play back . . . hard."

"I guess so. But I always saw politics as kinda like a pride of lions. Strong and brave out in the open and on the hunt, but back in the darkness of their homes where their deeds can't be seen—in the lion's den—they can become quite cowardly, depraved, and stupid."

"That's a mighty odd assessment." The commissioner's complexion altered from ashen to crimson. He seized my hand and squeezed extra tight. "Sorry I couldn't have been more help. I hope your case works out for you."

"You've been a great help, Commissioner. More than you know." I gimped out the door and back to the elevators. I was quite pleased with my lion-pride analogy, because it allowed me to call him stupid and mention the Lion's Den in the same sentence. Not too bad, if I do say so myself.

I probably should have informed the stalwart public servant that while I'm no politician, I don't just fight smart—I fight to win. He hadn't even begun to see "hard" yet.

32

I TOOK A LONG WHIFF of the ripe beast. Resting my glass on my apartment windowsill, I shifted position on the bar stool outside, hoping to give the leg at least a little comfort. The night air didn't even stir; the pool stench hovered unchallenged around me.

I'd brought my Sudoku book out with me, but I wasn't sure if I'd be able to finish this puzzle. It didn't matter because I needed some time out of the apartment to process everything. I'd had a busy day and needed to sort through all the information.

I was still flying under the radar with Oscar and Pampas, but I wasn't sure how long I could keep that going. My meeting with the commissioner and his lapdog went well, but I really didn't learn more than I already knew. I was just able to confirm the phone number and have a whole lot of fun at their expense. Maybe if I shook them up enough, they would make some mistakes in the future. I'd see about that.

Dante Hill had spoken with conviction. He gave

information rather freely, which was unusual for most cons. Maybe he was just reaching out because he had nothing else to help him. It didn't make sense that he would ambush Trish and me and then go back into his house and call 911. Then he didn't even remove the cocaine and two pistols from his house before the police arrived. I had to agree with him about that.

But Dante confirmed another disturbing element of this whole ordeal: a cop was definitely involved. Jamie seemed to be making her rounds —from Dante Hill (scumbag extraordinaire), to a phantom cop, to County Commissioner Vitaliano, to a pastor. She demonstrated a rather eclectic taste in men, to be sure. But why the connection to me and my shooting? Just a coincidence? A random chance that I would be investigating David's and Jamie's deaths? Or was there something more calculated in the equation that I'd yet to consider?

Another swig of Jim cooled my thoughts. No way was I going to finish my puzzle, so I let the pool funk chase me inside. I logged on to my laptop and pulled up a picture of Jamie. She was a beautiful yet troubled girl. Everything so far in this case, or these cases, seemed to revolve around a twenty-three-year-old girl who danced for men at night . . . among other things. I needed to know more about Jamie, about the Lion's Den. I needed to know a lot more about a lot of things. The deeper I dug in this case, the more I felt like I buried myself.

I reviewed my notes on the J & M Corporation. On a hunch, I ran J & M through the property appraiser's Web site. I was more than a little surprised to discover that J & M owned three properties in Orange County—all purchased within the last year. I saved and printed those pages and would sort through them later.

I pinned some more items on my living room wall and stepped back to admire my work. My mosaic of murder suffered from the disjointed, nonsensical patterns that would make it a great piece of modern art, but it was a poor representation of an allegedly ordered police investigation. Many pictures. Many lines. Much speculation. Few hard facts.

The knock on the door wasn't unexpected. Pam had arrived. She wore white pants and a nice green blouse, not that I'm all that into clothes. She smiled as I held the door open for her.

We said our hellos. As I directed her in the latest chorus that was this case, I made sure the more gruesome crime scene photos on the wall were covered. I filled her in on the games I'd played with the commissioner and Kurfis. She seemed to appreciate it.

Pam sat down at the kitchen table. "So how'd it go with Dante Hill?"

I shrugged. "He's a tough one to figure. He's got every reason to lie to me about the shooting. If they can pin it on him, he'll be on death row for killing a cop."

"But is he lying?"

"My gut tells me no. His story made sense. He thinks he's slick, but I don't think he would have called 911 to report the shootings, given his real name and address, then waited for the cops to show up and not gotten rid of the drugs and guns in his house."

"Did he know anything about Jamie?" she said.

"More questions than answers." I joined Pam at the table. "He and Jamie were on the outs around that time. She started dancing at the club and was bringing in a lot of money, and she was seeing . . . a cop."

Pam raised her eyebrows. I was beginning to get a feel for the lady. "She was dating a cop while dating Dante? He must have been furious."

"Not this guy. He couldn't care less, as long as she was bringing him money."

Pam crossed her arms and shook her head. "I'm so lost here sometimes. I can't believe people live like this."

"Believe it. Dante is a parasite and would leech off anyone he could. Women are just objects to him. Jamie was a moneymaker and part-time lover. That's it."

She seemed to agree with my assessment of the marvelous Mr. Hill. "So if she was seeing a police officer at the time when you were shot . . ." She paused.

"I don't know what it means, if that's what you

were going to ask. And how does it relate back to David? The obvious answer is Jamie. The only other connection between them is me."

"What case were you investigating with Dante to begin with?" she said. "Maybe there's something else there that connects the events."

"I needed to talk to Dante about a shooting that happened the week before at a rival drug dealer's house. The guy wasn't seriously hurt, but Oscar ordered me to follow up anyway so a drug war wouldn't open up with us having to clean up the mess. We typically worked homicides and suspicious deaths, but Oscar insisted. He wanted to head off any problems. Trisha and I parked a little ways down the street, as usual. The sun was setting, and it was getting dark. There weren't a lot of people out. We were talking as we turned up the walkway to his house."

I stopped for a breath and hid my hands from Pam because they were trembling. It's not that I haven't relived that night. I did every single day, many times a day. But I hadn't given it voice since I made my statement during the initial investigation.

"A tall hedge ran parallel to the walkway to Dante's front door. As we were heading to the porch, I heard something to my right. The first shot was so close I felt the flash of the gunpowder on my face. The round pierced my arm and then the side of my chest and both lungs." I rolled up my sleeve and revealed the scar just underneath my shoulder on my triceps. "The second tore through my hip and pelvis. I was down like a rock after that."

My voice cracked. "Memory is a funny thing. The seconds are etched in my mind as if they were in stone tablets, but I can't trust everything I saw, or believed I saw. I don't know if the medications later or the trauma did something to my mind, my judgment. But as I went down, I looked up at Trisha. My arm was broken, and I couldn't get my gun from my holster. She'd pulled her pistol and stepped to the side, like we're trained to do. It seemed like she was on target for a long, long time, but she didn't pull the trigger. I thought at one point her gun lowered, but I can't be sure. Then I heard the shot and she went down."

"I'm very sorry." Pam squeezed my forearm. "I can't imagine what you must have gone through."

Her kindness did little to stem the flood of raw emotions pouring out of me. "But then, as I lay there knowing I was going to die, someone came up to me and . . ."

"Someone was there? What did he look like?"

"I have no idea. I know this sounds crazy, but I was curled up, trying to crawl over to Trish and fighting to stay conscious, struggling to breathe. Someone stood between us. As sirens sounded in the distance, that person knelt and placed a hand on my shoulder. Whoever it was had to have been there for the entire shooting. Dante said he didn't see anyone, but I know what I felt. There's a witness out there, and whoever it is watched Trisha's murder and knows the truth."

"Trisha was more than your partner, wasn't she?" Pam said.

I knew Pam had a good right, but I just found out she had a pretty solid left hook as well. I didn't see it coming. I couldn't answer her right away because if I had, my voice would have splintered and I would have fallen apart on the spot. I stood and turned my back to her. I fiddled with a napkin on my kitchen counter.

"What makes you say that?" I said in little more than a whisper.

"It's how you say her name. *Trisha*. Your affection carries in your voice."

Could she hear the guilt that carried in my voice too? The shameful knowledge that when Trisha needed me most, I wasn't there for her? I watched her die and was helpless to stop it. For all my training and experience, I didn't see the ambush coming. I was her partner; I was supposed to protect her and watch out for her. I failed, and she died.

She paid the ultimate price for my mistake, and that had haunted me from the second I woke up in the hospital until now—with no indication that it would ever leave me in peace. I steadied myself with the kitchen counter and kept my gaze as far from Pam as I could.

"No one was supposed to know," I said. "If some-one discovered that we were dating, one or both of us would have been removed from the unit. We wouldn't have been allowed to be partners any-more. Neither of us wanted to leave Homicide."

I still couldn't face Pam, or she'd see my red, moistening eyes. No way was that going to happen. She wasn't going to see me cry.

"We were getting ready to tell everyone. I had just asked her to marry me two days before."

33

AFTER PAM LEFT the apartment, I drained the life out of Jim, leaving him empty on the counter in the early-morning hours. I watched an oldie but a goodie in *The Fighting Seabees*, starring Master Wayne, and then *Sands of Iwo Jima*. I hoped the war flicks would assuage my foul, tortured mood. It must have worked because I didn't remember much after midnight.

I awoke in the late afternoon and began my ritual. There was a lot to do, regardless of how I felt. We needed to know more about the Lion's Den. Since it was unlikely Chance Thompson would sprout a tree of conscience and tell me everything I needed to know, intentionally anyway, I felt it my duty to tease it out of him by whatever means necessary.

I picked up Crevis at his house and briefed him

on the plan. We pulled into the parking lot of Club Venus. Chance's tank of a Hummer was parked in the back. His Roidness was in the house.

We found a spot where I could watch the back door and most of the parking lot while I was in the shadows. The club was jumping. Cars streamed in and out, circling for parking spots. Since Chance knew what I drove, I had borrowed Pam's car. I turned on my scanner and went to work.

I checked Chance's cell phone number from the log I had made. I'd purchased a prepaid phone earlier in the day. I needed something to distance myself from some calls I'd have to make. If a cop were in the mix somewhere, eventually these calls could be traced to me. I wasn't going to make it easy for them. I dialed Chance and handed the phone to Crevis.

"Chance," he said, the gravel voice dripping with bravado.

"May I speak with Maddy Martin, please?" Crevis said in a British accent.

"You've got the wrong number."

"Are you sure, old chap?" Crevis grinned. "She did give me this number just last night."

"Look, you got the wrong number."

"Really, good man," Crevis said, "I do hope that she's not put you up to something dastardly."

"Listen, freak, don't call this number again."

I finally tuned in to his frequency and nodded to Crevis.

"Very well. Have a lovely evening." Crevis hung up.

"You're enjoying this a little too much," I said. "Now let's see if we hear anything worthwhile."

We waited in the dark as the traffic flow didn't cease for nearly two hours. No calls from Chance. People are creatures of habit, and even though the chromosome test might be close for Chance, he was still human. He had called Jamie about once a day using his cell phone. If his connection to Jamie was what I suspected, Chance wouldn't risk calling her on the business phone at Club Venus. His calls were usually between 9:00 and 11:00 p.m. That would be the time Chance would check on his girls from the Lion's Den. If he called Jamie then, who else did he call? And would we get the opportunity to track them down?

As midnight approached, Chance's bellowing voice blared over the scanner. "Hey, Brigitte. How's everything going?"

"Doing great," the female said. An alluring, sensual voice to be sure. "I'm getting ready to head over to Ben's. Marie is out of town. Should be a fun weekend. I'll let you know how things go."

"Good. Tell Ben I said hello."

"Hello, Brigitte." I made some hasty notes. It was time to shut down the Club Venus surveillance because we had some good info to start on, and the pulsating purple was giving me a headache.

34

THE NEXT AFTERNOON I called Ashley, and she seemed glad to hear from me. I was a little leery about trusting her, but she'd already taken some risks telling me what she knew. Plus, I didn't have a lot of options.

I asked if she knew a Brigitte who worked for Club Venus in the last year. She said she did, and like Jamie, Brigitte was stunning and made a lot of money fast, then disappeared from the club scene. Her last name was Mathis. In short order, I had an address in Winter Park. She owned two cars—a Lexus SUV and a motorcycle. Her driver's license picture could have been a work of art. Chance had the ability to draw in some of the most beautiful —albeit naive—young women I'd seen in a long time. That gave me more incentive to nail him.

Brigitte was going to see "Ben" for the weekend. It sounded like Ben's wife was out of town. I'd probably ID'd another dancer in the Lion's Den, but now I had to find out who the other lions were besides the commissioner. I had a lot of guess-work right now but needed more names to make the important links.

Crevis and I arrived at her street in Winter Park, a well-to-do town just north of Orlando. Brigitte owned an impressive, older three-bedroom ranch house on Lake Sue Avenue near Rollins College (my alma mater). The path around the lake was lined with oaks and royal palms. The homes were older but well cared for and stately. If she was going to see Ben, she probably wouldn't take the motorcycle—I hoped, anyway. So the Lexus would be our target.

"Hold on to this." I handed Crevis the GPS tracking unit.

Crevis played with the rubber flap. "What's this?"

"I glued a rubber flap over it to help conceal it. It should blend in with the bumper. Now you have to glue it down just like I showed you. On the inside of the front bumper so the GPS can locate its signal but still be out of sight."

We'd practiced a couple of times on my truck before going out. The faster he could get it on and get out of there, the better we would both be. We didn't need a repeat of our trash-search fiasco.

I gave Crevis his last-minute instructions and sent him on his way. He hurried along the sidewalk and passed her house, as I had told him. The silver Lexus was parked in the driveway. He walked about three houses down, then turned back around. As he approached the house again, he ducked down next to the car, dropped to his back, and wiggled underneath. Good thing he was lean and gangly. In my condition, I couldn't imagine trying to shimmy underneath the car and back up again. I was beginning to appreciate the little monkey.

I scanned up and down the roadway. A car approached from the north, then passed by. No problems. Crevis was in a good spot. It was unlikely anyone would see him underneath the SUV.

A few moments later, Crevis's head peeked out. He checked around and then hopped to his feet. He was back to my truck in no time. No neighbors, no dogs. Not a bad mission. Maybe Crevis and I were getting this partnering thing down.

I started the truck and drove away. I instructed Crevis on how to use the laptop to get to the Web site we needed. We'd see if our little present was up and running right. He found the site and the larger Web map. The GPS must have already acquired its satellite because our red dot was pulsing away at Brigitte's house. Now she would lead us to Ben and/or the Lion's Den.

Crevis and I made it to the Coral Bay just in time for our shift. I set up my laptop and kept the mapping page open. Crevis made his rounds. At 10:12 p.m., Brigitte's Lexus left her driveway and traveled south toward Orlando.

I wolfed down a ham sandwich as she wound her way through the city streets. When I first started in police work, surveillance like this would require at least four or five detectives, switching off the lead as they went, always with the risk of losing contact with the suspect or getting burned. Now, all I needed was the GPS tracker, a laptop, and a Crevis.

After a twenty-minute ride, Brigitte's vehicle stopped in a neighborhood in Windermere, where several professional golfers lived. *Extravagant* didn't do the neighborhood justice. I minimized the screen and checked the address with the property appraiser's office. The owner was Benjamin Scott. I knew the name from somewhere, but I couldn't be sure. I ran a name check through Google for "Ben Scott Orlando" and found Benjamin Scott, Esquire, attorney for the Orange County Board of County Commissioners.

I sat back and drew a breath. Brigitte Mathis had just headed to commission attorney Benjamin Scott's house for a weekend of . . . fun.

I searched for Scott's name paired with Vitaliano's. Another score. An article in the *Orlando Sentinel* detailed their relationship. It seemed that Scott and Vitaliano were working together to strengthen the county's adult entertainment ordinance. Lovely. A picture of the two guardians of virtue was displayed prominently, both smiling and shaking hands. Ben was about three inches shorter than Vitaliano and had sandy blond hair receding toward the back of his head.

I saved the article and rocked back in my chair. Two dancers from Chance's club, both "entertaining" two of Orange County's largest power-brokers, who just happened to be working on an adult entertainment ordinance. Chance's fleshy fingers were wrapped all around this ordinance. I needed to find out more about it and what he was up to.

I had time to kill, and I needed to finish some of the early work with Jamie and David. I reviewed more of their e-mails.

Dave,

   i was thinking about u last night. i was with someone i know i shouldn't be with, doing things i know i shouldn't be doing. i just keep asking myself how i got here. When i was kid, i wanted to go to college and get a decent job and have a life. i used to write poetry when i was a little girl. Now? My life is so out of control and not the one i ever imagined for myself. i feel so dirty and ashamed. And then u said that god sees everything and knows my heart. That thought terrifies me more than anything. i wish there was some way i could hide from his all-seeing eye. Some way that your god could not see me in my filthiness. i'm trapped with no way out. There's no way i can come back from the things i've done, from the life i'm entangled in. i don't mean to dump all this on u, but i'm really struggling with so many things. Please pray for me.

   Jamie

I checked David's reply.

Jamie,

God does see all and knows our thoughts, motivations, and actions. And in our wicked, depraved state, He still loved us enough to send His Son to die for us. That fact alone boggles my feeble mind. Please know that there is no such thing as too far for God, and there's no sin that is too deep. He yearns to forgive you and heal you. You just have to get to that place where you're ready to ask Him. I'm here if you need me, 24/7. I *am* praying for you and will continue to. Take care and God bless.

David

I didn't know whether to laugh at David's ignorance or weep for his loss. I couldn't tell if he was being played by a dancer used to manipulating people, or if she was a hurting young lady reaching out for help. Either way, this case troubled my sleep.

35

THE PRIOR NIGHT'S SHIFT was productive and exhausting. I went straight home and tossed and turned until I finally managed a couple hours of rest. I was up around noon because I had an appointment with dear, sweet Helga. Since I'd missed a couple of sessions, she said she'd have to "work" with me a little longer to make up for the time. Of course "work" to her meant that she beat me like a bad dog and pulled my leg like it was taffy at a county fair. I took my punishment without too much complaining. I figured I had it coming. After therapy, I hustled to the PD.

I hobbled my way down the corridor of the homicide unit on my way to see Oscar. I'd come in the front door so I didn't have to run the gauntlet of detectives in the back. I didn't have time and wasn't up for that. The trepidation of entering the building was less than it was the first time, but it still unnerved me. Too many memories here to contend with and keep my head sane at the same time. But I had to do this. I needed some answers fast.

I had committed a cardinal sin in a homicide investigation by allowing the circumstances to dictate the pace and direction of the investigation. I had been all over the chart for a while and needed to get back to basics. I tapped on Oscar's door.

"Come in, Ray." He laid a file on the desk. He took off his glasses and hurried them into his shirt pocket.

I'd never seen him wearing glasses before. I suppose a person can age a lot in a year.

"Twice in a week," he said. "Seems like you're getting around a little better."

"I wanted to check on the gun from the guy who attacked me. I hoped the ATF report would be back by now."

"I just got an e-mail back from them. I was going to check it out and then give you a call, but since you're here . . ." He opened his top drawer and handed me the printout. "The gun was first sold by a gun store in Clermont to a guy named Russell Morton about three years ago. I have a good address on Morton, so I planned on taking Bowden with me to pay him a visit."

"Mind if I go with you?"

"Do you think that's a good idea?" Oscar steepled his fingers and swiveled in his chair.

I hated when he answered a question with a question, using detective tricks on another detective. If he didn't want me to go, I would prefer that he just tell me so.

"I'm assuming you don't want me to go with you."

"Someone tried to mug you," he said. "I'd be irresponsible to let you accompany me on that interrogation. Maybe the guy sold the gun to someone else. Maybe it was stolen and never reported."

"Or maybe he's the guy."

"Or maybe he's not the guy. I know you too well, Ray. I can't have you taking a swipe at someone who tried to mug you."

"I'll behave myself. I just want to hear what he has to say."

Oscar nodded and pursed his lips. "If you can behave and keep your mouth closed, I'll think about taking you with me."

I checked my watch. "Great. When do you want to make that happen?"

"Can you give me thirty minutes to clean up some of this mess?"

"Sure." I nodded. "I'm going to visit some folks while I'm here."

I told him I would be back in time to leave. While I was interested in tracing the thug's gun, I really wanted to see what we could find out about the pistol that killed Jamie and David. I figured since the case had been closed, Pampas didn't send the gun off to be tested or to try to lift the serial number. That was about to change.

I headed down to the crime scene section. Dean Yarborough and Katie Pham's office was small and cluttered with a variety of crime scene trimmings; both were sitting at their desks. Must have been slow the night before.

"Hey," I said.

Katie turned toward me. "Oh, hi, Ray. What brings you here?"

"Just thought I'd see how things are going."

Dean sighed and turned back toward his desk. "What do you want?"

"Do I have to need something to say hello?"

"Yes, as a matter of fact, you do," he said.

Frodo was going to make this more difficult than it needed to be. He always protected his little kingdom. He flexed his minuscule muscles anytime I came into his territory.

"Since you're asking, I was wondering if we could send the pistol from the shooting at the Coral Bay off to the FDLE lab for a NIBIN search. The lab also has a guy who can try to lift serial numbers that have been ground down."

I'd made a couple of strong cases in the past by submitting pistols to the National Integrated Ballistic Information Network. The techs there document shell casings collected from shootings and homicides around the state. Each pistol leaves distinct markings on a shell casing, much like a fingerprint, which can be matched to shell casings from other crimes. It's a good tool and could tell me more about the gun. If we could lift the serial number, that would be a strong lead as well, but I needed to wiggle the request past the crime scene gatekeeper.

"It's a closed case," Dean said.

"True, but Pampas and I were curious where the suspect picked up the gun and if it had been used in any other crimes." I stretched the truth a little again, but this time I imagined that if Pampas actually thought about the case at all, that would be one of his considerations. The request needed to sound like it came more from Pampas than me.

"I can send that off." Katie gave me a nice smile. It was one of those smiles I'm becoming accustomed to getting since I walk with a cane, more a flash of pity than kindness. If it took pity to get the job done, I'd take it.

"We've got a lot going on to be sending guns to the lab on closed cases," Dean said.

"Maybe it will help close other cases."

Dean and I have history. He'd never do anything for me unless I filled out one of his stupid request forms, and even then, I suspected he placed my requests at the bottom of his stack. Anytime I needed something fast, I'd send Trisha back to talk with him. Dean would puff his chest out and fall all over himself to help her. Everyone liked Trisha. She just had that special quality—one I couldn't seem to imitate.

"It's a waste of time and resources." Dean pushed his glasses up on his nose and crossed his arms. "That gun's going in for destruction. If you're not happy with that, take it up with Sergeant Yancey. He approved the order."

"Why don't we get him down here right now so we can settle this?" I drew my cell phone and simulated punching in some numbers. "Then you can explain to him face to face why you don't want to send a vital piece of evidence off to the lab that could potentially solve other violent crimes. I'm sure he'll be sympathetic to your precious time constraints, seeing as this request will take you less than five minutes to complete."

Dean grimaced. "All right, I'll send the thing off if it's such a big deal to you."

I closed my phone and reholstered it, quite pleased that Dean didn't call my bluff.

"I'll take care of it, Dean," Katie said.

"No. I'll do it." He slapped the fingerprint card on his desk and prepared to stand.

Katie was on her feet and already at the door. "I'm on my way down to Property and Evidence anyway. I'll have them ship it today."

Dean regarded me and then Katie. "Fine."

She slipped past me and winked.

"You need to fill out the paperwork anyway, Quinn . . . on your way out." Dean didn't have the decency to look me in the face. Some things never changed.

I signed his request form and left his office. As I hiked back to Homicide, I caught Oscar in the hallway.

"Ray, I've changed my mind. I don't think it would be a good idea for you to talk with Russell Morton about the gun."

"I promised to behave. What more do you want from me?"

"It's just that if we do come up with something and have to go to court later, it'll look bad that we had the victim in the case doing the investigation. And if I have to show you a lineup, it can't be tainted because you saw this guy ahead of time. I gotta think how this will look if we take this to court. I want the people who jumped you arrested, and I won't risk messing that up."

Oscar had me in a difficult situation. I'd told him it was a mugging, nothing more. If I pushed this too hard, he'd be pushing back for answers.

He knew me well enough to suspect something could be up. I'd let Oscar take care of this gun issue while Katie took care of the other.

"Okay," I said, coaxing a little disappointment from my tone. Just enough to be convincing, but not over the top. "Just let me know when you get a chance. I'm curious what's up with this guy."

"No problem, Ray. I'll take care of this personally."

36

LETTING OSCAR TAKE CARE of running down the gun turned out to be a good thing. It gave me more time to deal with some of the fresh questions arising in the Hendricks case. I was stalled in trying to find out any information on the officers of J & M Corporation, but now I knew that Ben Scott and the Commish were working together to draft the new county adult entertainment ordinance. At least I was getting somewhere with the Lion's Den. I doubted their dalliances with Jamie and Brigitte and the ties to Club Venus were an accident. Maybe it was just research? Again, unlikely.

Scouring some archived articles from the *Orlando Sentinel* on the topic, I found four related stories. Imagine my surprise when I discovered that the ordinance drafting committee was created a little over a year ago, just about the same time as my shooting. And retired judge Raphael "Ralph" Garcia and Orlando business giant Mort Connelly were also on the committee with Scott and Vitaliano.

Orlando's biggest and brightest stars gathered together for this task. One thing I found rather interesting is that they all volunteered to sit on the committee. Most of the article was puffery about using the ordinance to limit the places these establishments could operate under and such. The Florida Supreme Court had ruled that cities and counties couldn't all-out ban adult entertainment, but they could place strong restrictions on the methods of operations and where those businesses could be located, which was the alleged mission of this committee. The establishments already in place would be grandfathered in, but if they ever moved, they'd be subject to the ordinance.

"We intend on drafting the strongest ordinance in the state, maybe even the nation, to keep Orange County's image one of family-friendly entertainment," Commissioner Vitaliano was quoted.

The emphasis on *image* struck me because that was what the man seemed to be all about. Didn't seem to matter about the substance of what they were doing. I felt I'd discovered the charter members of the Lion's Den. I added Judge Garcia and Mort Connelly to my list. Just because they were on the committee didn't necessarily mean they were part of the Lion's Den, but it certainly didn't exclude them either.

I decided to take a little field trip and map out the properties in Orange County listed to J & M

Corp. With my handy little GPS unit, I plotted out my course and ended up at the corner of West Gore Street and South Division, where a closed-down restaurant was located. I hit the second property, which was about twenty-five minutes away on International Drive. An abandoned Army Navy store. The third was downtown, not terribly far from Outreach Orlando Ministries. I took photos of all three.

None of the properties had For Sale signs posted or any construction work in progress. They were just sitting . . . waiting.

Since I was out and about, I took a swing past Ben Scott's place. It was Saturday, and his wife wasn't due back until Monday. According to the tracking unit on Brigitte's car, she hadn't left Ben's house since she arrived Friday night. Nice digs—a two-story brick palace with towers on each front corner, like a castle.

His driveway was gated, and you had to call to be let in. So much for the lifestyles of Orlando's rich and naughty. The driveway circled around behind the house. A wall of well-maintained palm trees covered the entire front of the house, and I couldn't see it well from the street. I couldn't see Brigitte's car, but I knew it was still there. It didn't matter; I'd already downloaded a satellite photo to get a better view of his property. I was really turning into a geek with all my gadgets. I was feeling pretty slick.

37

HAD I REALLY HEARD SOMETHING, or was I just dreaming? My window-mounted air conditioner hummed on full throttle as I blinked and then scanned the room.

My bedroom door was open a crack; sunlight from the living room and kitchen windows broached the darkness and illuminated the hallway. I checked the clock: 11:43 a.m. I wasn't supposed to be up yet, but something wasn't right.

I heard it again: the rustling of papers in my living room. A shadow passed outside my door, and soft footsteps shuffled along the carpet at the end of the hallway. I reached to the nightstand and removed my Glock from its holster. My heart pounded. I was two-pots-of-coffee awake now.

Flat on my back in bed was not the fighting position I desired. I didn't want to make too much noise getting up, because whoever was in my living room was trying to be quiet. They must believe I was still asleep. I inched to the side of my bed, keeping a watchful eye on the door.

My leg throbbed as I used my left hand to drop it off the side of the bed. I sat up quickly, maybe a little too quickly, and my hip warned me not to do it again. I needed to get to my feet. Leaning over, I snatched my cane and used it to push myself up. Cane in my left hand, pistol in my right, I crept toward the door. Someone was close; I could hear him breathing.

I eased open the door a few more inches and scooted to the side to peek down the hall.

Crack. A flash of light and an explosion of wood blew me back as a round struck the door frame by my head. I staggered backward but caught myself before I fell. Two more reports thundered down the hall, striking the door frame on the other side of me. Wood splinters peppered my chest.

"Ahhh!" I charged through the door, pistol raised. Charred gunpowder and a gray haze permeated the hallway. My front door slammed open and feet smacked the pavement as my attacker was in full sprint out of the apartment.

I hobbled as fast as I could out the door and into the pool area. The complex's gate clanked shut, and I limped toward it, my sights trained on the corner. I rounded the corner slowly with my pistol at the ready. I didn't want to rush into an ambush.

"Mr. Ray, Mr. Ray," Hector called from behind me. "Are you okay?"

"Call 911." I pushed through the metal gate and into the parking lot. I used my gun hand to screen the bright sun from my eyes. The parking lot was awash with brilliant sunlight; my eyes hadn't adjusted enough to see anything. The constant drone of cars rolled along John Young Parkway. No one in sight.

I eased next to a row of cars, the glimmering

reflections off the windows playing havoc on my vision. I came to the edge of the first car and shuffled around it, pistol at the ready. Nothing. I moved to my truck, which was parked next to it. Again nothing. I scanned the entire parking lot. The dirt bag was long gone. Hector was on the phone behind me.

"The police are coming, Mr. Ray." He stared at my pistol and stepped back. "Did you shoot someone?"

"No," I said, realizing for the first time that I was standing in the parking lot in only underwear and a T-shirt. "But someone nearly nailed me. Did you see him?"

"I'm sorry, Mr. Ray. I was in my apartment when I heard shots. I ran out and saw you out here. I did not see who it was."

Stabbing my cane into the asphalt, I knocked a chunk out of the crumbling, pitted parking lot. It could have been a kindergartner for all I knew, and he would have still outrun me.

I gimped back to my apartment, the door still wide open. Pebbles from the parking lot stuck to my feet. I wiped them off with the tip of the cane before I entered the apartment. A sick feeling hit my gut as I absorbed the scene. Papers littered my living room floor. My case notes had been ripped from the wall, and many of them appeared to be missing. My pictures, my camera, and my laptop—all gone.

I checked the Duke's portrait. He was still there, but he didn't look happy either. The only things not rummaged through or missing were the evidence items from the trash search—the steroid containers, Ziploc bags, and the J & M property receipt I'd secured in a lockbox in my room—and my external hard drive.

The call of distant sirens announced OPD's approach. I laid my pistol on the kitchen counter. I didn't want some overzealous rookie whacking me in my own apartment in my underwear—a very undignified way to die.

"Hector, can you go out and tell them it's all clear and lead them back to my apartment?"

"I can do that. Are you sure—?"

"I'm fine. I just need to get some clothes on. I think it's going to be a long day."

38

IT TOOK OSCAR all of twenty minutes to make it to my apartment; I figured he'd be coming. The officers on the scene had taken my statement, which didn't consist of much. I found three .45 cal casings on the living room floor. A lot of cops carry .45s. That reality hadn't escaped me.

The suspect must have fired from the beginning of the hallway to my room, maybe fifteen feet away. It was close, especially the first round. Missed my head by inches. My ears were still ringing. I supposed the other two shots were to keep me in the room while he made his escape. No signs of forced entry, and I know I locked my door. I always do.

Katie and Dean arrived and worked their way around the crime scene.

"Are you okay?" Katie slipped on a pair of latex gloves.

"I'm fine."

"So someone tried to kill you," Dean said as he breezed by. "What a surprise."

"Good to see you too, Yarborough."

I showed them the scene. I had already marked the locations of the spent shell casings with three paper cups from the kitchen. Some habits were hard to break.

Oscar stepped under the crime scene tape. Oscar, like most people, can be read as soon as he enters a room; he wasn't much for concealing his emotions. Oscar was livid. He had a file tucked underneath his arm.

A patrol officer named Rodriguez approached Oscar. "Sergeant Yancey, could you please sign in?" He held out a clipboard with the crime scene log on it.

"Leave us for a minute," Oscar said.

"But the crime scene log—"

"Leave!" Oscar's exhale rumbled like an agitated grizzly bear's. Something was up.

Officer Rodriguez made a hasty retreat out of

the apartment. Doug and Katie scurried down the hallway to my bedroom, leaving Oscar and me alone in the living room.

He examined my wall and what was left of my homicide flow chart. A deeper growl emanated from his innermost being as he squared up on me. "Guess who I talked to this morning?"

I shrugged, figuring silence was my best ally at this point.

"Doug Farnham. He wanted to make sure that your restored e-mail account and computer access were working well."

Remaining mute, I raised an eyebrow in protest.

"He said I had sent him an e-mail to activate your account, which happened to be sent the exact date and time you were in my office." Oscar stabbed my chest with a raging finger. "You used me and lied to me!"

Technically, I only used him, but quibbling over semantics wouldn't help. "There's more to the murder at Coral Bay than everyone thinks. It was no murder-suicide. It's a double murder, and the killer is on the loose."

"You've really lost it, Ray." He waved his hand across my murder mosaic. "You need to go back to the psychologist. This isn't healthy."

"The Coral Bay murders are linked to Trisha's and my shooting too. I can prove it." I had no choice now; I had to share more than I wanted to.

"You're crazy. The shooting messed up your

247

head, big-time. And why would I believe any-thing you say? You lied to me!"

"That's the second time you've said that."

"Because it ticked me off," Oscar said. "You've always been difficult to deal with, nearly impossible to manage, but I could always trust your word and your motives—without question. You always did the right thing, although in strange ways."

"Jamie DeAngelo was dating Dante Hill when Trish and I were shot at Dante's house. Check it out yourself."

He tossed his file on my table. "I had Doug run a report to track everything you ran through *our* system. I saw the report with Dante and a girl named Jamie. Do you know how many Jamies there are in Orlando?"

"Dante confirmed it was Jamie DeAngelo."

"He did what? How in the world did he do that?"

"I went to see him," I said. "He confirmed they were dating, and he said he didn't shoot Trish or me. I believe him. What he said made sense."

Oscar paced in front of me. "How did you manage to get in to see him?"

Feeling a sense of impending martyrdom, I saw no good reason to toss Porter under the Big O bus heading straight for me, so I shrugged. A nonanswer if I've ever given one.

"I bet you wiggled your way into the prison just like you've been sneaking around the department. That's going to end. Now."

"Oscar, whatever else has happened, I know what I'm talking about. These are not two independent, unrelated cases. They're deeply intertwined, and I'm on the verge of breaking the whole thing wide open. I'm asking you to trust me on this."

"Trust you," Oscar said. "You manipulated our friendship and used department resources for your own witch hunt. Not only am I *not* going to trust you, but I'm considering going to the state attorney's office and pursuing charges against you for obstruction in an official investigation."

"The Coral Bay case is closed, so that won't work."

"But Trisha's murder is still an active case." Oscar clamped his hands on his hips. "If you don't back off and get some professional help, I'll find something to charge you with and lock your butt up. That's a promise."

"The only activity in Trisha's case has been what I've found out. I lied, manipulated, and whatever else you think, and I don't really care. I've also found solid information to move the case forward."

"You've found nothing but speculation. You're on some vendetta against Pampas or a crusade to redeem yourself or whatever."

"If that's true, why has someone tried to kill me . . . twice?"

Oscar's eyes narrowed. "You said the first time was just a mugging."

I paused, not feeling so slick at the moment. "Okay, I left a little bit of pertinent information out of the first report." I raised my hands. "You got me. I admit that. But the guys who attacked me knew my name and told me to back off from asking any more questions. I'm sorry I didn't tell you that to begin with, but it's true."

"What's happened to you? It's like I don't even know you anymore. You've let this thing destroy your life."

"Look at my apartment. Obviously, someone is so concerned about what I've uncovered that they'd risk a daytime burglary to steal something I've come across and try to murder me in the process. Doesn't that count for something?"

"Ray, anyone who's spent even five minutes with you would want to murder you, so that isn't evidence of anything. How do I know you didn't set this whole thing up for some sick, unknown reason? I'm ordering you to stay out of both of these cases."

"You can't do that."

"Why not?"

"Because I don't work for you anymore," I said. "Your orders don't mean a thing to me."

Oscar lunged forward with his fist loaded, stopping short of popping me in the mouth. I didn't move. It gave me no pleasure to fire up Oscar like that, but I wasn't going to quit now—not for him, not for anyone.

"You're so selfish." Oscar eased back and straightened his tie. "I've held off saying this to you because of everything that happened, but now you need to hear it. You think you were the only one devastated when Trisha died?" His voice cracked.

He paused and then regained his composure. "I'll let you in on a little secret. A piece of all of us died that night. Every single day I've wondered what I could have done differently. How I could have stopped what happened to you both. I've been sitting back for a year now hoping you could move past this, get a life outside of police work. But your head's way too messed up. And you're too stubborn and arrogant to get the help you really need."

"My head might be messed up, and I know I'm difficult and a liar, but forgive me if I don't feel too sorry for you. You might have lost a little bit of you that night, Oscar, but *every* bit of me died on that sidewalk next to Trisha. The cases *are* linked. Just look at the evidence."

"Stay out of this, Ray, or you're going to jail." Oscar got in my face. "And you *can* trust my word."

"All I can say is, you better reopen the Coral Bay murders and find the person responsible for both these cases, because if I get to Trisha's killer before you do, you'll have a very good reason to arrest me."

39

OSCAR, DEAN, AND KATIE cleared my apartment, and I made vain attempts at straightening the mess. As I surveyed the disaster that was my living room and the hub for my investigation, I seethed at the notion that whoever did this thought they had stopped me and sidelined the case. Not by a long shot. They only ensured that I'd never, ever quit until I found them . . . and made them pay.

I had to replace my stolen items as soon as possible, so I thrust myself headfirst once again into the ever-swelling excesses of my credit card debt. I purchased an upgraded laptop with an aircard, a camera, and a battery-powered wireless security system to attach to my doors and windows—all at an interest rate that gave me a migraine. But I wouldn't be taken off guard like that again.

I picked up Crevis at his place and filled him in on the goings-on. We had a shift to cover soon, but there was much to discuss. I couldn't tell if my attacker was one of the two who jumped me in the parking garage. I suspected so but didn't have anything to back it up.

"If I get my hands on whoever did this, they're toast." Crevis punched his fist into his hand.

I admired his guts, but he didn't have any idea of what we were facing. The Lion's Den grew in scope and stature, and a rogue cop was at work in the mix. Sometimes ignorance truly was bliss.

Pam was waiting at the apartment as I arrived; the crime scene tape remnants lay on the ground just under my window. I opened the door and let us all in, then placed my new laptop on the counter. I would have been crazy upset with losing my other computer, except I'm neurotic about backing up my information. My external hard drive was in my room with all my case notes and copied files still intact.

I didn't reveal that to Oscar or the responding officers. It was better for whoever stole my stuff and shot at me to think he slowed me down by stealing my notes, pictures, and reports. I guess if Oscar discovered I left that part out, he'd consider it just another lie.

"I'm sorry I've dragged you into this," Pam said. "I had no idea people would try to kill you."

"I'm a big boy. You didn't drag me anywhere. I went willingly. Besides, a little murder attempt can keep a guy on his toes."

"I don't understand you at all, Ray Quinn," she said, my attempt at humor bouncing off her. "But this is getting out of control. I want you to catch David's killer, but I'm scared that something's going to happen to you, and it would be my fault for asking you to help me."

"Pam, we can't quit now, even if we wanted to. Whoever did this will not stop until anything that can link them to the murders is destroyed—

including all of us. The only way we can protect ourselves is to catch this person and stop them forever."

She agreed, although this was taking a toll on her. She felt responsible for me like I felt responsible for Trisha. It never seemed to end.

"We're going to have a more difficult time from this point on," I said. "Oscar caught me using the department database and resources, so I'll be even more limited in the information I can access. I imagine that I'm persona non grata at the station as well. I'll have to figure a way around that."

I shared with them that I believed the Lion's Den was made up of at least two of the four members of the adult entertainment ordinance committee.

"But what difference would that make?" Pam said. "It's just a county ordinance."

"If Chance Thompson has his hooks into these committee members through his girls, he can control how the ordinance is written and the locations these clubs will be restricted to. Suppose Chance can corner the market on adult entertainment in all of Orange County by buying up land he knows will be zoned for this purpose—his clubs would dominate the prime locations. He could do this through different corporations and silent partners so no one would catch on. That's a huge market, and Chance and his associates could stand to make millions of dollars."

"So Commissioner Vitaliano can talk about

limiting the impact of these . . . clubs while he's having an affair with one of these girls on the side and lining his pockets with the money?" Pam said.

"That's about it." I nodded. "He's playing both sides of the fence. Looks like Ben Scott is doing the same thing."

"How do we stop them?" Crevis said, the hubris of youth ringing in his voice. "They can't get away with this."

"The only way we can stop them is to somehow set them up."

"How do we do that?" Pam said.

"I'm working on it," I said, which was my pat answer for "I have no idea."

40

BY ANY REASONABLE STANDARD at this point in my investigation, I should have met with the Florida Department of Law Enforcement agents in Orlando, turned over the evidence I had uncovered, and let them take over the investigation—while I remained in my happy world as the night watchman of the Coral Bay Condos, waging my valiant battle against boredom and sobriety. Maybe they would catch the suspects and someone would go to jail for the murders, county kingpins would be toppled, and the political landscape of Orange County would be in a cataclysmic upheaval.

While it all sounded good in theory, several

255

problems presented themselves in practice. For one, I wasn't sure if the FDLE would take me seriously, considering my relationship with Trisha, and that I was one of the victims, although the extent of our relationship wasn't public knowledge.

But there was still a greater concern. Even if FDLE found the people responsible and they went to prison, would they truly pay for the pain they caused? Could a comfortable prison cell, three squares a day, an exercise yard, free medical and dental care, and a fully stocked library be the payment for crippling me, murdering an innocent pastor and a young woman, and butchering the only woman I ever loved?

In my economy and what was left of my so-called life, I was inclined to say it wouldn't be nearly payment enough. A much heavier toll must be exacted for that kind of evil, and comfort played no part in my vision of how this thing would end. I wasn't turning this case over to anyone.

I checked my e-mails and received a Google alert for the names "Ben Scott and Michael Vitaliano." I had set my e-mail account to notify me if those names appeared together on fresh postings anywhere on the Internet. A story appeared in today's *Orlando Sentinel.* A public hearing was being conducted tomorrow night at the Orange County commissioners' chambers regarding a reading of the newly drafted ordinance and a rezoning hearing on the possible locations of the adult entertainment district. Since it was open to the public, I figured I'd have to drop by and say hello.

I also reset my new computer to see if my connection with the GPS unit on Brigitte's car was still running. Not only was it working, I had a good bead on her. She and Ben must have ended their weekend rendezvous because she was back at her house. The battery life on the GPS unit had about three more days on it.

Crevis had stayed the night on my couch. We were up well past sunrise and watched *Rio Lobo*, an amazing John Wayne flick if there ever was one. It was my duty to introduce Crevis to the greatest hero of all time. They seemed to get along. I nearly fainted when Crevis said he'd never seen a John Wayne movie. I informed him that you did not simply "see" a John Wayne movie, you experienced it.

We had popcorn, and I tossed back a fair amount of Jim, enough to wash away most of the concerns from earlier in the day, while Crevis stuck with soda. I think Jim was insulted, but he'd get over it. It was a bizarre slumber party, but Crevis said if he didn't stay on the couch, he'd sleep on the patio in front of my door. He wasn't going to let anyone attack me again. In the long run, he might be cheaper than a guard dog. And I think Crevis has had all his shots.

Crevis had already eaten and was taking a shower. I flipped on the coffeepot and grabbed a bowl from the cabinet. As I poured some cereal, I considered the foolishness of whoever broke into my apartment. He spent a fair amount of time gathering the laptop, my notes, and camera first, instead of trying to kill me in my sleep. If he would have entered my room without making all that racket, he would've had a fair shot at finishing the job, assuming he's the same one who shot me the first time and attacked me in the Coral Bay garage.

But why did he just want to steal the stuff? I could retrace my steps and glean the same info anyway. It didn't make sense.

I chomped on my cereal. What had I learned so far? Ashley's information was a boon to the case and had turned me on to the Lion's Den. I paused and then dropped my spoon in the bowl, milk splashing onto the table. I was such an idiot. He wasn't simply stealing my notes to slow my investigation. He wanted to know what I knew and who I talked to—so he could silence them too.

"Crevis," I hollered, pushing my chair back. "We've got to go. Now!"

In less than two minutes, Crevis and I were tearing out of the parking lot. For the first time in my life, I prayed. I prayed I was wrong.

41

IT TOOK EIGHTEEN AND A HALF excruciatingly long minutes to make it to Ashley's apartment from mine, as I serpentined through traffic with no regard for the laws.

Crevis struck his head on the roof as I didn't slow for the speed bumps in her parking lot. I called her home phone and cell several times and left messages for her not to open the door for anyone but us.

I slid to a stop in front of her building. Her car was parked in its spot; she had to be home. Crevis bounded up three flights of stairs. I lagged behind him but carried my lame self up the stairs as best I could, practically hopping on one leg from the second to the third floor. Once at the top, I fought for oxygen; my lungs were spent. I nodded to Crevis, who pounded the door.

"Ashley," I called in between gasps. "Open up."

Nothing.

Crevis beat the door again.

Still nothing.

I drew my pistol. "Kick it in."

Crevis smiled as he retrieved his brass knuckles from his pocket and slid them onto his hand. He launched his foot into the door, cracking the frame. The door swung in and smacked the wall.

I stepped through, my pistol raised high.

"Awwk!" Big Bird squawked at us. The apartment was dark. A light was on in the back. I followed it.

"Ashley!"

My call was met by silence. I hurried toward the back room; Crevis trailed me with his fists up. Her bedroom door was open a crack. I eased it open the rest of the way with my cane while training my Glock on the room.

"Ashley, it's Ray Quinn. Is everything all right?"

I entered her bedroom and answered my own question. Ashley lay facedown on her bed with a pink belt wrapped around her neck.

I lowered my gun and gimped closer to her. I touched her elbow. She was room temperature. She'd been down for a few hours, maybe more. I looked around the room. Nothing else appeared disturbed.

"Crevis, call 911."

"I can't," he said, covering his mouth. "I'm gonna be sick." He sprinted into the bathroom off the hallway, where he promptly purged what little cereal he'd eaten earlier. I would have to explain that to the crime scene techs.

I made the call. And for the second time in two days, I waited as the sirens approached. No way was I getting out of this. If Oscar was hot yesterday, I couldn't imagine what he'd look like today. I pulled out my cell phone and snapped a picture of Ashley and the room. I knew I wouldn't be able to come back inside or have access to the file. I snapped a few more of the living room and front door. I snapped away until the patrol units arrived.

"Ray Quinn," Oscar said as he scaled the last flight of stairs. "You are the last person I wanted to see today."

I just gazed at him. The sky was darkening as an afternoon storm was rolling in, a common occurrence around Orlando this time of year, but the weather merely mimicked my mood—gloomy and foreboding. Crevis and I stood out on the third-floor walkway.

"What?" he said, hands out. "No witty comeback?"

"I'm not feeling real witty today. A dead girl is in there, and she's dead because she talked to me."

"We'll find out about that. I'm going to get a statement from you about this and everything else. If you hold back on one thing or lie to me, Ray, I'll charge you with every statute under the sun. No more of your games or stupid comments."

"I'll shoot straight with you."

"You'd better." Oscar pulled out his notepad. "Where were you last night?"

I could see the small red light flashing through his shirt pocket. He was recording me; this was official.

"I was at home."

"Alone?"

"No. He stayed over at my place." I pointed to Crevis, who was leaning over the railing, looking as if he'd hurl again, his face the color of curdled milk.

"He a friend of yours?"

I paused. My life was such that now Crevis was not only my friend, but my best friend. "Yes."

"He'll vouch for you?"

"Yeah, but go easy on him. He's just a kid, and I don't think he's ever seen a dead body before. He's not doing so hot."

I ran Oscar through the series of events that led up to Crevis and me finding Ashley. I told him about talking to her before about Jamie and her working at Club Venus. I didn't mention the Lion's Den or other aspects of my investigation that didn't involve Ashley.

I didn't care if I did some time for it. I wasn't revealing everything I knew to anyone at OPD, even Oscar. I didn't know who would get ahold of my statement. And with that look in his eyes, it wouldn't have mattered what I told him. There was nothing in his gaze but utter contempt for me.

"Raise your right hand," he said. "Do you swear that everything you told me is the truth, the whole truth, so help you God?"

"I do."

He reached in his pocket and flicked off his recorder. "I bet."

He ambled over to Crevis, still leaning on the rail. He led Crevis farther down the walkway and looked back at me. He wanted to be sure he was out of earshot.

As they talked, Pampas, Stockton, and Bowden all showed up. No one came my way; it appeared orders had been given not to talk to me under any circumstances.

I couldn't blame them. Pampas smirked and hissed as he passed. I kept quiet. I had too much on my mind to get worked up by such a lowlife like him.

Oscar and Crevis talked for about ten minutes, and then they both headed back my way.

"You can leave . . . for now," Oscar said. "Keep your cell phone on, should I need to get in touch with you."

"Who's lead on the case?" I said.

"Given all the drama already around this thing, I should be the one working this." Oscar stowed his pen and notepad back in his pocket. "I'll have Bowden as backup. Anything else you need to tell me?"

I shook my head. In all the years I'd worked with Oscar, he'd never taken lead on a homicide. He always managed them but never assigned one to himself. A twinge of hope wiggled into the back of my mind. Maybe Oscar had listened to some of what I said and would try to link the cases. The thought faded quickly as he shared a disgusted look with me.

"Then you both can—and I would suggest that you do—leave," he said. "We've got a lot of work to do."

"Sorry about the mess, Oscar."

"Aren't we all."

Crevis and I headed down the stairs as Katie and Dean hiked up with gear in tow. Again, no one spoke. I was being shunned—officially.

"What did Oscar have to say?" I said as we got into my truck.

"He was pretty nice." Crevis stared out the window. "He just asked what happened, and I told him."

"That's it?"

"Pretty much."

"Wanna grab something to eat?" I said. "My treat?"

"I'm not very hungry."

Neither was I. A young girl's life had just been snuffed out because she committed the heinous crime of talking to me, thinking no one else would ever know. She trusted me and even called me "nice." I didn't feel so nice. I couldn't feel anything but the deadness of my soul.

Oscar, the only person on the planet who stood by me after the shooting, now considered me a scumbag and a liar, someone to loathe and detest. Maybe he was right.

42

THE ORANGE COUNTY commissioners' chamber was less than a quarter full. The five-hundred-seat auditorium was in a half-moon shape and faced the commissioners' seats, which were raised, of course.

I'd dropped Crevis back off at my place. After everything with Ashley, he needed some time alone. I could cover most of this meeting and then make it back in time to pick him up for our shift.

A dozen reporters lined the first row with their cameras situated for the best view. Other civilians dotted around the room. The proceedings would be about as fun as watching an algebra competition and seemed to be a nonevent to most people. It was the most important public meeting I'd ever attended.

Ben Scott sat off to the right of the commissioners. Mort Connelly and Judge Garcia huddled together up front near the journalists. Commissioner Vitaliano was perched in a prominent place on the dais—right in the middle. His gray hair was perfectly combed, his suit tailored, his smile as phony as his life. He folded his hands in front of him and listened to the speaker at the podium. He nodded his head at appropriate times and feigned concern and attentiveness.

The image of Ashley's lifeless body, as well as

David's and Jamie's, kept scrolling through my thoughts. Every time I'd focus back on Vitaliano's smug mug, I wanted to just hobble up to him and bludgeon the truth from him with the business end of my cane.

Chance's buddy Carl filled a seat on the right side of the room, attempting to keep his gargantuan frame from being conspicuous. It was a bit like hiding a bear in a bathtub. I didn't see Chance anywhere, which shouldn't have surprised me. He'd had an inside track on the goings-on since long before this public meeting was held, so he sent his minion to keep an eye on things, probably to gauge public reaction to the announcement.

The speaker at the podium prattled on about the water district's concern over potential flood levels in the county. They were getting the normal business out of the way before they discussed the ordinance.

I stayed near the back. A person came from behind me and posted to my right—Gordon Kurfis, the good commissioner's chief of staff. He tucked his hands in his pockets and rose to his tiptoes and then back down.

"You seem to have an ever-increasing interest in politics, Mr. Quinn." He faced the podium, not even looking at me. His bulbous middle peeked out from his blazer, as if he were carrying a beer-belly baby to full term.

"Just keeping that public service thing going,"

I said. "You never know, I might run for office someday."

Kurfis chuckled and shook his head. "That would be a sight. I don't think you have any idea of everything that goes into managing a county like this or what goes into being a great leader. But you're in for a treat tonight. You get to watch one up-and-coming politician at his finest."

"Really?" I panned the table with my finger. "Which one are you talking about?" I had to jab him a little.

"I know what you think, Quinn. And you're dead wrong about the commissioner. That man is one of the most moral and genuine people I've ever had the privilege of knowing. I'm not the only one who recognizes his potential either. He's going places."

"Well, if he's the most moral person you know, then you need to hang in better circles. Because the only place that man is going is prison."

Kurfis snorted like a bull preparing to charge. "You played that line when you came to our office. I don't know what your game is, but it's my job to run interference for the commissioner against troublemakers—even if they're disturbed ex-cops. You're way off base here, so I would suggest you get some medication for your post-traumatic stress disorder and stay far away from Michael Vitaliano."

The man at the podium must have said something funny because the room erupted into laughter. His Haughtiness Vitaliano laughed, clapped his hands together, and regarded his comrades at the head of the chamber. He then glanced our way, and his smile evaporated the moment he noticed Kurfis and me together. He trained his gaze on us for a few seconds, then turned back to the speaker, his pseudo smile returning.

Maybe it was a lucky guess about the post-traumatic stress disorder. Or maybe Kurfis had been digging into my police file or talking with someone at OPD. I was betting on the latter. Kurfis did what I would do: he checked up on me.

"Whenever your boss wants to sit down and tell me all about Jamie and his relationship with her, then maybe, just maybe, I'll get out of both of your lives. But now I'm looking for a killer. If the good commissioner had anything to do with Jamie's or anyone else's death, I'm going to hang it around his neck for the world to see."

"If you want to get into the private-investigator business, I would suggest you stick to chasing cheating husbands and serving subpoenas. You are way out of your league right now, Quinn."

"I've been there before. And don't think for a second your Ivy League education can keep you from being an accessory to murder. That doesn't look good on a résumé."

Kurfis faced me. "If you think—"

"Shhh." I held my finger over my lips. "Your meal ticket is about to speak."

Kurfis straightened his power tie and marched toward the other side of the auditorium, flashing me a look that murdered me a hundred times. I was beginning to think he didn't like me.

"I'd like to thank everyone who has come tonight," Vitaliano said. "As you know, County Attorney Ben Scott, Judge Raphael Garcia, Morton Connelly, and I have worked diligently over the last year to draft the most restrictive ordinance in the state to limit the adult entertainment industry in Orange County. The supreme court has ruled that we can't exclude these businesses from coming into our towns and counties, but we can certainly limit where they operate and restrict their business practices. I think we've done that here."

The applause was less than thunderous, more of a pat.

"I'd like to propose the following ordinance with a severely limited section of the downtown area and two other locations, off the main thoroughfares. We've also limited the signs and advertising those businesses can produce. When visitors come to this county, we want them to remember us for wholesome entertainment and the best of what central Florida has to offer." As he unveiled the map of the proposed locations, he posed for the camera shot from Channel 6 News.

Several small squared-off sections of the county and the Orlando metro area were plotted on the map. It was no coincidence that among the portions of the county set aside, J & M Corporation just happened to own properties there. Outreach Orlando Ministries was also within the boundaries—an unexpected surprise.

I had motive: a lock on all the adult entertainment locations within the county. The competition would be all but eliminated. Chance and his group knew well ahead of time where the limited locations specified by the ordinance were going to be, because they picked them out. They then gobbled up the properties with different corporations and subcorporations. They'd rake in the money.

Smart business planning, until something went wrong and people had to die.

43

"IT TICKLES," CREVIS SAID as Pam rubbed his bristled head with the hair dye. His rust-colored hair had been transformed into a slick black pelt that resembled a boot brush more than a haircut. His tiny mustache had grown out for a day or two; Pam painted the dye there as well. My sink was mud colored and probably permanently stained. I didn't think I would ever get it clean.

"We're just about finished." Pam brushed a last light coat on Crevis's lip.

"My undercover name will be Creavas Pierre," he said in a French accent. The kid had some real issues. He ran a finger over his pencil mustache. He did look different, at least enough to throw someone off who might have seen us together before.

Ashley Vargas's funeral was scheduled for 2:00 p.m. at Dobbs Funeral Home on Kirkman Road. Given the circumstances, I didn't think it would be wise for me to show up . . . inside, anyway. Crevis and Pam had stepped up to help me on this again. I was disturbed that I couldn't pull off most of the investigation by myself, not even a good trash pull. But, I had to admit, our little investigative unit was at least starting to have some fun.

Crevis cracked a few French jokes and made faces in the mirror with all the maturity of a ten-year-old.

"Crevis," I said.

He contorted his face in the mirror all the more and stuck out his tongue.

"Crevis." I grabbed his chin and forced him to look at me. "Focus!"

"I heard ya, Ray," he said, his jaw still cupped in my hand. "I was just having fun."

"I need you to listen to me and take this seriously. You're going to be inside there by yourself. I don't think anyone will recognize you, but we can't be too careful."

"Does that mean I get to carry a gun?"

"Absolutely not. That means you have to listen to everything I tell you. I don't have so many friends that I can afford to lose any."

Crevis grinned. "I'll be okay."

I explained how the small camera would work. I attached it to the inside of his coat with the pen camera portion facing outward. He could record —audio and video—everyone he could see in front of him. The battery life was several hours and would certainly last through the service.

Pam slipped Crevis's coat on, and we tested the system, which worked on a wireless connection to my laptop—another rousing purchase that should just about bankrupt me. But if Oscar got his way, or whoever'd been trying to murder me got theirs, I wouldn't be around to worry about paying those bills.

With our wired-up, tricked-out Crevis in tow, we all loaded into the freshly rented minivan, the finest vehicle ever created for surveillance. Eight out of every ten cars on the road seemed to be minivans. You could park them anywhere and they just seemed to fit in. I had Crevis remove the middle seat, and we set up our surveillance station there with my laptop tied down on a box, a digital camera, a digital camcorder, notepads, and water bottles. You never knew how long stakeouts could go, so you had to be prepared.

Pam drove and Crevis sat in the passenger seat. I remained in the back. I didn't know who would attend Ashley's funeral, but I wanted to get pictures of everyone there as well as write down the tag numbers. I needed to identify some of the other girls who could be in the Lion's Den with Brigitte. And, although they say it on television all the time, sometimes the killer really does come back to the scene. Maybe he'd show up at the funeral. We'd be foolish not to be prepared for that. We pulled into the parking lot, which was already filling up. I instructed Pam to park near the front entrance.

"Crevis, I want you to try to face as many people as you can, so I can zoom in for some closeups. If anyone asks, just say you were a friend of Ashley's and leave it at that."

"Got it." He flipped a bony thumb in the air.

"If you have any problems, just walk out or run as fast as you can," I said. "Or yell over the mike that you need help. We can hear you."

He hopped out and hurried to the front of the funeral home. A line was forming to get in. Pam's little makeup job worked well. I flipped on the wireless connection and tuned in to Crevis's clothes rubbing as he walked, but the audio was still strong. The camera jiggled as he moved but still provided a clear signal to my computer. I called him on the cell phone for a voice check.

"Creavas Pierre," he said.

"That's enough, genius. I'm just checking the range and voice. Everything sounds good. Keep your phone on vibrate."

"Oui, oui, monsieur." Crevis hung up.

He wasn't taking this as seriously as I'd hoped.

A fair amount of cars flowed in before the

service. A majority of the young women appeared to be in the "entertainment" industry. At 1:50, Chance's monster Hummer advanced on the funeral home like he was taking hostile territory. He gunned it until he coasted into a parking space.

Chance exited his macho machine and straightened his jacket, which seemed like it would split down the middle at any moment as it tried to cover his swollen frame. Carl extricated himself from the passenger side of the vehicle with such difficulty, I thought I'd have to call the fire department to use the Jaws of Life to get him out. I shot some good video of them swaggering into the red brick building.

The organ started playing a tune I probably should have known but didn't. I was sure Pam did though. She hummed along, confirming my suspicions. The camera continued to bounce until Crevis focused on an attractive blond girl in line in front of him. He must have been staring at her because the video stream remained locked on her curvaceous body for an inordinate amount of time.

I called him again. "Crevis."

"Oui, oui."

"Quit staring at the girl and shift around so we can see everyone inside."

"Oh," he said. "You noticed that. She's hot."

"Ogle her later." I regretted my idea to put him in there in the first place. "This is business, so for now, move and look around."

"Oui, oui," he said and hung up.

I forced a cleansing breath and monitored the screen. He was moving around a bit more now. I got some good closeups of individuals as well as photos of the crowd.

I turned to Pam. "Are you okay?"

"Yes . . . well, maybe not so much."

"What's bugging you?" I figured we were getting a little more comfortable with each other. I didn't think she'd mind me probing a bit.

"My heart just goes out to these girls." Pam leaned in closer to the screen. "That's what they really are . . . girls. They seem so pretty, yet so lost. Why do they let these men take advantage of them like that?"

"I wish I had an easy answer for you. All I know is that somewhere in there lies the answer to your brother's, Jamie's, Ashley's, and Trisha's murders. And for what it's worth, I don't understand it either."

As the pastor started speaking, a black Honda Accord screeched into the parking lot and raced past our van. The driver hurried into a spot, and a female hopped out. She wore a sleek black dress that clung to her shapely body and a black hat with a veil over her face. She scanned the parking lot before sprinting toward the sanctuary. She stopped at the doors and checked the lot again, then headed in. The best I could tell was that she was tall, slender, and in a hurry.

"I couldn't get a good look at her," I told Pam. I called Crevis again.

"What?" he whispered.

"A lady in all black came in, and she had a black hat and a veil over her face. Get a shot of her when you can."

He hung up without saying anything. The camera slid around as he was twisting. He stood and got a shot of the woman, now sitting in one of the back rows. I zoomed the camera in on her. The veil remained over her face. I didn't like that.

The pastor's eulogy was about fifteen minutes long. Much about sin, redemption, and everlasting life through Jesus Christ. He touched on Ashley's brief life without ever speaking about her current profession. Classy. I think he even got an amen from Pam.

After the service, Crevis met us back in the van, and we followed everyone to the grave site, about a ten-minute drive, which was completely taken up with Crevis giving me a blow-by-blow of the sermon and then telling me which of the girls he thought were gorgeous.

As we arrived at the cemetery, everyone took their places. A middle-aged couple held hands next to the site. They must be Ashley's parents. The sickness in the pit of my stomach overtook me for a moment. To imagine their little girl had been murdered by some scumbag . . . because she talked to me. If I had any decency, I would meet with them and explain. I didn't think that would happen today. Maybe sometime in the future.

Chance and Carl stood respectfully on the other side of the grave, a harem of striking young women dutifully surrounding them.

The mourner in the black dress arrived at the graveside service, although she stood behind everyone else. The service was unremarkable in every way—except in its sadness. After five minutes everyone said their good-byes. The lady in the black dress had kept her veil on the entire time. The veil seemed more of a disguise than an instrument of grief. She hung back away from everyone else and was going out of her way to be inconspicuous, which made her conspicuous to me.

She hurried to her car and exited with the same speed that she had entered.

"Follow her," I said.

Pam pulled in behind her as she turned onto I-4. She flipped her veil up on her hat. I still couldn't get a good look at her. I had her tag number, but I wasn't sure if I'd be able to run a check on it since I'd been booted from OPD's computer system. Besides, I needed to see her face.

"Get alongside of her."

"I'm trying to get over." Pam veered into the other lane, but a truck cut us off and forced her back. The driver laid on the horn.

"We need to get next to her."

"I'm trying." Pam whipped out again and sped up.

I could see the side of her head but still couldn't get a good shot of her. "Pass her!"

Pam stepped on it, and we started to pass. I aimed the camera down at the woman through the tinted windows and understood why she had worn a veil.

Katie Pham's attractive face came clearly into the frame.

44

WE FOLLOWED KATIE to her apartment complex just outside of the Orlando city limits. She went inside her first-floor apartment, then returned about fifteen minutes later wearing her blue crime scene jumpsuit. I had to move if I was going to catch up with her.

"Stay here, out of sight," I said to Crevis and Pam. They didn't need to be seen with me. I might need them at a later time.

Negotiating through the parking lot, I hurried to intercept her before she got into her car. "Katie," I said, as she unlocked her car door.

"Ray? What are you doing here?"

"We need to talk."

"Sergeant Yancey gave orders that none of us are supposed to talk with you. I'm sorry about that. He's really mad at you."

"Does Oscar know you used to dance at Club Venus with Jamie DeAngelo and Ashley Vargas?"

Katie's normally soft, inviting facial features pulled taut, and she worked her car keys in her hand. I had no idea if she really did dance at the clubs, but it made the most sense of why she was at that funeral in disguise.

"What business is that of yours?" she said. "It's not like it's illegal or anything."

"I just want to know if you told Oscar about your ties to two murder victims you processed the crimes scenes on? Under the circumstances, it's not an unreasonable question."

Katie paused for a moment. "I needed money for college, to pay off some of my loans and get the classes I needed for this job. The money was good, so I danced for a while and put myself through school. I did what I had to do. That part of my life is behind me now, and I don't like you coming here and throwing it in my face."

"If that part of your life is over," I said, "why did you attend Ashley's funeral today?"

"I knew her. I felt bad about what happened. Do you know how hard it is to work a crime scene where the victim was a friend and then not be able to tell anyone? I just wanted to pay my respects."

"I'm going to guess that you didn't tell Oscar because you didn't put your time at Club Venus on your work history when you applied at the department. That could have caused you some trouble." I mentioned that for two reasons: it was my best assessment of the situation, and I wanted to encourage her to ignore Oscar's shunning order and talk with me. Katie was a sharp girl and seemed to get it.

She nodded. "I only worked there part-time and on a mostly cash basis. And, no, I didn't list it on my application."

"How well do you know Chance Thompson?"

"As well as anyone else," she said. "He was nice to me, let me work when I wanted to, and didn't keep me on the schedule."

"You freelanced, then?"

"Yeah, something like that," she said.

"How well did you know Jamie?"

"Like most of the girls, we crossed paths. We'd talk some in the dressing room, but we didn't hang out. She was kind of private and kept to herself. I hadn't seen her in a while . . . until I showed up at the scene."

"What about Ashley?"

"The same," she said. "I purposefully didn't get too close to Chance or the other girls. Besides, some of the girls did things I didn't even want to know about. I minded my own business and kept to myself. It was a temporary job to get me through a tough time."

"Did you ever hear about anything called the Lion's Den?"

She cocked her head back. "No."

"Ever see any important people come into the

club?" I said, being intentionally vague. She needed to fill the rest in.

"Lots of people went there. There was no lack of business."

"Do you know who killed Jamie or Ashley?"

"No." She looked at her watch. "Anything else? I'm going to be late for my shift."

"I need help with my investigation."

"From what I'm told, your 'investigation' is dead." Katie worked the keys in her hand. "Sergeant Yancey shut you down."

"Not hardly. But you and I could go and discuss this with him, if you'd like. Maybe with your insights on Club Venus, Oscar would be more likely to help me."

"And to think I used to try to be nice to you. I felt bad about what happened. Now I know why no one likes you, Ray. You're a bully who'll do whatever it takes to get what you want. No matter who it hurts."

"I watched Trisha die, and I've seen the carnage this killer has caused." I caned closer, invading her personal space. "So you're right. I'll do whatever I have to do to get him. You can help me or get crushed in the middle. I don't really care anymore."

"What do you want?"

"I want you to check the ballistics test on the pistol taken from the Coral Bay murders that you sent off to the FDLE lab, then forward the report to me. And I want you to wear a wire and go under-cover into Club Venus to help expose the killer."

"I'll get you the report," she said. "But under no circumstances am I working undercover for you. As a matter of fact, after I get you this report, you better not ever talk to me again. We're finished, and I don't care who you go to about my past."

I hesitated long enough to make her squirm. I really wanted her to get inside the club, but that wasn't going to happen. I should have approached her differently, but I was making this part up as I went along. I took out my pen and scribbled down my e-mail address on a notepad and tore it off.

"E-mail the report to me, then we're finished."

She took the paper and opened her car door. "Don't ever come back here again."

She slammed the door and revved the engine as her Honda scurried out of sight.

45

MY TALK WITH KATIE certainly brought up more questions than answers. I had always assumed Jamie's connections to the police department had to be through a man. Unfortunately, in the world we live in, that doesn't necessarily have to be true. Were Jamie and Katie closer than she indicated, or was there an entire set of circumstances I was missing altogether?

Pam and I dropped Crevis off at my place, so he

could get ready for our shift. He'd meet me at the Coral Bay later.

Then we drove to Outreach Orlando Ministries. I had some questions for Mario the Weeping Felon with regard to the Lion's Den's plans for new adult entertainment sites. I hoped he could pay attention to me long enough before he started bawling again.

We parked on the street outside the ministry, which looked about as desolate as a derelict ship left wrecked on the shore for everyone to see.

Mario greeted us, or I should say Pam, at the front door. He hugged her and then merely tipped his head in my direction. It almost hurt my feelings . . . almost.

I toted my case file with me and sat in Mario's office. "I've got a few more questions."

"I figured." Mario took a seat, then reclined in his chair.

"The ministry owns this building, correct?"

"Yeah, we purchased it about three years ago."

"Anyone offer to buy it recently?" I tapped my pen on the pad.

Mario eased forward and rested his elbows on the table. "Yes. But that's not unusual."

"Do you remember who was interested?"

"A representative for an investment group contacted David and me to set up a meeting."

"How long was this before David's murder?"

"Couple of months maybe."

"What was the outcome of the meeting?"

"They made a more-than-generous offer for the building." Mario wiped the sweat from his shiny brow. "Much more than I thought it was worth."

"But David didn't take it?"

"He wasn't interested," Mario said. "He said the location here in this district was more important than money. He believed the money to support the ministry would come, but there were needs to be met right here."

"I take it you didn't agree?"

"It was a lot of money. We could have taken that and purchased a whole new building and equipment and still had some left over. David should have considered it, but he wasn't going to budge."

"Have you heard from these people since David's murder?"

Mario worked his gaze toward Pam, then shifted back and crossed his arms. "They called last week to set up another meeting."

"You can't be seriously considering this," Pam said. "David's dreams were all here. This is where he wanted to serve. You just can't give up on that."

"I'm not giving up, Pam. But sometimes changes have to be made. The ministry is dying here. If we sell the building, we can move into a smaller facility and have more than enough left over to cover expenses for a couple of years. That will keep us afloat for some time until more donations come in. A change of location might . . . shake the reputation we have right now too. It could be the best decision for the ministry."

"You can't do this to his life's work," she said.

"Unless some miracle happens, Pam, we won't have any choice."

Pam lowered her head and turned away. I don't think she wanted me to see her crying.

I turned back to Mario. "Does the name J & M Corporation sound familiar?"

Mario shook his head.

I perused the printouts. "Does the Relk Corporation sound familiar?"

"Yeah, I think that's it."

I shouldn't have been surprised. If J & M Corporation had holdings in all the areas listed in the ordinance, it could have piqued someone's interest. They appeared to be spreading the properties out to different subsidiaries. Very shrewd. Someone put a lot of time and thought into this.

I showed Mario the *Orlando Sentinel* photo of the Lion's Den Four, as I chose to call them. "Are any of these guys the person you dealt with?"

"No. No one in this picture."

I showed him a photo of Gordon Kurfis.

"Yeah. That's him." Mario tapped the picture with his fingertip. "He met with David and me before. And he's the one who contacted me again. Do these people have anything to do with David's death?"

"I don't know," I said, not wanting to be definitive with him. Pam gave me the look, knowing that I wasn't telling Mario what I really felt. I couldn't help that I didn't trust him, and now he was ready to make a profit on ministry property. His true motivations were as much a mystery as anything else in this case.

"These people who want to buy the building intend to turn it into a strip club," Pam said. "Cancel the meeting with them and pray that God keeps this place going."

Mario hissed and caught his head in his hands. "I'm doing everything I know how, Pam. But it seems at every turn I'm messing everything up. I don't think I'm the one God wants to lead this ministry."

For once, Mario and I agreed on something. While I'd never met David, and still didn't have much use for his religion, at least I could see by his conversations and actions with Jamie that he had really believed what he was preaching. He extended himself to a woman needing help—a woman most people would have judged as unworthy of help, including me. With Mario's record, I didn't think he was cut from the same cloth as David.

"Mario," Pam said, "I don't care if we have to get a loan or something. We can't just quit David's dream."

"Nobody's quitting," he said. "We're just running out of options."

"When is your meeting with Kurfis?" I said.

"Next week. He's supposed to call me Monday and let me know the time."

"When he calls, I want you to let me know."

"I will." He wiped his eyes, the waterworks flowing again.

46

I MANNED MY POST at Coral Bay Condos and sent Crevis on an errand (a legitimate one this time). I had him go to the store on his lunch break and get us more supplies. I needed printer paper, an ink cartridge, a memory card, and a sub sandwich in a bad kind of way.

I downloaded the photos of the scene at Ashley's apartment from my phone to my laptop. I was glad Oscar didn't pick up that my cell phone had a camera in it. I had to snap those photos. It's not like I didn't care; I just needed to catch the person responsible for her death. While it seemed callous, it had to be done. She was no longer Ashley Vargas; she was a valuable piece of evidence. At least that's what the cop in me was supposed to think. I still felt dirty for doing it, though.

On every crime scene I'd ever worked, I could distance myself from the victim and keep my emotions out of it. Ashley was different. Whoever killed her did it because of me. I sat at her kitchen table and talked with her. She said I was "nice." But in truth, I wasn't being nice to her, any more than I was being mean with Chance in his interview. I evaluated them quickly and formulated an approach that would give me the most success. It was good police strategy, but I've been doing it so long that sometimes I forget which person I'm supposed to be.

Ashley's pictures booted up, and one of her fully clothed body on the bed came into frame. The pink belt was wrapped around her neck, from behind, apparently. The murder definitely wasn't a sex crime, and nothing obvious had been stolen from the scene. The belt appeared to have been from her closet, because there were several others similar to it still hanging there. I figured the killer used a different method to throw off the investigators. Since he had my notes, this guy had to know that I was a pariah among my peers. Nothing I said could be trusted in law enforcement circles.

My e-mail alarm chimed. Katie had sent a copy of the report. Her response was terse and to the point: "Here it is, jerk." Finer words hadn't been spoken to me in a while. I guess we were now finished too. I was running out of police contacts.

I checked the report, which compared the shell casings and ballistics of the weapon to other crimes around Florida. The FDLE expert determined that the Ruger 9mm had been used in only one other crime. The case number was an OPD case—it leapt out at me as I read it.

The pistol that killed David and Jamie was the same weapon that murdered Trisha and crippled me. The shell casings were an exact match to those left at the scene of our shooting.

My mind went numb. Somehow I doubted that Pastor Hendricks waited near a shrub line at Dante Hill's house to ambush Trisha and me a year ago, especially since he hadn't even met Jamie at that point. I was hitting overload.

I massaged my hip, as I had a new ache there, one of solidarity with David Hendricks and Jamie DeAngelo. Had Katie even read the report before she forwarded it to me? This was going to rip the case from my hands. Once everyone discovered the gun link, FDLE would step in. I had to work quickly if I was going to find the killer. This investigation was getting way out of control.

The rest of the report was about the gun's serial number. While it had been ground down, the expert was still able to lift off the number. I jotted it down. I wished I still had my computer set up to check NCIC/FCIC to see if the gun was listed as stolen. Oscar had taken care of that, though. I was locked out of any database that could help me find where that gun came from and who it was last registered to.

How could this have slipped through? An alleged murder-suicide is swept under the rug, and the murder weapon from Trisha's death and my shooting is nearly destroyed? The connections to me and the police department were now undeniable, even for Oscar. But I didn't know if I could or would approach him yet. My mind was in full-blown chaos. I needed to relax.

I logged off the computer and closed my eyes for a moment. I pulled out my Sudoku book and attempted to work it, to rejuvenate my scattered thoughts.

It didn't help.

Crevis returned with our stuff, and we caught up on the latest doings over sub sandwiches. I shared with him the knowledge about the gun, the implications still battering my brain. He was going to stop by his house to pick up more clothes. He'd been staying at my apartment since the attack. I figured I'd be hard pressed to get rid of him now.

The sun crawled over the horizon. The day-shift guy relieved me, and I hobbled my way to the parking garage to head home. Crevis had left early to get to his house before morning rush-hour traffic got thick. As the tip of my cane striking the concrete called out my cadence throughout the garage, I didn't feel right. Since my attack there, I'd been a bit leery of the place. Now without Crevis, I felt odd. I figured it was just another casualty of my crippled psyche. Maybe Kurfis was right—I did need some meds.

I inserted the key in the truck door when shoes shuffled near the car next to me. I let go of the keys and whipped out my 9mm, coming on target to Rick Pampas's reptilian face.

"Settle down," Pampas said, his hands up. "You're awfully jumpy these days, aren't you?"

"You shouldn't be sneaking up on people. What are you doing here, anyway?"

"We need to get some things straight, Quinn, before I head into work."

"Well, I'm not feeling so chummy right now." I holstered my weapon. "So you're gonna have to make it another time."

"Why are you stirring all this up on the murder-suicide?" He braced his hand on the bed of my pickup.

"Murder-suicide? I'm not sure what you're talking about." I tapped my finger on my chin. "Oh yeah, you must mean the double murder here where you blew the investigation."

"You're really not that funny, Ray. You never have been. You just can't get over the fact that you're not a cop anymore and you never will be one again."

"At least I was a cop. I'm not so sure you ever were."

"Well, the way everyone else sees it, including Yancey, I'm the top guy in Homicide now," he said. "That must drive you nuts, but it's the way it is, and it's not going to change—no matter how much you try to gum up the works. Keep your fingers out of my cases. You've got no business messing with what I've already closed."

"Why did you remove Jamie's phone records from the report?" I was tired, but I doubted I'd ever get the chance to ask Pampas these questions again. "Why didn't you send off the gun to be tested? And why didn't you spend more than ten minutes assessing the crime scene? You dropped the ball on this or intentionally fouled it up. Either way, you're gonna eat it now. You're going down."

"In your dreams. I didn't take anything from the report. It's a murder-suicide and it'll stay that way. You're still a basket case about losing your girlfriend, Trisha."

I straightened and struggled not to give away too much body language that he'd struck a nerve. I didn't know how to answer him.

"You didn't think I knew about that, did you?" Pampas laughed and closed the distance between us. "See, that's your problem. You think you're so much smarter than everyone else. You worked in a room full of detectives, for Pete's sake. Didn't you think we'd notice you two taking long lunches together? How you looked at each other? Always disappearing together? C'mon. I knew you two were dating months before the shooting."

"What's your point?"

"Stay out of my way, rent-a-cop. I've put a lot of time into Homicide and have worked hard to be in this position. I don't need you going behind my back to tear me down."

292

"Just what do you plan on doing if I don't?" I said.

"Your tough talk might have worked at one time," he said. "I can't remember why I was ever intimidated by you. You don't seem so tough now." He reached up and grabbed the plastic badge off my chest, snapping it between his fingers.

My Glock appeared in my hand in a second, acquiring my target on his forehead—again. He stepped back and feigned a smile, but he couldn't hide the fear in his eyes. He was wondering if I'd really shoot him or not. I wondered the same thing.

"Don't push me too far, Pampas. I have nothing left to lose."

"It's against the law to point guns at *real* cops." He shuffled back.

"I know. But I'm not worried. No jury in the world would consider you a real cop."

"Stay out of my business." Pampas turned and walked away. "Or you'll get broken again."

47

PAMPAS'S THREAT WAS WAY DOWN on my list of concerns, although I couldn't write it off altogether. He was squirrelly enough to protect his own interests, like his job and position. But was there something more sinister to his threat than his fragile ego and a poor performance review? Did he remove the phone records or never put them in to begin with? And why didn't he send the gun off for testing? We did that with most firearms used in violent crimes, even if we thought it was a murder-suicide. If Pampas were stupid, I would actually cut him some slack. He wasn't, so he was on the suspect short list.

Since no respectable law enforcement officer in Orange County would talk with me anymore, I waited until 9:00 a.m. and reached out to Tim Porter again to beg for more favors—to send subpoenas to the phone company for all the cell phones registered to the Relk Corporation and their subsidiaries and to run an ATF serial number check on the pistol that had caused so much devastation.

The Lion's Den, J & M, and its plethora of side companies were inexorably entangled. If I had all the phone numbers listed to them, I could check off the ones I knew and find a way to use the others, should the opportunity present itself. I wasn't quite sure what I would do with them yet, but at some point Tim Porter would stop taking my calls too. I needed to get the information while I still could.

"You're sure about the link between your shooting and the murders at the condo?" Tim said.

"FDLE's ballistics unit made the match. It's confirmed."

"You need to let Oscar know," Tim said.

"The lab is going to send a copy of their findings to Pampas, so they're all going to find out soon enough." I'd chosen not to reveal that fact during my little talk with Pampas. I didn't want to ruin the surprise when he got the report, or to tip off that I'd got a copy before he did. "I just don't know when he'll get it and what he'll do with it after that."

"This is the last stuff I'm sending off for you. It's Wednesday, and I can hold off telling my people over the weekend, but you're gonna have to find some way to let Oscar know or else turn this over to the Orlando FDLE office."

"I'm just trying to stay ahead of everything here. I can't believe where this case is going. They've got a bad cop close to the unit, Tim."

"Just keep your head down. We've got to forward this information to the right folks to do this right. I'm praying for you, Ray."

I hung up without thanking him, though I should have for kindness' sake alone. Tim was my only friend in law enforcement now, and I couldn't afford to be impolite. But if I wanted prayers, I could call Pam and get them ad nauseam. What I needed was information.

I had no idea how I was going to make the final connection between the Lion's Den, the murders, and the police department. At least the Lion's Den made sense. It was about money, pure and simple. But where did the police connection come in? Was there an aspect of this I was missing?

About ten minutes later, my cell phone rang, and I checked the number. Tim Porter, FDLE. "You miss me already?"

"No, just thought I'd tell you what I found," he said. "Are you sitting down?"

I didn't like the sound of that. "Go ahead."

"I ran the serial number through NCIC/FCIC and found out some surprising things about your gun. Then I called a friend at ATF to confirm what I had."

"Good deal," I said.

"We'll see about that. It was last sold four years ago to a Clarence Stowe out of Orlando."

"Excellent," I said. "He should be easy to track down."

"He should be real easy. Clarence committed suicide with that gun fourteen months ago."

"Okay . . . now for the punch line."

"The gun was placed into OPD's evidence for destruction. It should have been destroyed or still be in the evidence section at OPD. It shouldn't be out on the streets killing people."

"I'm so over my head right now."

"That's not the half of it. FDLE has already sent their report to OPD. Oscar and everyone in Orlando is gonna know the murder weapon came from the evidence room. This thing is blowing wide open."

I hung up on Porter again.

I didn't have a lot of options left, so I might have to meet with Oscar and try a new tactic—telling him the truth.

48

SINCE MY SHOOTING, I've been trapped in a peculiar world of disconnect between my body and my psyche. When I want to run, no matter how much I desire, struggle, or will it with all my might, I can still only hobble. When I desperately need my balance, I sway at the will of a breeze and gravity.

This case mimicked my personal dilemmas. As a homicide cop, I had the power and resources to make things happen, get information, or turn up the pressure to get that information. Now, I was at the mercy of circumstances and limitations I felt powerless against. All my resources were cut off, just as I was so close to breaking the case wide open. The case was as hamstrung as I was.

I had re-created my murder collage as best I could. Pictures of suspects dotted the wall with lines crossing from the Fab Four of the Lion's Den to Chance Thompson to a large question mark that represented the unknown at Orlando PD. David Hendricks's driver's license picture was smack in the middle of the wall, with Jamie's and Ashley's on either side of him. David's smile appeared warm and genuine, one of the people in my life I've regretted not meeting. He was gaining my respect.

Pam passed by my living room window, and I

met her at the door. I told her about the gun being used in both my shooting and David's murder, a morbid twist of fate I couldn't shake.

"Now they'll have to reopen the case," Pam said.

"When this comes to light, OPD won't open anything. FDLE will take it over. But until then, I'm running out of ideas, contacts, and steam. I don't have a lot left."

"You've done more than I could have ever asked for." She rested her hand on my shoulder. "You proved David's not a murderer and that he was just trying to help Jamie. You've linked your shooting to David's case."

"And I all but killed Ashley with my own hand. I was sloppy and stupid, just like I was with Trisha." I was dancing in that gloomy place again and was powerless to stop myself; the veil of that awful darkness shrouded me. "You might not want to hang around me too long. I'm hard on the women in my life."

"I'm not going anywhere until we're finished." Pam walked into the living room and sat on the couch. "I don't know why all this has happened, but you're fighting evil, and the devil does not fight fair."

I didn't want to argue with her about devils or evil, mainly because I was sure she was at least right about evil. Pam was earning some serious respect as well. I guess I thought she'd crumble at the first sign of trouble or violence. I felt her religion would make her weak and vulnerable to such things. Not this lady. She was tough as they came. Trisha would have liked her a lot.

"Regardless of what we've uncovered so far," I said, "all we've really done is raise more questions. With everything we've found, we still don't know who shot Trisha and me, who killed David and Jamie, and who murdered Ashley. We know a lot about the Lion's Den and how they're somehow linked to the adult entertainment ordinance, but we still can't prove that theory. We're still missing something—the critical piece of evidence that will tie all these things together."

Crevis emerged from the bathroom all fresh. "Ray, I'm gonna run by my house and get more of my stuff. Do we need anything while I'm out?" He punched the heavy bag with a solid right.

I stopped it with my hand as it swung toward me. I'd coached Crevis through a workout earlier. He had some sharp punches and kicks. I showed him how to lean in just a bit more to maximize his power. He caught on quickly. He had good potential.

"We don't need anything. Be back in time to pick me up for our shift."

Beaming, Crevis looked at Pam. "Ray and I are roomies now." He jabbed the bag again and headed out the door.

I shrugged. "I was feeling sorry for him, so I let him move in here for a while."

"Be careful what you say to him," she said. "He's young and impressionable, and he idolizes you. Don't abuse that."

Pam's warning was fair. I didn't let her know that Crevis was growing on me. He made the cave seem not so dark. Besides, he was becoming more of a John Wayne junkie than me—and that was hard to do.

As I walked into the living room to sit with Pam, I caught my foot on the edge of the couch, unleashing a raging inferno up my leg. The dizzying pain stopped me as I didn't want to scream out in front of her. I held it to a growl.

I took the cane and whipped it around in a baseball swing, smacking the handle into the dry wall—knocking a hole right in the middle of the murder collage. I jerked back on my cane, but it was stuck. I yanked hard and a chunk of dry wall flew out and skipped off the coffee table and onto the floor.

"I'm so sick of this!" Leg spasms wreaked havoc on my balance. I buoyed myself on the back of the couch. "I had everything going for me—I was strong and healthy; I had a great job . . . and a woman I loved. My life had never been as good as it was a year ago. Then just when I had everything I'd ever wanted—*bam*—in three seconds it was all stolen from me."

Pam was quiet, letting me finish my temper tantrum. I hadn't vented any of those emotions since the shooting. I'm not like that; the Duke's not like that. But it wasn't fair. My life was supposed to be totally different. I'd had a plan.

"But you're still alive for a reason, Ray. God has a new direction for you . . . if you'll listen."

"I don't want a new direction. I want my life back. I want Trisha back!"

"Can I pray for you?" she said.

"Pray to whom? If your God exists, *He* did this to me. Or He sat back and just let Trisha die. Either way, He's responsible. Doesn't your God know what's going on down here? Doesn't He know that people are suffering and dying? Or doesn't He care?"

"His own Son was tortured, nailed to a cross, and stabbed with a spear. And Jesus died there . . . for us," she said, her voice soft. "God knows all about suffering. He's experienced all that and more. He cares more than you can imagine."

"I don't see it." I squeezed the top of the couch as the agony ricocheted throughout my body. "I don't see it at all. I only see pain and misery."

Pam got up and walked around the couch to where I was standing. "Please let me pray for you."

I wanted to scream out but didn't. I wanted to tell her, "No way!" But I couldn't. I was physically, emotionally, and spiritually at my end. I had nothing left to resist with. A feeble nod was all I was capable of.

She rested her hand on my shoulder. Her touch

was gentle. "Heavenly Father, Ray needs You now. Please heal him and be with him. Let him see You in this. In Jesus' name, amen."

I didn't say anything when she finished. I needed to get ready for my shift.

49

AFTER PAM'S IMPROMPTU PRAYER MEETING, she reluctantly headed home, and I got ready for work. I left early so I could drive out toward Ashley's apartment on my way. I couldn't believe I had a meltdown in front of Pam. The good part was, I knew Pam wouldn't bring it up again or use it against me—like I'd probably do if it were someone else.

After swallowing four aspirins on the ride there to ease the ache in my leg, I chased them with a soda. The pain meds make me too sleepy to take before a shift, so I'd have to grunt through it with over-the-counter stuff. I scrolled through my options in my head, and I knew just how desperate my situation had become when I broke down and called Dean Yarborough for help.

"Yarborough," he answered.

"Dean, Ray Quinn. Don't hang up."

"What do *you* want?"

"I need your help," I said.

"So what? I could get in trouble for even talking to you. As usual, you've really stirred things up."

"I need you to look up a suicide report from fourteen months ago," I said. "Clarence Stowe."

"What makes you think I'd do anything to assist you? You've always treated me like garbage. You'd bark orders at me, poke fun at me. Why should I do anything for you now?"

I might have been a bit terse with Dean at times and maybe had some fun at his expense, but I didn't have time for all that now.

"Don't do it for me," I said. "Do it for Trisha."

Dean hesitated, but I could hear him breathing. "You think this is related to her murder?"

"Yes. If you'll burn me a copy of the report, I'll meet you at Ashley Vargas's apartment and explain everything. I'll be there in an hour."

"I'll think about it." He hung up.

I was exhausted from doing double time at Coral Bay and working this case and extremely late mornings with Jim. Not that I slept much before, but I was stretching it now. As I turned into Ashley's apartment complex, I recalled the last visit I'd made here, only to discover her lifeless body.

How would things have been different if I hadn't agreed to help Pam? Ashley would still be alive. I'd be better rested in my world as the night watchman.

What Pam had said was true, though. Evil didn't fight fair. I didn't need a teacher to tell me that. I'd seen enough evil in my career to clearly identify it out of a lineup. Even though I knew the wickedness people were capable of, the last few swipes stung like nothing I'd ever felt in my life.

Lying on warm pavement watching Trisha die, powerless to even crawl toward her.

Now, because I tried to help and actually do something right, Ashley Vargas died, and I might not be any closer to finding the person responsible for both. The more I dug in, the more questions popped up and suspects came on the radar.

I parked in front of her building and took my time getting to the third floor. My leg wasn't letting me forget the stumble at my apartment. I didn't know what I would accomplish by coming here. Maybe relieve some guilt, if nothing else.

The blinds of her apartment windows were cracked enough for me to cup my hands on the glass to see in. The furnishings were still there. The door and frame had been replaced from Crevis's kick. I rested my elbows on the metal railing of the walkway, embracing the breeze on my face. Surprises never ceased as Dean's crime scene van negotiated the speed bumps in the parking lot. I would have bet he wouldn't show.

He skipped up the steps with an ease I envied and had a manila envelope in his hand. He was wearing his usual blue CSI jumpsuit.

"This is the report." He pushed his glasses up on his nose; the hair from his comb-over flapped in the wind like it was waving at me. "You could have gotten a copy from Records. It's a closed case."

"I know, but I didn't want to wait. I need to review it tonight. Besides, I don't think showing my face at the police department to pick up a copy of a police report would be a good idea right now. Oscar would probably have me arrested for loitering or something."

"So you think this has something to do with Trisha's death?" Dean said.

"Yeah. This was the same gun used to shoot both Trisha and me and kill David Hendricks and Jamie DeAngelo."

"So that's what this is all about. There have been a bunch of closed-door meetings today. Everything has been real hush-hush. Sergeant Yancey had Internal Affairs in his office. That's never good."

"I can imagine it's getting pretty hot there," I said. "It's not my problem now. The only thing I have to do is to find out who got this gun out of Property and Evidence and used it for the murders. After that, it should be a walk in the park."

"I'm sorry I gave you grief on the phone, Ray. I didn't realize everything that was going on. If I knew this would help find Trisha's killer, I would've jumped right to it."

"Well, I'm sorry . . . for a lot of things. Do you remember this case, Clarence Stowe's suicide?"

Dean nodded. "Katie and I were on call, and we picked up the case. We thought it was a homicide at first. The guy was facedown on his living room floor with a gunshot to the head. We couldn't find the gun until we rolled him over; it was lying underneath him. Pampas cleared it as a suicide."

"Do you remember who was there? It should be on the crime scene log."

He flipped through the report. "Me, Katie, Pampas, Steve Stockton, and Oscar, who showed up late. Patrol officers S. Whitman and D. Ruiz were there as well."

"Who logged the gun into evidence?"

He paused. "Katie and I. I don't remember the order of collection, but we were both responsible. I know that gun made it to the property and evidence section. After that, I can't say."

Property and Evidence was locked down pretty well. You had to sign in and out. But people were in and out of there all the time. Given the right opportunity, someone could have passed it on the shelf and picked it up. Unlikely in this case. The ties seemed to be pretty secure— someone in this group was the suspect. Katie Pham jumped out at me.

"How well do you know Katie?" I said.

Dean shrugged. "We spend a lot of time together at scenes and such. But to be honest, I don't know her that well. She keeps to herself a lot. Doesn't talk about what she does off-duty. She wouldn't steal a gun or anything like that."

I didn't tell Dean about my knowledge of her

prior nocturnal activities. There was a huge difference between a CSI and a detective: The CSI
works in the logical world of techniques and rules
of evidence collection. They don't deal with the
vagaries of the human condition. Katie wasn't off
the list.

"I'm gonna ask you straight up, Dean. Did you
have anything to do with this?"

"Would I be here if I did? I don't like where
Pampas is taking this investigation. Trisha
deserves better. I've never much liked you . . . but
I did respect you. If you can make this thing
happen, I'm in."

"I want to look around Ashley's place. I might
need to get with the management."

"I can get us in." Dean looked around, then
pulled a lock-picking set from his pocket. He
worked the lock a minute or so and then opened
the door.

Ashley's apartment looked and smelled the
same as I remembered, except the bird was gone.
We moved to the back bedroom. The sheets on
the bed were missing.

"Did you take the sheets into evidence?"

"Of course." Dean squatted down and examined
the edge of the mattress.

"Can you get me a copy of Oscar's report?"

"You're kidding, right?" Dean swallowed hard.
"Between Sergeant Yancey and Internal Affairs,
they're monitoring everything we do on the

computers and everywhere else. He'd skin me alive if I did that. I'm risking my job doing this."

So much for jumping right in. I was glad he brought me the report and got us into the apartment, but Dean lacked any real chutzpa to help with the case. As far as gallantry went, I think I'd seen Dean's limit.

I tried to imagine what the killer must have seen and did while he—or she—was at the scene. How did he get Ashley in the back bedroom? She was fully clothed, so she wasn't asleep. Did he ambush her in the parking lot and force her to her apartment? Maybe if he was armed. She might have been too afraid to cry out. Hard to tell.

Nothing jumped out at me in Ashley's place but bad memories. I still needed to view it, though. I snapped more photos of the layout. I didn't know how helpful they'd be, but since I had the chance, I took it.

As I stood in Ashley's room, haunted by her memory, I developed a plan.

50

DEAN AND I PARTED WAYS, and I made it to my shift just in time.

The suicide report made for some bland and depressing reading. Clarence Stowe, a sixty-three-year-old male, took his own life with a single gunshot to the head. He was terminally ill and apparently felt he'd meet the Grim Reaper halfway. But how did his gun get in the hands of a killer? It's not like there was a burglary to the police Property and Evidence section.

The buzzer at the front door chimed. I looked up, but my eyes betrayed me. Katie Pham was staring at me.

"You gonna let me in or what?" Her hand still covered the wall-mounted intercom. Her hair looked unkempt, for her anyway.

"Are you armed?" I said, half joking. Of course, the other half of me was dead serious.

"We need to talk."

I hit the buzzer, and she opened the door and hurried in. She wore a pair of blue sweatpants and a navy blue jacket with a light blue lining.

"Thanks for the report," I said.

"You've got everyone at the PD running crazy right now."

"So I heard. What brings you around? I didn't think you were that fond of me anymore."

"I'm not." She slipped her hands into her jacket pockets. "You treated me like dirt yesterday. Just because I used to dance at clubs doesn't give you the right to do that."

"I'm looking for a killer, Katie. Sometimes I forget my manners."

"The cases are linked, aren't they?"

"You read the report?"

She bit her lip and shook her head. "I can't believe

I'm going to do this. But I want to help you."

Not exactly what I expected from her. "Why the change of heart?"

"I don't think the PD is going to give this the attention that it needs. Everyone seems more concerned about finding out how the gun left Property and Evidence than the link between the shootings. Internal Affairs was down in Sergeant Yancey's office most of the day today. They're looking to hang someone out to dry for the gun thing . . . and I get the feeling it's me."

"Do you have anything to worry about?"

"Don't be stupid. But I was the most junior and inexperienced person at the scene, and Dean and I logged that gun in. If they ever find out about my dancing at Club Venus, they'll assume I did something with it, and everything I've worked for is finished."

"So you're looking to head them off at the pass? If you can help solve the case and find out about the gun, you might save your own career."

"I know it sounds self-serving, Ray, but I really want to find this person too. I think we can help each other out."

"Are you sure you want to do this? I have no idea where all of this will lead, and if Oscar finds out you're helping me, your career is definitely over."

"I'm working on borrowed time as it is," she said. "If you found out about Club Venus, Internal Affairs is going to find out. They'll terminate me for lying on my preemployment interview. I've seen them fire people for less. I'll do whatever you need me to do."

"Will you go back into Club Venus for just one night?" The plan already churned in my head. "Maybe only half a night?"

Katie nodded. "I'll do it. And I know that I might just live to regret those words."

"She's really hot, Ray," Crevis whispered, mesmerized by the dancer-to-be.

Katie showed the good sense to wear a long trench coat to cover herself as we were planning our night at my apartment. Her tan, curvy legs peeked out as she sat on the sofa. Her hair was primped up and immaculate, with two flowers tucked just above her ears. I didn't think I'd be able to look at her in her crime scene jumper the same again.

Katie had called Chance earlier and asked if she could dance again a couple nights a week. Chance bit, saying they were short a few "entertainers" and would love for her to come back anytime. Katie had never told Chance that she went to work for the police department when she left. She liked to keep all of her cards close. Neither Katie nor I mentioned that the reason they were probably short on help was Ashley's death. We didn't need to give life to that thought, although I'm sure she considered it.

Pam was loading some software we would need on my laptop. "Thank you for helping us," she said to Katie. "I don't know if we could pull off this crazy plan without you."

Katie drew the belt of her coat tight. "We just need to get this done. But I have to tell you, Ray, this is easily the most insane plan I've ever heard."

"I'm open for suggestions, if anyone has a better idea." I evaluated my crack team and knew deep down in my heart that Katie spoke the truth. Everyone remained silent. I didn't have a better plan, and apparently, neither did anyone else.

"Katie," I said, "I want you to clip this to your . . . bikini bottoms." I handed her a small flower I'd made to fit the Eagle and Hawk audio and video receiver, as small as a pencil eraser. I gave her another matching brooch to clip on the other side. The OCD side of me needed some balance and symmetry. "Now switch it on as soon as you can when you get in, so we can tell what's going on."

"No problem. I should be able to turn it on as soon as I'm in the dressing room."

"Excellent." I smiled. "Crevis, if this is going to work, you'll have to have perfect timing."

Crevis stared at Katie but didn't reply.

"Keep up with me here, Crevis." I snapped my fingers in front of his face.

"I heard you," he said. "Perfect timing. Got it."

"I need you all to understand something." My team's attention drew to me.

For a moment, I felt like I was on a cop operation again, briefing everyone on a major case. Then Crevis stared at Katie, and I was reminded that I was working with amateurs who I feared wouldn't be able to react well if something went bad. And the only thing consistent about police operations is that something almost always goes wrong.

"We need to be at our best tonight. This might be our only chance to get this right. I don't want to mess this up . . . and I don't want anyone here to get hurt."

"Katie will be fine," Crevis said. "I'll be in there with her, and nothing, I mean nothing, will happen to her."

Katie rolled her eyes.

"I'm not so worried about her," I said. "Now, does everyone have their assignments?"

"Yes," they said in unison.

"Crevis, you need to act like any other patron in there. Pretend you're having a great time, but keep the mission in focus. You need to be ready to move at the right time. Understand?"

"I got it, Ray. But I'm still not gonna drink or anything. You know how I feel about that."

"You don't have to drink," I said. "Just buy a beer and carry it around. Then go to the bathroom and pour it out and buy another. Buy at least two while you're there. If you look like you're not drinking, it could draw suspicion."

"I never thought of that." He nodded. "I can do that."

I checked my watch. "Well, let's get this plan moving."

51

THE THURSDAY-NIGHT CROWD was hopping at Club Venus. But I hadn't been by the place any night that it wasn't packed. Chance knew his business well, and the burgeoning belly of Orange County served up plenty of customers.

Pam and I found a spot near the front and backed the van in. I made sure my equipment was up and running. Everything looked good. We were to arrive first, then Katie, and finally Crevis. If all went well, we wouldn't be here too long.

Katie arrived just after we got settled, and she hurried into the back door.

Crevis's wire turned on, and music I couldn't identify came blaring through, with Crevis singing along. "I'm here, Ray," he screamed into the bug. His engine and radio shut off, and his heavy steps approached.

My laptop went live as Katie turned on the camera in the dressing room. She waved her hand in front of the hidden camera.

"It's a go now," I said.

Pam was quiet, looking like she was praying.

"I need to see Chance before I head to the stage," Katie said.

I assumed no other girls were in the dressing room and she said that for my benefit, but I couldn't be sure.

The tunes from the club pounded through the speakers, so I made some adjustments to handle the two signals coming in. I turned Crevis's signal down some. I just needed it to monitor him. As Katie zigzagged through the crowd, I could see much of the goings-on. The camera worked better than I thought. I loved it when the tech stuff worked.

Katie arrived at Chance's door, which I recognized from my first visit. She knocked as she let herself in. Chance was at his desk. He was as ugly on-screen as in person.

"Katie." Chance stood and walked toward her. "I'm so glad you've come back to work with us."

"Thanks for taking me on such short notice. I really need the work."

He took a step back. "You look great. Have you been working out?"

"I run some. Try to eat right. I keep busy. I guess I always knew I'd be coming back."

"The best girls always do." He grinned. "Knock 'em dead tonight. We can work out any future days later."

"Thanks, Chance. You've been great."

He hugged her for a long time. Katie headed out of the office.

"I guess that wasn't what I expected," Pam said. "I thought he'd be an evil villain or something. He treated her like . . . an employee."

"It's just business to him," I said. "But you don't get in the way of his business. That's for sure. Katie's a freelancer to him. She's unusual for these types of clubs. Most of the girls dance to support their drug habits or to keep their boyfriends in cash. Guys like Chance couldn't care less about these girls, unless they're not making him money."

Katie went and talked with the DJ. I couldn't hear everything she said, but it was apparent that she was on next.

Katie aimed the camera right toward the stage, just where I needed it. The dancer was taking her last bows and bucks, and she pranced off the stage. The DJ announced Katie, or Loloni, straight in from the Hawaiian Islands. I guess it didn't matter that she was Katie, Asian American from Orlando. The whole club scene was about an image they wanted to portray, a fantasy for the men to cling to, so they wouldn't cling so tightly to their cash. Loloni took the stage.

The camera scanned the room as Katie danced to a throng of drunkards. Pam wrapped her arms around her stomach.

"I can't believe she's putting herself in this situation just to help us," Pam said.

I hadn't told Pam all of Katie's motivations, but I too appreciated the lengths she was going to to make this work. "Like you said before, 'Evil doesn't fight fair.' Neither do we."

I checked my watch. It was time.

Katie gathered several dollar bills from some college-aged guy and then danced to the side of the stage. In a stunt that would rival any Charlie Chaplin film, Katie caught her heel on the side of the railing and flipped over, smacking a table on her way down.

"Now it gets good," I said.

Katie's camera faced straight up as several men gazed down at her. "Are you okay? . . . Do you need an ambulance? . . . Somebody get a doctor!"

Katie made an attempt to stand but screamed out in pain. "My ankle! I think I broke my ankle!"

In less than thirty seconds, Chance's mug filled the screen. "Are you okay, Katie?" he said, like he cared. What a guy. He was nearly as good an actor as Katie.

"I think my ankle is broken," she said. "I've broken that one before. I'm such an idiot." She said it with such conviction that I was convinced.

As Chance was leaning over, Crevis's head appeared right over his shoulder—just on cue. As Chance attended to Katie, Crevis looked left, then right. "Hey! Stop pushing me!" Crevis yelled and then fell on top of Chance.

Crevis and Chance toppled out of sight of Katie's camera. Crevis appeared again and pointed to a guy behind him. "That guy pushed me."

Chance scrambled to his feet and snatched the unsuspecting pawn by the neck and shook him. "You're outta here! There's no call for behavior like that in this club."

"I didn't do anything," the helpless guy screamed as Chance dragged him out of view.

Crevis glanced at Katie's camera and held up Chance's cell phone as he smirked. Crevis had lifted it from the carrier on Chance's belt during their tumble.

"He got it." I clapped my hands together. "Now get out of there, Crevis. We've got some quick work to do."

Chance returned and Crevis disappeared out of view. Chance reached down and picked up Katie. The camera went fuzzy, then out.

Katie's signal was gone. Chance must have somehow switched it off when he picked her up.

I turned up Crevis's signal, but I couldn't get anything from him either. I didn't know if he did something to his transmitter when he fell, but they were both silent. I scoped out the front door with my binos but didn't see him come out. I waited about a minute and then called his cell phone. It went straight to voice mail.

"I don't like this, Pam." I tapped my finger on the laptop and then scanned the front door again. Nothing. No Crevis. No Katie. Not good. I rationalized the communications problems away, but I couldn't get rid of the nagging feeling that something had gone horribly wrong inside that club. And I was in a comfortable van . . . just waiting.

"He should have been here by now."

"It's only been a couple of minutes," Pam said. "He knew the plan. He'll be here."

"Something's not right. I can feel it." I called Crevis again. Straight to voice mail.

A terror overtook me that I hadn't considered. Katie had been a bit too free in coming to me. I should have suspected something was off. Was she working for Chance the entire time? Had we just been set up?

52

I TOSSED MY KEYS TO PAM. "Move the van. If it is a setup, they'll know you're here and will be coming for you. Get off the property and park across the street. If I'm not back in ten minutes, call 911 and get out of here."

Pam hopped into the driver's seat. "What else can I do?"

"Pray." I was out of the van and heading to the front door lickety-split. I slid my hand back and adjusted the Glock in its holster. I pulled out my wallet while I was on the hoof and got the cover-charge money ready.

Was Crevis fighting for his life right now as I was traveling at a turtle's pace to get to him? Was Katie filling Chance in on the whole plan as they tortured Crevis? I wished Helga had pushed me even harder in therapy.

Two goons covered the door at my approach. I made a mental note of what I would do if they didn't let me in. It involved some cane whacking and a little gunplay, but no matter what, I was getting to Crevis.

No problems at the door as I laid the cash down quick. I scanned the packed room. I didn't see Chance, but his office door was shut. Katie and Crevis were nowhere in sight. I looked toward the bathroom just as another club thug walked out and looked around. I'd try there first, but then I was bursting into Chance's office.

I pushed through the crowd, my pulse pounding to the beat of the music. I opened the men's room door as another patron came out. No one else was in the bathroom. I looked under the stalls and saw Crevis's feet cocked funky. He was down.

"Crevis!" I nailed the stall door with my shoulder, knocking it in.

Crevis covered himself up. "Ray! Use the other stall. I'm not done yet."

"Are you insane?! Why didn't you answer the phone?"

"I'm not talkin' on the phone when I'm on the toilet. That's just wrong. Besides, I told you on the bug that I was going to the bathroom."

"The bug went out." I holstered my pistol. "Now hurry up!"

"Can you close the door, please? This is embarrassing."

I slammed the door hard and smacked the wall. My adrenaline was spiking out of control. Maybe Kurfis was right and I really needed some meds, or I needed to slow down on the Jim and get some rest.

"Hurry up!" I considered taking the phone from Crevis, but if Chance saw me in the club and his hoodlums shook me down, they might find it. Crevis would have to get it back to the van.

Crevis finally finished. "The van is across the street. Get out of the club and meet me there." I let him leave first and waited about a minute until I left the bathroom. I had made a huge mistake coming in here. Now I wasn't sure how to correct it.

I splashed some water on my face and regarded my pathetic countenance in the mirror. I had to be losing my mind. I'd just freaked out like a spastic rookie. My cell phone rang.

"I'm out, Ray," Crevis said.

"I'll meet you there." I opened the door and moved outside the restroom, scanning around. The crowd was heavy, pulsing with the maddening beat of the DJ. I made a beeline for the front door, which was about one hundred feet away. I kept my head down and tried to be inconspicuous. The cane didn't make that easy.

When I was about ten feet from the door, Chance Thompson cut me off.

"What are you doing in my club, Quinn?" His chest puffed out, and he worked his fists at his sides. He wasn't happy to see me.

"Just getting a look around. I have a lot of free time on my hands these days."

Carl swooped in, his hulking frame eclipsing my view of the door.

"We need to talk," Chance said. "Follow me to my office." He pointed to his office on the other side of the floor.

Did he actually think I would follow him there? "I've had enough fun for one night. So I'll have to pass on your kind invitation."

Carl slipped his hand underneath my left armpit, lifting me up. "You're coming with us."

I drew my pistol and pressed it against his rock-hard stomach. "Over your dead body. Let go of my arm and get out of my way, or you'll become just a memory, scumbag."

Carl and I locked gazes that must have communicated I was two seconds away from pulling the trigger. His eyes widened and he stepped back. He turned his body so I could head out of the club.

I kept the pistol close, so as not to draw any more attention than need be in the darkened club. I eased the Glock back in its place, no one around us the wiser.

Chance worked his jaw, as if he were chewing iron. "I don't know what you're up to tonight,

Quinn"—he aimed a thick finger at me—"but get out of my club and stay out."

I walked sideways, like a crab, as I passed them, not wanting to turn my back. A breeze blew through the open door. It felt great on my face. I passed the door goons, and Chance and Carl were about ten feet behind me.

"This guy is barred from the club," Chance said, loud enough for me to hear him. "If you ever see him here again, deal with him, and then call me."

53

PAM OPENED THE VAN DOOR at my approach, and I crawled into the backseat. Crevis was in the front. Katie wasn't around; I didn't want to call her. I'd be a little more patient this time. I felt like an idiot for moving too quickly with Crevis. But I couldn't bear one more person close to me dying in this investigation.

I drew a cleansing breath to calm my tattered nerves, so I didn't bludgeon Crevis about the head and neck for scaring me half to death.

Aiming my cane at Crevis's head, I said, "If you ever deviate from our plans again—be it a bathroom break or a heart attack—I will kill you myself. Do you understand me?"

"You were worried about me." Crevis smirked. "You were afraid something was happening and you came to help. That's pretty cool."

"I was worried about the integrity of the case, that's all. Don't do it again. Now give me the phone."

Crevis handed me Chance's phone. I opened the back and removed the battery and the tiny SIM memory card, which was square, flat, and about the size of a penny. It stored all of Chance's call data, his address book of names and numbers, and his caller identification. His phone was useless without it.

I inserted his card into the port of the SIM card reader and copier I just bought. It resembled a pager, with a cord that plugged into my phone. It would copy Chance's card information directly to the extra phone I purchased for that purpose.

Now I would have access to his address book. But the best part was that when I used a cell phone containing his copied SIM card, his number would show up on the caller ID—a tool I planned to use. The red light blinked as the information was being copied, about a three-minute process.

My personal phone buzzed; Katie's number showed.

"Are you out?" I said.

"Yeah. It took a little longer than I thought. Chance took me to his office and had me ice my ankle."

"Did he seem suspicious?" I didn't reveal my little meltdown, thinking she'd turned the tables on us. I tend to keep to myself the really embarrassing stuff I do.

"Not at all. I told him I would try to pick up a

couple of days next week and let my ankle heal. He seemed to buy it."

"Good. I'll call you tomorrow."

"Okay," she said. "Let me know whatever else I can do."

"Katie," I said before she could hang up.

"Yeah?"

"You did real good tonight. We couldn't have done this without you."

"Thanks, Ray."

She hung up just as the light on the SIM copier flashed green. Good to go. I removed the card from the port and snapped it back into Chance's phone. Now on to the rest of the plan.

I handed Pam Chance's phone and the audio wire, so I could monitor her conversations. She hopped out of the van, crossed the busy highway, and strolled through the parking lot. I watched her with the binos until she moved just out of my sight at the front door.

She said to someone, "Is your manager here?"

"I'm the manager," Chance's gravelly bass voice came over the wire. He must have been keeping an eye out for my return.

"I found this in the parking lot," she said. "Someone must have dropped it."

"Hey, that's mine," he said. "How'd it get out here?"

"I just found it out by the street."

"Thanks, lady. I'd be lost without this."

54

THE DUKE STARED DOWN at me and seemed to be empathizing with my current plight.

I paced around my couch, putting all the last-minute details in my head. In three weeks' time, I'd gone from two dead investigations to now being on the cusp of blowing both wide open. I don't remember being this anxious as a cop. But I also don't remember anything this personal either.

I'd spent most of the afternoon wiring our location and making sure my equipment was ready. I could have used that time for more rest, but I was too amped for that to happen. I had called Mr. Savastio and told him that both Crevis and I were not coming into work. He wasn't happy, to say the least, but I couldn't care less. The Coral Bay Condos would survive a night without Crevis and me.

Crevis waited in the kitchen for my summons of his help. He did possess certain skills that even when I was healthy, I couldn't do—namely, mimicking voices. He'd been practicing all morning in preparation for this.

I was more nervous than anticipated. Everyone was in place. The plan had been made, and I promised myself I wouldn't spaz out like I did at Club Venus. I had the team I had, and I was going to trust them.

"Are you ready?" I said.

"Let's do it." Crevis gave a thumbs-up.

I handed him Chance's cloned phone. Crevis made the first call.

"Hey, buddy." Vitaliano's voice came through clearly. Because of the copied SIM card, the number Vitaliano would have seen was Chance's.

"We've got a problem," Crevis said in a gruff, testosterone-mocking voice. "Meet me at Lake Eola Park by the amphitheater at eleven thirty. Don't tell anyone. We've got business to take care of. Don't call me back, and turn off your phone. We're being watched." Crevis hung up right away.

"Nice." I patted Crevis on the shoulder. "Now only a few more to go, and we can neuter some lions."

At 11:00 p.m., Lake Eola Park was mostly deserted, with the exception of a small group of homeless men huddled at the small amphitheater's entrance directly on the lake, about a hundred yards north of where we were setting up. The sliver of the quarter moon peered down, as if it were winking at me, a hopeful omen for a successful hunt. The air was crisp and electric, almost alive.

I parked our van on North Rosalind Avenue less than a football field away from where I'd wired our location. I had chosen the concrete deck between the amphitheater and the grass park because it had a couple of benches and rows of palm trees around—open enough to film and see clearly, yet secluded enough to have a private meeting at night and feel comfortable.

Crevis helped me wire the trees with two cameras to look down on our meeting place; the audio was set near the benches. I could look out the passenger windows and get a good view of the square, as well as the illuminated fountain in the middle of the lake in the background, but the wireless cameras provided the best observation point of the complex.

A black Cadillac coasted in off East Washington Street and eased up to the curb on North Rosalind across from the amphitheater. The driver turned off his lights. Judge Garcia, wearing a Hawaiian shirt and with a stogie embedded in his mouth, meandered over toward the benches where we were to meet. Just a few minutes later, Morton Connelly arrived in a sweet red BMW, parking on the street as well. The Lion's Den had a thing for fancy cars as well as fancy women.

Ben Scott showed up next in a silver Lexus. But the guest of honor, Michael Vitaliano, cruised in last—along with Gordon Kurfis—in Gordon's Suburban, a nice addition to the show.

"So what's all this about?" Mort said. I zoomed in on the pride, the old lions gathered together in the open.

"I don't know," Judge Garcia said. "But I don't

like it. We agreed that we wouldn't be seen together outside of the commissioners' chambers."

Katie approached the group from the shadows with an armful of papers, right on time.

"Gentlemen, Chance will be here in a minute. He wanted me to hand these out to you before he arrives." She gave each a sheet of paper with a picture of me printed on them.

I'm smiling in the photo. A nice touch, I thought.

"You are by no means to talk with this man," she went on. "He knows about the land purchases and the Lion's Den. He's going to make a lot of trouble for us."

"I already told Chance about this guy." Vitaliano smacked my picture with the back of his hand. "We've talked about him."

"Oh no," I said, watching for Katie's reaction.

She paused. "Yes . . . but he's been digging more and has found out things we were worried about. He's been able to connect J & M Corporation to all of us."

"How can that be?" Vitaliano tossed his hands up. "Chance gave his assurances. He made promises."

"Like this, dirt bag," I said in the van. "I made the connections just like this. Vitaliano helped me lock him in."

"We were told there was no way anyone could connect us with that." Judge Garcia pointed his gnawed cigar stub at Katie. "We were supposed to be silent partners. Chance better get here right now and explain this."

I hadn't had more than a circumstantial link between J & M and Relk and the Lion's Den . . . until now.

"I don't think we should be talking about this," Kurfis said. "I don't like the feel of this. Something isn't right."

"I don't like it either," Ben Scott said.

"Neither does Chance," Katie said. "He's working on a solution right now, but what he needs is for you all to be calm . . . and quiet. This Quinn character can cause a lot of problems for us."

"Tell me about it," Mort Connelly said. "I didn't risk this investment to end up the subject of some grand-jury investigation. We'd better find a way around this guy, and I mean now."

"I'm telling you all, stop talking about this." Kurfis held his hands out like he was directing traffic. He scanned the area. "Chance wouldn't call us all here like this—not all together. We were all clear about that. This smells like a setup. And we don't even know who you are." Kurfis pointed to Katie, who froze.

She turned her attention to the camera in a tree just above the fray and flashed a get-me-out-of-this look. "My name is Katie. I'm Mr. Thompson's personal assistant. He'll be here shortly to answer all your questions."

"I agree with Gordon," Ben said. "We all need

to head home. Discuss nothing and meet with Chance one on one."

"You can meet with me now," Chance said as he and Carl emerged out of the shadows from the park.

"What's all this about?" Mort demanded.

I wanted to know the same thing; I hadn't called him. I wanted to trap the Lion's Den and then work my way to him, through them. This was not part of the plan.

"It's about all of you being morons," he said. "I got Gordon's e-mail from his BlackBerry telling me he might be late here. I've been trying to call all of you ever since. And whose idea was it to meet like this, anyway?"

"Yours," Vitaliano said, the others chiming in. "You told us to meet here and turn off the phones, that we were being watched."

"You're all crazy." Chance scowled. "This whole thing reeks of one person—Ray Quinn."

"I love when they recognize my work," I said to Pam and Crevis.

"And what are you doing here, Katie?" Chance said, more an accusation than a question. Katie pivoted and started toward the roadway. Carl snatched her by the back of her neck, pulling her toward him as he lifted a pistol from his waistband.

"That's it!" Crevis yanked open the van door. "I'm coming, Katie."

"Crevis, wait." I grabbed his shirt, but he was already three steps away and at a dead sprint across the street. "He's got a gun!"

"Call 911," I said to Pam. I pulled my pistol and crawled from the van. "This is going to get ugly."

55

BY THE TIME I had my footing, Crevis was approaching the group. Carl still clutched the scruff of Katie's neck, holding her firm, with his pistol at his side. Carl didn't seem to see Crevis barreling right toward him.

I pegged at top speed, but there was no way to catch Crevis. I was about fifty feet back when he tore through their circle. Since I couldn't fire on the run with Katie, Crevis, and the others standing around, I holstered my pistol so I could move quicker.

"Hey!" Crevis called to Carl as he leapt in the air. Carl turned just in time to catch a flying side kick in the chest, knocking him and Katie to the ground, his pistol skipping across the pavement and into the grass.

"Run, Katie!" Crevis rolled to his feet, hands up. Katie darted into the night.

"Mike, we need to leave now!" Kurfis screamed as the desperate feet of the Lion's Den scampered away.

Carl jumped up. Crevis launched a roundhouse

kick at his head, but Carl blocked it and caught Crevis with a haymaker to the face. Crevis went down hard.

Carl kicked him in the ribs twice before I stabbed him in the back with the tip of my cane, sinking it deep in his kidney. Carl yelped and collapsed to his knees.

I butt-stroked him in the back of the head with my cane handle, then drew the cane back for a home run when Chance tackled me full force. Smacking the ground hard on my side, I twisted to my back and used my momentum to slip my Glock from its holster.

Chance straddled me and caught my wrist, forcing the gun to my side. His right claw locked down on my throat. "You're a dead man, Quinn."

He smacked my arm on the ground twice, my gun flipping onto the grass. Chance and I grabbed the pistol at the same time. I yanked it back toward me. Chance fell forward with it and went to jerk it back again when I jabbed my thumb in his eye.

"Aaah!" Chance shook his head but kept hold of the pistol. He connected on my cheek with a solid left that rocked me. I lost my grip. He ripped the Glock from my hand and stuck it in my face, still sitting on top of me.

He was too strong, and I couldn't roll him off. I pushed the gun away with my left hand and reached for my backup pistol. I couldn't get my hand in my pocket, so I grabbed the .380 cal from the outside of my pants, forced the barrel against Chance's thigh, and pulled the trigger.

The muffled thud of the round piercing Chance's thigh caught him by surprise as he screamed and fell off me. The powder burns from the pistol scorched the skin down my leg, and the backup gun was tangled in my pocket because the slide had locked back. It was useless now.

Chance scurried to his feet, blood pouring from his leg wound, and trained the gun on me. Staring down the barrel of my own pistol was not how I envisioned this ending. I was out of breath and options. I'd been shot before and only hoped he'd make it quick. Pam should have called the police by now. At least they could solve this homicide—it was on tape.

"You've caused me a lot of grief, Quinn." Chance sucked in wind as he held his thigh with one hand and my favorite pistol with the other. "And now you're gonna pay for it."

Crack! Another shot echoed around us. I flopped around on the ground, anticipating the blazing pain. It didn't come.

Chance flashed a blank stare and dropped the pistol to his side. He took one step, collapsed to a knee, and crashed facedown in the grass.

Crevis stood behind him with Carl's gun in his hand—smoke rolling out of the barrel. "I had to do it, Ray. He was gonna kill you. I didn't want to shoot him. I swear I didn't!"

"Ray! Crevis!" Pam crossed the deck at a sprint. "The police are coming." She hurried to me and knelt by my side.

"Help me up, quickly."

Pam handed me my cane and did her best to lift me from the ground. I wobbled but remained standing. She slid her arm around me to keep me steady. Chance had nailed me good.

Crevis's mouth was frozen open. He alternated his gaze between me and Chance, who was still facedown in the grass. Carl was unconscious behind us. Katie emerged from the shadows and hugged Crevis, who seemed catatonic now.

"It's okay, Crevis," I said. "You did everything right. You saved my life. Now get me over to Chance."

Chance moaned, and his legs fluttered.

"Roll him over," I said.

"I . . . I can't," Crevis said.

"Roll him!" There wasn't time to explain.

Crevis rolled Chance to his back. His breathing was labored, and he gazed at me with a glassy, distant stare that said he wasn't too long for this world. I tore off my shirt, balled it up, and handed it to Pam. "Put pressure on his wound until the ambulance gets here." Katie knelt on Chance's other side, a crimson puddle forming from the exit wound on his chest.

"Chance, you're hurt really bad, and you might not make it. This is your only opportunity to clear your conscience. Why did you have Trisha killed? Who's the cop working for you?"

He shook his head and smirked, blood trickling from his mouth. "You'll never know, Quinn . . . jerk." He coughed and groaned, clenching his meaty mitts on top of Pam's hands as she kept pressure on the wound.

"Hold on," Pam said. Chance convulsed and moaned louder this time. "Help is coming. You're going to be okay." Pam started praying over Chance, who went unconscious in her care.

The distant call of the sirens hauled me back to reality. The pavilion lit up as the Orange County sheriff's office helicopter thundered above us, the spotlight bathing the area in near daylight.

I held my hands up in the air. Strobes and sirens came from several different directions. It was going to be another long night.

56

I USED TO LOVE interrogation rooms. They were a playground where I could psychologically strip suspects' emotions and thoughts, like peeling an onion, until they crumbled into weeping heaps, confessing to uncountable, unconscionable crimes.

But now it didn't have the same comfortable feel to it. The gray, drab carpet in the closet-sized room made the impact on me it was designed to do: to steal my confidence and make me vulnerable to my interrogator.

Chance Thompson died on arrival at Orlando Regional Medical Center without answering my questions.

Crevis was in the room next to me, about to be interrogated for the shooting. Pam and Katie were in the building somewhere. They had us all separated to get our statements. Good police procedure, but maddening when you're on the receiving end. I imagined how scared and messed up Crevis must be right now.

At the scene I had briefed Oscar and the other detectives on the basics of the case. But now, in this interrogation, would be the official version where I had to decide how much I would or wouldn't disclose—possibly to my peril.

Oscar sat opposed to me, in more ways than just the position of our chairs. His glasses were down on his nose as he reviewed his case notes on a legal pad. His once-chiseled features showed some serious slippage and wear, like a wax figure set a little too close to a fire.

"I want you to go easy on him, Oscar." I adjusted the T-shirt Oscar got for me before the interview. Mine was blood soaked and in evidence by now. "I don't care what you do to me. You can lock me up, beat me up, whatever. But I want Crevis taken care of. He did what he had to do."

"You dragged him into all this drama," Oscar finally said, glancing over his notepad.

"I know. And I'm sick about it. But he shot Chance to save me. It's all on the laptop. Just review the recording and you'll see."

"Since when did you start caring about anyone but yourself?"

"This isn't a psych eval." I leaned forward. "It's a police investigation of a fatal shooting. I know how that goes. It's an easy narrative to follow—I shot Chance in the leg to keep him from killing me; Crevis picked up Carl's gun and used deadly force to defend me, so don't put him through all the rigmarole just 'cause you're angry with me."

"I've already reviewed your recording. I saw it all. Your friend will make it through this. But I don't know about you. You were taping conversations without consent. You wouldn't back off when I told you to. I can't guarantee anything."

"I was taping in a public place and working to expose an ongoing criminal enterprise," I said. "I can make the argument in court."

"You might have to. We've got a businessman shot dead in the park, four other prominent county leaders conspiring to commit numerous felonies, and an ex-Orlando detective caught in the mix. I can't imagine what the headlines are gonna look like for the next few days."

"I'm not worried about any of that." I probed the hole in my pant leg, the powder burn numbed

338

over for now. I'd feel it more tomorrow for sure. "I'm more worried about piecing together this group and tying them to the murders of Trisha, David and Jamie, and Ashley."

"Well, I need your official statement first. The truth would be good right now, Ray. Your butt is on the line. We'll get into the other stuff later."

Since I wasn't in custody for any crime, Oscar didn't have to read me my rights. I didn't give him any grief or play any games. I wasn't in the mood. I gave a mostly straightforward account of my investigation, leading up the point where Crevis shot Chance.

The only thing I left out was the police angle, but I'd tell Oscar at the right time—which could be soon. I didn't care if the statement would be used to burn me later with any of the legal gray areas I danced in. I came clean, and it felt surprisingly refreshing.

"Raise your right hand," Oscar said, for the benefit of the videotape. I did. "Do you solemnly swear that everything you told me is the truth, the whole truth, so help you God?"

"I do. Now I want to see Crevis."

Oscar nodded and escorted me out of the room and to the television monitor for Crevis's interview. He was sitting at the table next to Steve Stockton, leaning forward, his elbows resting on his knees. The left side of Crevis's face was swollen, and a dark, discolored lump appeared just under his eye. Carl must have clipped him hard.

I caught the tail end of his statement, where he recalled seeing Chance with the pistol, ready to shoot me. He grabbed the gun in the grass, pointed it at Chance's back, and fired once. Stockton used some soft follow-up questions but was easy on him. I owed Steve one too.

Oscar remained quiet as the interview progressed. I couldn't read what was going on with him. We moved to Mike Vitaliano's interview. He'd been stopped from leaving the scene by one of the patrol units. He reluctantly agreed to come to the station. Bowden was doing the interview.

"Detective, I've told you for the last time," Vitaliano said, "I don't know anything about any shooting or this Chance character. And I certainly don't know what you're talking about with this 'Lion's Den.' I'm being harassed here for political motives."

"Really?" Bowden said in a snarky way I appreciated. He pushed Play on the laptop and adjusted it around so the good commissioner could have the best view—the recording of the entire event scrolled out before him. Vitaliano was mum for several minutes as he watched the incriminating clip.

After the video, "family values" Commissioner Michael Vitaliano crumbled in a matter of seconds, wept, and vomited out every filthy detail about the Lion's Den—the land deals, the ordinance manipulation, and vulgar fine points about the girls, as well as his love for the now-deceased Jamie DeAngelo. The kind of love that cost him about four grand a month to procure.

He might have been sincere about his affections for Jamie (although I doubt it), but it really didn't matter at this point. His normally pristine hairdo was an unkempt silvery mess, jutting out in different directions like a sandspur. I knew he was weak at heart and would crack with the right pressure.

According to Vitaliano, it started out when he, Ben Scott, Gordon Kurfis, Morton Connelly, and Judge Garcia all went to Club Venus for a night out a little over a year ago. Knowing they were important county officials, Chance arranged for them to have a back room for privacy for their "entertainment" needs. The night was such a hit that they decided to meet regularly. They dubbed themselves the Lion's Den that first night.

It was in those late-night ventures in the back room of Club Venus that the plans for the county ordinance germinated and grew. Chance paired up his best girls with the men of the Lion's Den, an early payment for cornering Orange County's adult entertainment market. Vitaliano locked himself and his compatriots into a rancid deal that would have potentially netted him and his delinquent friends millions to add to their already-swollen portfolios.

It didn't make a lot of sense in my book. The men of the Lion's Den had everything most people would want—great jobs, lots of money, wives and families who cared about them, but they were still tempted for more—sexier women, more zeros in their bank accounts, and the mesmerizing thrill of abusing their power. Now they stood to lose it all and pile up some pretty impressive prison time as well.

Vitaliano confessed that he had called Jamie several times on the day she was murdered to talk her out of leaving him and their arrangement. She told him that she'd had enough and wasn't going to be his or anyone else's girl. She had found God and wasn't going to live like that anymore. Vitaliano called her that day while on a business trip in Atlanta, with plenty of witnesses to boot. He swore he had nothing to do with her murder or any others.

All that would have to be verified, of course. His statement was remarkably void of any police involvement.

57

BEN SCOTT, GORDON KURFIS, Mort Connelly, and Judge Garcia were rounded up within the hour. Ben and Gordon played hardball—at first. Until they realized that the Commish had flipped on them and the little fact that there was video of our encounter.

When each investigator played my tape for them, the alpha males of the Lion's Den turned cannibalistic, each blaming the others with vigor and passion. The entire tasteless mess spilled out into the interview rooms. There wasn't enough bleach in the station to sanitize those rooms now.

They all shared one common element to their stories: each cast Chance Thompson as the mastermind of the Lion's Den, the adult entertainment ordinance, the girls, and the land purchases. While that might have been true, it was also quite convenient for them to put the majority of the blame on the dead guy. Names of two more girls involved were revealed. Oscar's crew would pull them in later.

Carl jabbered on at length to Pampas about his involvement. At one point, the behemoth bawled and asked for his mother. Not the most masculine thing for a professional tough guy to do. He confirmed the details of the Lion's Den as well, but there were no connections to any of the murders. But there was much more to his story, and I knew it. He was Chance's number one guy. He had to know.

"Let me ask him one question, Oscar," I said while watching Carl blubber.

"You're joking, right? Your involvement in this investigation is over. We've got it from here, and you're gonna be lucky if you're not indicted for something."

"Just one question. That's it."

"What's the question?" Oscar said.

I told him, "This is the last thing I'm ever going to ask of you. Just one question."

Oscar hissed. "I'm getting too old for this." He opened the interview room door. "One question. Then you're out."

I gimped in, my body sore and bruised. It was sad that I was getting accustomed to being beaten up on a daily basis.

"What's he doing—?" Pampas said.

"Don't go there." Oscar held his hand out to Pampas's face. "He's gonna be quick, and then he's done. It's getting late, so don't give me any grief over this."

Carl gazed up at me and then lowered his head and sniffled.

"Make it quick," Oscar said.

"Carl, you're looking at a lot of time and some serious charges," I said. "So you need to think about helping yourself out."

He didn't respond, but I could tell he was listening.

"Who's the cop working for Chance?"

"What are you talking about?" Pampas jumped up. "You're trying to mess this investigation up even more. Oscar, get him outta here. He's crazy."

"I should have known better." Oscar grabbed my arm. "Get your butt out of this room before I knock you out."

"Let him answer the question." I shook away from Oscar's grip. "Tell me, Carl! Who's the cop on Chance's payroll?"

"I don't know." Carl made eye contact with Oscar, then Pampas, then me, a look of abject fear crossing his face.

Oscar and Pampas shared stymied gazes; Carl's admission of a dirty cop stopped them for the moment I needed.

I caned closer to him. I had to press him before Oscar tossed me. "Who's the cop, the one who's killed for him? Who is it?!"

"I swear I don't know. Chance always said he'd never get in trouble; he'd know if the cops were looking at him. He had someone on the inside of OPD, but he never told me who it was."

"You're lying!" I smacked my cane on the table for effect. "You're his number one guy. You knew about the land deals, the girls, and all the other things, but he didn't tell you who the cop was? You're full of it. You're gonna go down for the whole thing."

"If I knew, I'd tell you," he said. "Chance was smart. Maybe he thought if I ever got caught up with something, I'd snitch on him, especially talking about murder. Maybe he figured right. But I didn't kill anyone. Chance ordered me and one of the other bouncers at the club to jump you in your parking lot to scare you when you started shootin' up the place. But I didn't have anything to do with those girls getting murdered or any of that. I swear. I'd never do somethin' like that."

"Did he order you to kill me at the apartment?" I said. "Now's your chance to help yourself."

"No. Chance was angry about the garage thing. He said he had something better to take care of you. I figured it was his OPD guy."

I pressed him for more, but he stuck tight to his story. And, unfortunately, I believed him about that. Chance was just devious enough to keep his hired gun close to him, so no one would know. Just like he was committed to die with his mouth closed to spite me.

Oscar and I left Pampas to clean up the rest of the interview.

"When were you gonna tell me about the cop?"

"There's a dirty cop, Oscar. I've had to walk carefully."

"Since you started your crusade, we've got two more people dead now. I wouldn't call that walking softly."

"One of our guys was connected with the Lion's Den and is a killer," I said. "We've got to find out who it is."

"Easier said than done." Oscar removed his glasses. "Because it looks like that secret died with Chance."

58

STEVE STOCKTON WALKED Crevis out of the interview room and released him to me. They'd put together a packet for the state attorney's office to review. Crevis would survive it—legally, anyway. It was a clear-cut justifiable use of deadly force. He stared down at the floor and hadn't spoken since he came out into the hallway.

"You okay?" I said.

Crevis shrugged. "I just wanna go home."

"I'll take you there as soon as we're finished up here. Do you want me to call your dad?"

"No." He shook his head. "I didn't mean my home. I meant your home. Just take me back to your place. I'm worn out."

Crevis and I met with Pam and Katie in the lobby. Katie hugged Crevis hard as she cried. I couldn't tell if she was weeping for Chance, for Crevis, or for everything that had happened.

I was weeping on the inside, but for a much different reason. I needed to attend to Crevis first. I'd worry later about what was left of the case.

Pam made sure Katie got home safe, and we all agreed to meet up later and discuss where we were in the investigation. I didn't dare put into words what I knew to be true.

The investigation was as dead as Chance Thompson.

I got Crevis home at a little after 4:30 a.m. and gave him some ice for his face. I cleaned and bandaged the burn on my leg and swallowed some aspirin. We talked for quite a while, just Crevis and me; Jim and the Duke weren't invited.

I shared with him my experiences after my shootings and other violent encounters—the loss of sleep, anxiety problems, flashbacks, nightmares. He needed to know what to expect. Maybe he wouldn't experience any of those things. Maybe he'd be just fine. But you could never tell. At least this way he'd know that what was happening in his head was normal after such a traumatic event. I shared more with him that night than I'd ever told anyone. But I had put Crevis in that situation. He was my responsibility. I wouldn't mess that up.

Around 7:00 a.m. Crevis slipped into a comalike sleep. No such luck for me. I stared at my murder mural as Crevis snored on the couch. I'd blown it. I took my best shot and failed . . . again. I had no idea what I was going to tell Pam.

I went out, got the paper, and read the headline: COMMISSIONER VITALIANO UNDER CRIMINAL PROBE. Since the incident happened late in the evening, they didn't have much info, but the gist of the story was accurate. The meat of the crude tale would be revealed soon enough as the coming days would be filled with an all-out exposé. It was simply the first of many swipes the press would take at this investigation. The *Sentinel* could keep this going for weeks.

A much smaller story appeared in the local section: NIGHT CLUB OWNER KILLED IN PARK. Four prosaic lines and a quote from Oscar that the case was pending a review from the state's attorney. He'd left Crevis's name out. Maybe Oscar wasn't as mad at me as I thought.

While I was pleased that Vitaliano and his minions were getting their due attention, I was lost as to what to do next.

I folded the paper and dropped it on the floor. I was exhausted but I couldn't sleep. I stayed in the kitchen for a while until Pam showed up.

"You look terrible, Ray."

"Well, I'm glad to see you too."

"That's not what I meant." Pam frowned. "You don't look like you slept at all."

"I didn't. Too much on my mind."

Crevis snorted but continued in la-la land.

"So where do we go from here?" Pam asked the dreaded question.

I paused. I wasn't about to lie to her. Not Pam. "I'm at a loss. We've locked down the links to Club Venus and the Lion's Den, but we're no closer on the murders. It's driving me crazy."

Pam sighed and crumbled into my kitchen chair. We sat together in my kitchen for a long time, neither of us knowing what to say.

My shift at the Coral Bay Condos was exceptional only in its silence. Crevis stayed home. He wasn't up to coming back to work, and I didn't push him. I glanced through some of David and Jamie's e-mails.

David,
   i couldn't sleep last night. i've been feeling that God has been stalking me, placing me in situations and meeting people like u so i could learn more about him. i did something this morning that i haven't done since i was a little girl. i prayed. i asked God to forgive me and for Jesus to save me from myself. i feel odd . . . but good. i'm at the end of my rope. i can't live like this anymore. i'm leaving this life. i'm walking away. i want to follow God—whatever that means. i need your help now. i have to cut some people out of my life, but then i'm outta here. i'll probably need a new place to stay. i don't want any of these people to ever find me again. i won't go back. i'll call u later today. i just thought u would want to know. Thank u for believing in me.
   Jamie

Something had happened with Jamie. Maybe she had indeed come to the end of her rope. I read David's reply.

Dear Jamie,

I praise God for what He's done in your life. The angels in heaven are rejoicing and singing praises with you now. Tears of joy fill my eyes as I write this. I'll do whatever I can to help you. We'll find a place for you to stay and get you on your feet. If you feel it's not safe, call me. I'll be here for you, Jamie. I promise. Call me later today. I can't wait to see you! God bless.

Your brother in Christ,
David

David Hendricks's last e-mail in life was to a dancer-prostitute who I wouldn't have spent ten minutes to do anything for. Because he cared and extended himself to her, Jamie DeAngelo was walking away from being a pretty play toy in men's hands into a different life altogether. David hadn't bribed her, hadn't wooed her with love or riches. He told her about his God and displayed a rare kindness to her.

I didn't believe in David Hendricks's God, but I couldn't help but see the impact that belief had on David's life—and Jamie's. Whether I believe in God or not, David was sold out to his faith like his sister. Pam and David lived it. Jamie could see it. I could see it. I mourned for people I never knew. I grieved that I couldn't find their killer.

My thoughts tortured and conflicted, I shut

down my computer and pulled my Sudoku puzzle book out for some diversion. I continued with the exasperating puzzle I'd been on for a couple weeks. Even though I hadn't had much time to work it, I should have been through it by now. It didn't make any sense that I couldn't solve it because it wasn't even in the most difficult section of the book. My head was just messed up, and I couldn't put any cogent thoughts together.

I tossed the book to the ground. "It's no use." I spun in my chair and worked my fingers through my hair. The monitors were quiet. No Crevis around. I was alone with my thoughts. I couldn't solve multiple murder cases, and I couldn't figure out a simple Sudoku puzzle. It made no sense.

What was I missing? Did my logic get crippled with my leg? I took a deep breath. *What am I missing?* I ran the formula as far as I could. I thought about the formula I was working with and toyed with an idea that was a breach of everything I believed in, everything I held dear. But if I was right, this would be the only way to verify it.

I caned around the desk. I flipped the cane around and used the handle to hook the book so I could grab it without bending over too much (something I was getting better at by the day). After checking my puzzle, I thumbed to the back and compared it with the answer key, a gross violation of puzzle law. But something was wrong.

I flipped back to the puzzle. There was a typo. Only one number, a five was in place instead of a two. A next-to-nothing mistake from the publisher made it impossible to solve the puzzle. It had no answer with that set of numbers. I could have worked it to my dying day but never solved it because I had the wrong formula. I had the wrong starting point. I corrected the error and finished the puzzle in less than five minutes. Now it was back to my case.

I revisited the details of the investigation. The murderer worked only for Chance, and the cop's name died with him. But that didn't mean I was without resources and options. I took out a pen and listed the events in chronological order. The gun from the suicide was taken from the evidence items. Those present—Pampas, Dean, Stockton, Katie, Oscar—were listed on the crime scene log. Two other patrol officers were present, but they didn't appear anywhere else in the case and wouldn't have handled the evidence.

The night Trisha and I were ambushed, I got orders from Oscar to follow up on the Gerald Pitts shooting, even though it wasn't fatal and the victim was uncooperative—very unusual. Oscar didn't want a drug war to erupt. I checked out on the board, writing down that I was heading to Dante Hill's address. Whoever ambushed me would have had to see the address and make it out there before me, or had to know I was going there.

I didn't go to Dante's immediately. I went out to the parking lot and met with Trisha; we talked for a few minutes, and she asked to come along.

We arrived at Dante's house. Parked two houses down and approached. We turned up the sidewalk to his house when the suspect fired three shots, two striking me, one Trisha. For someone to have ambushed us, they had to have read the board or heard Oscar tell me to follow it up. But that could have been anyone in Homicide, or Dean and Katie walking by. Steve or Rick. The list was short.

Now David's and Jamie's murders. The odd trajectory of the bullet, the scuff wound to David's knee, and the embedded pillow stuffing in his head wound. No forced entry. The gunshot residue was and had always been a problem. Maybe the suspect put the gun in David's hand and fired a shot, but there were only two rounds and two casings found at the scene. That didn't make sense.

Then the suspect shot at me with a .45 cal and missed at pretty close range, less than fifteen feet. When Trisha and I were shot, the suspect was just a few feet away from me and hit me in the hip and arm—which means the suspect is either a lousy shot, or he just wounded me on purpose.

I pinched the bridge of my nose. Why David and Jamie? Who else was she seeing? Why did he kill her? Why kill Trisha? The suspect was familiar with all the goings-on in Homicide and had the ability to tweak evidence and reports.

I sat straight up in my chair as a moment of clarity raced through my head. I couldn't believe I hadn't put it together before.

59

I FINISHED MY SHIFT and probably my career as the night watchman at the Coral Bay Condos.

Crevis awoke as the credits were rolling on *The Shootist*—easily John Wayne's greatest achievement on the big screen. Not that I hadn't watched the film a hundred times before, but on this day it had a deeper meaning than ever. The Duke, beginning to show his age and a hint of frailty, portrayed John Bernard Books, a larger-than-life gunslinger dying of cancer. Books decides that rather than let the disease take his life, he would challenge the three best gunfighters in town (some lowlifes to begin with) to one last duel to the death. He dresses in his fanciest duds and meets his foes at the local saloon. Books dies but takes the three with him in an incredible final gun battle. John always did everything with style and guts. I needed to get ready if I was going to finish this thing once and for all.

I located my nicest suit, the one I used to wear for court, in the back of my closet. I removed it from its protective plastic with great care. It was navy blue, and I had a red, white, and blue tie to go with it. The pants fit a little snug around the waist, but I could still make it work. I clipped my OPD tie tack to my tie and made sure it was on straight.

Oscar had taken my Glock and my pocket gun and placed them into evidence for Crevis's shooting. I still had a smaller Glock 26 9mm that used to be my backup. It held eleven rounds, and I had a spare magazine for it. That should be plenty.

"What are you getting all dressed up for?" Crevis said.

"I have an appointment."

"With who?" He scratched his head.

"The killer."

"I'll be ready in two minutes." Crevis leapt to his feet and grabbed one sock off the floor and then the other. He hopped on one foot as he slipped the first one on. "Just give me a second."

"Don't worry about getting ready, because you're not coming with me."

"What?" he said. "You can't go alone."

"I won't be alone, but I don't want you to be there. I've put you through enough, Crevis. Stay here and hold down the fort."

"I don't understand." His brow furrowed. "Did I do something wrong?"

"No." I rested my hand on his shoulder. I didn't expect that he would understand. "You've been the best friend—and partner—anyone could ask

356

for. But I want you to stay home today. You'll understand later."

"I'm not staying, Ray. You're not going to face this guy without me. And if you try to leave me here, you're gonna have a problem getting out of this apartment." Crevis squared up on me, and the cretin meant business.

I didn't have time to reason or wrestle with him. I guess he was going with me, but I really didn't want him to experience any more and be as messed up as me. "Fine, but I'm leaving in five minutes."

"I'm moving." He grabbed his blue jeans and hopped in them, pulling them up to his waist in no time.

Time to make the call. I punched in the numbers. Dean Yarborough picked up on the second ring.

"Dean, this is Ray. I need your help again."

"What's up?"

"We missed some key evidence at the Coral Bay," I said.

"What evidence?"

"Meet me there in an hour and I'll show you. It's really important and will solve all these murders. Bring your processing kit. We'll be in the same room where David Hendricks and Jamie DeAngelo were killed. Bring Katie too."

"Do you know who did it?" he said. "Who the killer is?"

"If we do everything right, we just might find out." I hung up.

Then I called Oscar, Pampas, Stockton, and Pam to meet me there as well, relaying the same information.

It was going to be a little reunion no one would soon forget.

60

CREVIS AND I were fashionably late. Not that I liked those kinds of dramatic entrances, but it would amp up the tension for the suspect—and that's what I hoped to do. Draw out the stress on the guilty one.

The door to David's apartment was unlocked, so we let ourselves in. The condo hadn't been sold yet, and the carpet still hadn't been replaced in the master bedroom. Everyone was there in the unfurnished living room, waiting for us.

"Sorry I'm late," I said.

"What are you so decked out for?" Pampas said. "You look like you're going to a funeral."

"Just happy to be alive." I hurried past him. "We've got some evidence to collect."

"You'd better not be playing a game with me, Ray," Oscar said. "I don't have any energy for that today. It's been a long week already. Let's see your 'evidence.'"

"Well, let's get started," I said. "Can everyone follow me to the back bedroom?"

We huddled in the small master bedroom

where a hideous event took place nearly two months before.

"I was wrong about a couple of my initial assessments of David's and Jamie's murders," I said.

"You were wrong?" Pampas said. "What a surprise."

"Get to the point, Ray." Oscar placed his hands on his hips, pushing back his coat, exposing his pistol and badge.

"Please be patient." I held up a finger. As much as I was ready to pounce, this kind of thing had to be done with precision and a certain amount of finesse. "This evidence will answer all the questions we have about the murders."

"Ray," Oscar said. "The point."

"Oscar," Pampas said, "why do we have to listen to him babble on? All the other Lion's Den stuff isn't related to this. This was a murder-suicide. David Hendricks killed that girl here. The gunshot residue proves it."

Pam flashed him a warning look, but I spoke before she could.

"That, again, is where you're wrong, Pampas. The person who killed Trisha and wounded me was at the suicide of Clarence Stowe before all this went down. The suspect used his gun, which should have been in Evidence."

"But you still didn't answer the question," Pampas said. "What about the gunshot residue?"

"That's why I asked Dean to join us. Because in

your anemic and clumsy search of the apartment, you overlooked the one aspect that could have tied all these cases together." I turned to Dean. "There's a piece of evidence in this air-conditioning vent that will lead us right to the killer. Unscrew the faceplate next to my leg. It's in there."

Dean raised an eyebrow at me but didn't move.

"Go ahead." I pointed to the vent with my chin.

Dean got on his knees, pulled his Leatherman tool from his pocket, and flipped out the Phillips head screwdriver. He loosened the four screws and removed the faceplate. He reached into the vent.

"And in doing all this," I said, "I'm going to give Pampas a case so simple that even he can solve it."

"What's that?" Oscar said.

"There's nothing in here." Dean looked up at me.

"The murder of Dean Yarborough." I rested my pistol on Dean's pathetic cranium.

"What are you doing?" Dean said, his voice cracking. He inserted his hand back in the vent and searched frantically.

"There's nothing in there, idiot. I just had you do that so I could get an easier shot at you. I'm taking you out for killing Trisha, David, Jamie, and Ashley, you disgusting little reptile. You're gonna finally pay for what you've done."

"Ray, put the gun down," Oscar said.

"I will . . . when I'm finished. But don't come any closer."

"I didn't kill her, Ray, I swear!"

"You were at Clarence Stowe's suicide. You lifted the gun from Property and Evidence," I said. "Chance got you locked into his clutches using Jamie. When you saw that we were checked out on the board with Dante's address, you headed there to cut Trisha and me off. You saw your opportunity and took it. Did you kill Trisha because you were afraid she'd figure you out? Or are you just a vicious troll who likes to kill women?" I pressed the pistol against his head. I heard Pampas break leather. He'd be on target—my head. Perfect.

"Pampas was at the suicide too." Dean cowered at my feet, unable to look up at me. "He worked the Hendricks murder. He's always hated you. He's been jealous of you and your work. He wanted you dead. He had access to Property and Evidence. He's the one who did all this."

"That all might be true," I said. "But whatever else Pampas is, he's a very good shot. He would have killed me for sure, at least the second time, in my apartment. He would've never missed me at that range and would have finished the job. The person who shot me at Dante's and again at my place was sloppy with a firearm. That rules cops out. With everyone at the Stowe suicide, that leaves only you and Katie."

"But what about the gunshot residue on David Hendricks's hands?" Dean said. "It was confirmed by the lab."

"I was getting to that," I said. "The gunshot

residue tests did test positive. Problem is, that doesn't mean the tests you submitted actually came from David's hands. I'd bet everything I have that you dabbed the test kits on your own hands, then pretended they were David's so no one would be the wiser. But you didn't think anyone would ever figure this out. You messed up bad there. When they test the kits you submitted, we're going to find *your* DNA and hair follicles all over that test, not David's. His DNA won't be anywhere on them. You were the only one in a position to manipulate that evidence. And you killed *Trisha.*"

"I wasn't trying to kill her, I swear," Dean said.

"When you shot me, she drew down on you but paused." I pushed the barrel harder against his skull. I could feel him tremble. "I didn't imagine that. She didn't pull the trigger because the attacker was someone she knew—you! She couldn't believe that you were the one attacking us. Because she was good and decent, she hesitated just long enough for you to shoot her first."

"That wasn't supposed to happen," he said, his hands quaking.

"Then why is she dead?!"

"I was trying to kill *you,*" Dean hissed. "I didn't know she would be there. She wasn't signed out on the board, only you were. I swear I didn't know. I was going after you. When I saw that you were going to Jamie's and Dante's address, I thought you had found out about me. I called Chance. He told me to stop you . . . however I could. Chance made me do it."

"Are you going to blame Chance for killing David and Jamie too?" I said. "Jamie was just trying to get the trash out of her life—namely you and Vitaliano. Once you started killing, you couldn't stop until everyone who could put you behind bars was dead. It's time to pay, you toad."

"Chance made me kill them all," Dean whimpered. "I didn't want to do it."

"I don't really care who or what made you do it," I said. "Pam, Crevis, and Katie, you all need to leave. Wait outside in the hallway, please. It's payback time."

"Ray, don't," Oscar said. "You can't do this."

"What are you doing, Ray?" Crevis said.

I knew I shouldn't have brought Crevis; it wasn't fair to him. My peripheral vision caught some nervous shuffling, but no one dared approach. Nearly fourteen months and agony beyond anything I could have imagined boiled down to this one second.

I had fantasized again and again what I would do to the person who murdered Trisha and stole my life. Now he knelt at the business end of my pistol, one muscle twitch away from receiving the revenge I'd yearned to give. I savored the moment . . . until she spoke.

"Ray," Pam said in a calm and controlled voice. "You've caught David's killer. No one else could have done that. Now it's over. Let the police and the courts deal with Dean."

"This is what you wanted too," I said. "Revenge for the murder of your brother."

"I wanted justice, not vengeance." Pam took a step toward me. "Don't do this. You're not the person to carry out that judgment."

"I'm exactly the person to do this." I clenched my jaw tight enough to crack a molar. "I have every right to take out the man who killed so many people and destroyed my life. You gonna tell me now that God wouldn't want me to?"

"Yes," she said. "God doesn't want you to take vengeance. That's His job. But Trisha wouldn't want you to, either. You're alive, Ray. She'd want you to have a life, not end it like this. She'd want you to move forward, and you know that's true. Now you can."

Trisha's face flashed to my mind, and the time on the beach when she told me she loved me washed over me. I imagined her standing here next to me, watching this whole ordeal. What would she think of me now? Would she like what I'd become? I could almost hear her voice telling me, "Don't do it." I lowered my pistol and stepped back.

Pam rushed forward and wrapped her arms around my chest, squeezing tight. Her body rocked as she sobbed. "Thank you."

Steve Stockton hurried to Dean and grabbed his arms, standing him up. Pampas joined him but gave me an embarrassed look as he cuffed him.

"I'll take this." Oscar eased the pistol out of my hand. "You did well, Ray. It's gonna be all right." He rested his mitt on my shoulder.

Stockton and Pampas whisked Dean out of the room, probably fearing I'd have another meltdown. Pampas gazed at me with a disappointment I could only assume came from not being able to shoot me. Or, more important, what his own future held.

61

OSCAR LET ME WATCH Dean's interrogation at the station. Bowden did the interview, and a solid one at that. After hearing his Miranda rights, Dean gave a detailed statement of his murder spree, mostly while sitting in a near fetal position in the chair, his legs drawn up to his chest. A vile creature, to be sure.

He'd ambushed Trisha and me out of fear of being discovered, supposedly on orders from Chance, as if that mattered now. He killed Jamie because she was leaving him, Vitaliano, and her life, and she was the one link to Trisha's murder, as well as possibly exposing the Lion's Den. He couldn't take those risks.

He'd followed Jamie to David's apartment, broke in, and killed them both. He used the pillow to muffle the noise. David tried to fight to protect her but was shot while on his knees, which explained the abrasion. The trajectory of the round in the room made sense now.

Dean then tried to kill me . . . again. When he'd read about Ashley's statement to me, he broke into Ashley's apartment and murdered her because she told me about a police involvement. He feared that she knew his name but hadn't told me it yet. He couldn't risk that—one murder or many all added up to the same end if he was caught.

He removed Jamie's phone records to protect the Lion's Den and himself, and he had, indeed, tested his own hands for the gunshot residue.

After Dean was finished, Oscar drove me to Lakeside Alternatives, a mental-health facility where I stayed for three days and three nights for a mandatory mental evaluation called a Baker Act—against my will, of course, although I didn't put up much of a fight. I should have been angry with Oscar for that, but I wasn't. I didn't seem to have any anger left. It was probably still hanging around apartment 419 at Coral Bay Condos.

Besides, I think Baker Act-ing me was more of a tactical decision for the case as well. When the evidence of Dean's confession was challenged in court, Oscar could testify that I was acting on my own and had nothing to do with the department—making Dean's statements, even under duress, admissible. Time would tell on that one. He could also say that I was mentally unbalanced at the time and suffering from posttraumatic stress disorder, muddying the waters for any potential criminal charges coming my way later.

Crevis, Pam, and Oscar visited me each of the three days. Patients normally couldn't have visitors, but Oscar had some clout; he was getting things done.

The best part of my stay there was I got to read the paper every morning, uninterrupted. Dean's booking photo covered the front page in an exposé of Commissioner Vitaliano and the whole sordid story. A very satisfying read and some of the finest reporting I'd seen from the *Orlando Sentinel* in a very long time.

But it was the next day's edition that held my attention the most—David Hendricks's picture occupied the front page along with a story that vindicated him and his reputation. The Outreach Orlando Ministries was highlighted with some choice quotes from Mario and Pam. Her picture was taken next to him. It made me smile.

Later that day, Oscar sat on the concrete bench in Lakeside's courtyard, a serene little spot with a small walkway and several benches. "We wrote a search warrant for Dean's apartment," Oscar said. He still wore his work suit and had taken a few minutes away from the investigation to update me. "We found the .45 cal he used to shoot at you. Some ammunition matches the brand of the ammo from Trisha's shooting. The lab will have to confirm the actual ballistics, though. We also found some correspondence with Jamie confirming what he said, and a phone that was listed to J & M Corporation. He had press clippings from your first shooting there as well. And we sent the test kits for the gunshot residue off to the lab for a DNA comparison. You called that one right. We have a boatload of evidence now."

"That's great, Oscar." I was in my blue jeans with one of those pajama-type smock tops. I had a plastic bracelet around my wrist in case I fled the facility so everyone could tell that I was a maniac on the loose.

"You did good work, Ray."

"Thanks. I go home tomorrow. I think they fixed my head."

"So you won't be a smart aleck anymore?"

I smirked. "I'm not that fixed."

62

SEVERAL NEWS SATELLITE TRUCKS blocked the street in front of Outreach Orlando Ministries, and a throng of reporters crowded the front door. I had difficulty finding a parking spot. Pam and Mario were addressing the crowd. She caught my eye and broke away to greet me.

"Ray"—she hugged me—"I'm glad you came by."

"Wouldn't have missed it."

"This is even better than I could have imagined. The mayor and other city officials are getting a tour to see how they can help the ministry." She took my hand and squeezed it. "Nothing can bring David back or heal that wound, but I know I'll see him again. You cleared his name, Ray. And whether you realize it or not, when you caught David's killer, you saved his ministry. God is using you in mighty ways."

"So your God can use heathens too?"

"Absolutely. He once spoke through a mule. Using you wouldn't be that different." She grinned.

I placed my hand over my heart. "I'm sure you meant that in the kindest way."

Mario was speaking with several reporters when he glanced our way. He stopped his interview and hurried over to us.

"Ray," he said. "Thanks for coming."

"I'm glad things seem to be working out."

"You have no idea. Fox News and CNN have done nationwide stories about what happened to David. An investigative show has contacted us as well to do a follow-up story. Not only are they clearing his name, but donations have been coming in nonstop. It's amazing. I just can't believe what God is doing here." Mario, true to form, got choked up, and a tear ran down his ex-felon cheek. I cut him a little slack, though.

"I think David would be pleased," I said.

Mario wiped his eyes. A reporter called his name. "Well, I gotta get going." Mario hugged Pam, dipped his head toward me, and turned to walk away.

"Hey, Mario." I extended my hand.

He looked at it for a second, then seized it tightly. "Thank you, Ray. God will bless you for what you've done here."

In a rare moment of temperance, my filter remained on and kept me silent.

"I talked with Sergeant Yancey earlier today," Pam said. "He told me he found some of your stuff at the police department. He wanted us to come by and pick it up."

I nodded. "Sure."

Pam and I arrived at OPD, and I punched in the code to the back gate, surprised it hadn't been changed yet, even after my meltdown. The lot was packed, more than usual. I figured most of the detectives would be following up on the numerous leads with the Lion's Den and the homicides. Maybe they were having a meeting, which occurs all too often in major cases. But meetings keep the powers that be feeling like they're doing something.

I rapped on the back door because my security card wouldn't work; Bowden let us in. He wore his normal long-sleeve shirt and tie but had a black band around the investigator badge clipped to his belt.

The homicide unit was jammed with investigators sitting on tables. Uniformed officers were scattered throughout the building, all of them with black ribbons over their badges—the sign that an officer was killed in the line of duty.

"What's going on?" I said to Bowden, who dummied up and grinned. I had been led into some sort of ambush. I just wasn't sure what was happening.

"Ray." Oscar stepped from his office. "Come over here."

"I thought you said you found something of mine? What's really going on?"

"Oh, I did find something." He handed me a black stapler with my old ID number on it. "I think this was yours."

"You called me here for this?"

"You can use it at your new job," he said. "These things cost two or three bucks. You wouldn't want to waste that."

"Wow. I get to keep my City of Orlando stapler." I squeezed it once to make sure it still worked. "It's my lucky day."

The officers pressed in closer. Something was definitely amiss. Pampas was the only one who didn't gather around. He was in blue jeans and a T-shirt, filling a cardboard box with the personal items from his desk. I'd heard from a little birdie that he'd been transferred back to Road Patrol —midnight shift.

"There's one more thing." Oscar stepped into his office and returned with a plaque.

I hissed. I had been duped.

"You think you're the only one who can be sneaky?" He pushed his glasses up on his nose and cocked his head back.

"Did you have anything to do with this?" I said to Pam.

Her smirk told me everything I needed to know.

"'For heroism and investigative prowess above and beyond the call of duty. On this date, the City of Orlando Police Department recognizes Detective Ray Quinn with a Department Commendation for his part in the clearance of four homicides.'" Oscar handed me the plaque and shook my hand. "You did real well, Ray. No one else could have pulled that off. Trisha would be proud of you. I know I am."

I took the plaque as the room erupted in applause. It's rare when I don't know quite what to say. "Thanks" was all I could manage. I started for the back door. Time to go. I was hitting overload.

"No, no." Oscar stopped me. "You don't ever leave here by the back door again. You walk out the front, Detective Quinn, with your head held high."

Police radios and shuffling feet reverberated from the hallway just outside the door to Homicide, the hallway that led out to the front of the building. A crowd had formed there also.

"What's out there?" I said.

"There's only one way to find out." Oscar smiled.

Pam hooked her arm in mine and led me to the doorway. I hobbled out. Officers in their dress uniforms lined the hallway. The black ribbons must have been to honor Trisha's memory one more time. Her case could be closed now. So could mine.

"Company, attention!" Oscar said. All the officers came to attention. "Detective Ray Quinn is leaving the building." He turned to me. "This is how a detective should retire."

I lowered my head, lest I give a good Mario impression. Pam walked with me out of the building as the entire force stood at attention.

The constant tap of the brass tip of my cane on the terrazzo floor was the only sound in the hallway, save my heartbeat.

63

"PUT THAT IN THE CORNER," I said to Crevis, whose arms were loaded down with two cardboard boxes.

I swiveled around in my new chair, the aroma of fresh leather tickling my nose. I was surprised we found an office space on Colonial Drive for as cheaply as we did, especially with the view. My window faced the entrance to the Amway Arena, home of the Orlando Magic. It should be interesting on game nights.

The bustling downtown traffic roared by my window, and the LYNX city buses' brakes squealed by on a regular basis. We'd get used to the noise, but it did add a certain flair to the whole venture. This was a good place; I could feel it. The lettering on the window of our new front door said The Night Watchman Detective Agency. I hired a guy to airbrush our logo below the words: a man with a cane. A rather nifty symbol, if I do say so myself.

Crevis checked his look in the mirror on the wall next to the front door. He couldn't pass the thing without gawking at himself. He wore a dark suit, coat, and tie, with a black fedora I just bought him. I don't think he'd ever worn new clothes before. He slid his hand down the rim of his hat, a full-toothed smile crossing his face.

He strutted over to my desk and brushed his coat back, revealing the private-investigator badge clipped to his belt. The image of an ugly red-headed Humphrey Bogart came to mind. I didn't tell Crevis that I had already purchased his 9mm as a gift for when he passed his carry-concealed permit class.

"Crevis Creighton, Private Eye," he said in a not-too-bad Bogey imitation. "How does that sound?"

"Frightening," I said. "For the bad guys, anyway."

"What do you need now, boss?" he said. "I've

got everything at the apartment finished and loaded most of the stuff here."

"Why don't you run and get us some lunch?" I eased out my wallet and slipped him a few bucks. Whatever else could be said about Crevis, he wasn't afraid of hard work.

"I'll be right back. Then we can start snooping around somewhere. Can we pull someone's trash tonight?"

"We'll see." I chuckled.

"I got the rest of my stuff out of my dad's house today," Crevis said. "He still thinks I'm an idiot for doing this, you know."

"Crevis, don't believe the nonsense your father or anyone else tells you. You're honorable and brave, and you have the heart of a tiger. I'll teach you everything I know, and when you're ready, I'll help you get into the academy. You're gonna make a great cop someday."

"I'll give you my best, Ray."

"I know you will."

"I still don't write so good," he said. "So I don't know what I'm gonna do about reports."

I took the digital recorder from my top pocket and slid it across the table. "Just narrate into this whatever you do on a case. I'll transcribe it for you. That shouldn't be too hard."

"I can do that." Crevis slipped the recorder into his pocket, then headed out the door. He checked his look in the mirror again.

"And quit staring into that mirror before you break it and give us all seven years of bad luck." I couldn't let him get too cocky. He chuckled and tipped his hat to me.

He opened the door to head out as Pam entered our office carrying a large manila envelope.

"You look handsome in that suit, Crevis." She smiled. His face turned redder than his hair before he hurried out the door.

"So what brings a fundamentalist schoolmarm to a private investigator's office?" I steepled my fingers and twirled a bit in the chair. "You have a case you need solved?"

"I've been practicing something I wanted to share with you."

I nodded. "Okay."

"Be patient with me as I give this a try." She cleared her throat. "Here goes: Ray Quinn is a really nice guy."

"Very good. You didn't stutter, laugh, or pass out. I think you're getting that whole bluffing thing down. You pulled that off like a pro."

"I've been working on it for a couple of days," she said. "I thought you'd appreciate it."

"I do."

"Are you holding up okay?" she said. "It's been a crazy couple of weeks. I've been praying for you every day."

I checked my watch. "You've been here all of

thirty seconds, and you're already beating me down with the God-stuff."

"God's doing something in your life, Ray. I just want you to find His peace," she said. "Do you really believe everything that's happened is just a coincidence? You're a logical man, so can you really deny the obvious—God's hand was over this investigation the entire time?"

"I will give you that it certainly has been an unusual set of circumstances that brought us together and that the cases intertwined." I raised a finger, keeping her from a fundamentalist rant. "But that's it. I'm not sold on this God-in-control thing. It'll take a lot more than just one good case to convince me of anything."

"Oh really?" Pam placed her hands on her hips. "Do you have any leads on the mysterious witness from your shooting? The one who—"

"I know who you're talking about." I cut her off again. "I have a couple of ideas I'm working on."

"Let me know when you find out," she said with the annoying grin she has when she thinks she has you.

"You'll be the first to know," I said. She would be, but I had to do a lot more sorting out of my life before I got to any of that.

"I have something else for you." She handed me the envelope. The label read Department of Children & Families.

"What's this?"

"Your foster- and group-home records."

"How in the world did you find them? This stuff is supposed to be sealed and nearly impossible to get ahold of."

"You're not the only one with contacts," she said. "Since you wouldn't let me pay you any-thing, I wanted to do something for you. Maybe this can help you answer some questions about your birth parents . . . when and if you're ready."

I held the thick folder in my hand, not sure if I wanted to tear it open or not. I should have just let Pam pay me when I had the chance.

"Thank you, Ray Quinn. I'll never forget what you've done for me and David's ministry." She seemed like she had something else to say, but she stopped herself. We traded some awkward looks. "I have to go." She smiled and hurried out the door.

As she left the office, a sadness overtook me that I didn't quite expect. I was starting to enjoy seeing her every day and didn't like the thought of having Pam out of my life forever. An idea passed through my melon: maybe I could call her later in the week for lunch . . . to go over more details and cleanup on David's case, of course. Not a bad plan.

I opened my desk drawer and slipped the envelope into the Open Cases file. I wasn't quite ready to break the seal on that case yet and wasn't sure if I ever would be.

I took a seat on my bar stool underneath a muggy Florida skyline. My Sudoku book kept me company as I hoped to knock down a few puzzles before I called it a night. I'd spent most of the day putting together a business plan for the Night Watchman Detective Agency. It had a nice sound, and in spite of how insane of an idea it was, I was excited about getting started.

"Mr. Ray," Hector called from the other end of the complex. "We fixed the pool, no? Maybe you can swim now? Get some good exercise for your leg."

"I might take a dip sometime, Hector. Maybe tomorrow if I get a chance."

He waved and stepped back into his apartment.

I ambled to the edge of the pool, its glistening waters a foreign sight for me—pure, clean, clear, absent of any gooey debris. An antiseptic chlorine smell permeated the air, the stinky bog mist gone forever.

The light reflected through the translucent pool, tiny ripples shimmering on the surface as the pump churned away. I took out a nickel and prepared to pitch it in for old time's sake. As I went to flick it, I decided against it. I need every nickel I had now. I pocketed it again.

I had met with Helga earlier in the morning.

She informed me that my leg was probably as good as it would ever get and that she'd brought me as far as she could. Helga's real name was Jennifer, and she was a graduate student at the University of Central Florida, studying to be a full-time physical therapist.

We talked for a while after she finished. Jennifer said she wanted to help people like me get mobility back after an injury. I bought her a card, something with flowers and a nice saying on it; I can't remember. I think she really appreciated it. Maybe I've been hanging out with Pam too much.

Crevis and I were scheduled later to take in a movie that I hadn't seen in a couple of years: *The Quiet Man.* A good film that was a bit of a departure for John, and one I hadn't had on my top shelf until recently. The Duke portrays Irish-American boxer Sean Thornton, who walks away from the fight game after accidentally killing a man in the ring. In an attempt to resuscitate his crumbling life, he travels back to Ireland, the home of his youth, searching for a new direction in life. He falls in love with Maureen O'Hara and trades punches with her brother in one of the better fight scenes committed to the big screen. Good stuff. I might even microwave some popcorn for this one.

I wondered about Tim Porter's prophecy and what he had said about God not being finished with me yet. As much as I enjoyed giving Pam grief about God, I couldn't ignore some of the "coincidences" in this case and in my life. And, as she'd so aptly put it, I had yet to identify the witness to my shooting, the one who knelt down and comforted me. My ideas would have to wait until I'd put some order in other areas first.

Soaking in the refreshing air, I meandered back to my bar stool. Not much had actually changed in my life. In spite of me finding her killer, Trisha was still gone—a cavernous void in my life that I didn't think could ever be filled. I wasn't a cop anymore and had come to the place where I could admit that I would never be one again. I was submerged in debt the size of the gross national product of a small country. And my body would remain a wrecked vessel for the rest of my life. My leg throbbed and cried out to me to rendezvous with Jim later, the pain at its peak. Maybe I would, maybe I wouldn't.

But something else seemed to be at work in me as well. In spite of all these things, for the first time in over a year, I looked forward to waking up in the morning. I couldn't help wondering that when Pam put her hand on my shoulder and prayed for my healing, maybe, just maybe, her prayers had hit their mark.

READERS GUIDE

1. What purpose does Ray Quinn's sharp sarcasm serve for him? How does he use it to his advantage? How does it harm him?

2. Both Pam and Ray have suffered staggering losses in their lives, but Pam keeps her faith while Ray remains agnostic. What is Ray's objection to a loving God? Have you heard those same objections from others? Why is Pam able to stay strong in her faith?

3. Ray is suffering from posttraumatic stress disorder (PTSD) and severe depression. How do these affect Ray's relationships with others? Do you know someone who suffers from either of these conditions? If so, how does that affect your relationship with him or her?

4. Why was Ray so reluctant to help Pam at first? And why did he eventually agree?

5. What is Pam's motivation for asking Ray to reinvestigate the case? Is it more than just clearing her brother's name?

6. Why does Crevis desire to become a police officer? What does that say about his life? And why is he so loyal to Ray?

7. How does Mario's addiction to pornography hamper the investigation? Do you know people who have or are struggling with this? How has it adversely affected their lives?

8. Once Ray discovers his shooting and Trisha's death were linked to David Hendricks's murder, why doesn't he turn the case over to the authorities? What does he hope to accomplish by solving it himself?

9. Oscar and Ray's friendship goes back many years. What does Oscar do early in the story to try to help Ray? Why is Oscar so angry with him later? Describe a time when you've been angry with someone you were trying to help.

10. God's purpose in each of our lives is a major theme throughout the story. By the end of *The Night Watchman*, does Ray begin to see a larger purpose for himself? Did you?

Center Point Publishing

600 Brooks Road ● PO Box 1
Thorndike ME 04986-0001 USA

(207) 568-3717

US & Canada:
1 800 929-9108
www.centerpointlargeprint.com